I0668699

CHEROKEE STEEL

CHEROKEE PASSAGES BOOK THREE

also by

REGINA McLEMORE

Cherokee Clay
Cherokee Stone

CHEROKEE STEEL

CHEROKEE PASSAGES BOOK THREE

REGINA McLEMORE

FIFE
PRESS

an imprint of
YOUNG DRAGONS PRESS

OGHMA
CREATIVE MEDIA

Bentonville, Arkansas • Los Angeles, California
www.oghmacreative.com

Copyright © 2022 by Regina McLemore

We are a strong supporter of copyright. Copyright represents creativity, diversity, and free speech, and provides the very foundation from which culture is built. We appreciate you buying the authorized edition of this book and for complying with applicable copyright laws by not reproducing, scanning, or distributing any part of it in any form without permission. Thank you for supporting our writers and allowing us to continue publishing their books.

Library of Congress Cataloging-in-Publication Data

Names: McLemore Regina, author
Title: Cherokee Steel/Regina McLemore | Cherokee Passages #3
Description: First Edition | Bentonville: Fife, 2022
Identifiers: LCCN: 2022939607 | ISBN: 978-1-63373-782-2 (hardcover) |
ISBN: 978-1-63373-783-9 (trade paperback) | ISBN: 978-1-63373-784-6 (eBook)
BISAC: YOUNG ADULT FICTION/People & Places/United States/Native American
YOUNG ADULT FICTION/Historical/United States/20th Century
LC record available at: https://lccn.loc.gov/2022939607

Fife Press trade paperback edition February, 2023

Cover & Interior Designer: Casey W. Cowan
Editors: Laura Lauda & Amy Cowan

This book is a work of fiction. Apart from the well-known actual people, events, and locales that figure in the narrative, all names, characters, places, and incidents are the product of the author's imagination or are used fictitiously. Any resemblance to current events or locales, or to living persons, is entirely coincidental.

Published by Fife Press, an imprint of Young Dragons Press, a subsidiary of The Oghma Book Group. Find out more at www.oghmacreative.com

I dedicate this book to my two children,
Joel McLemore, and Alison McLemore Kinback,
as well as their Philpott and McLemore ancestors who paved the road
before them and helped make them into the fine people they are today.

I also want to honor the memory of my McClain cousin, the late
Cossena Powell, who always supported me in my writing endeavors.

TABLE OF CONTENTS

ACKNOWLEDGEMENTS

MANY THANKS TO MY EDITORS at Oghma Creative Media and Young Dragons Press, Chrissy Willis, Katheryn Lumsden and Laura Lauda, for all of their editing help and encouragement. Special thanks to Faith Phillips, Jonita Mullins, Donna Jones, Renee La Viness, Wanda Elliott, Lynda Hagar, Barbara L. Clouse, and JC Crumpton for graciously providing critiques, book blurbs, and encouragement.

I

BONITA

& ROSS

FIFTEEN-YEAR-OLD BONITA McKindle's morning proved disturbing. At first when she opened her eyes, she didn't know where she was. The musty smell of her grandmother's house permeated her nose reminding her that she had gone home from church Sunday night with her granny and had spent the night. The sun was barely peeking above the horizon, and Bonita rolled over, hoping to get another hour's sleep when the raucous cries of a flock of ravens, nesting in the oak tree outside her grandma's house, woke her fully. She sighed. There would be no more sleep with that racket going on. The reverberation of Granny's old shotgun sent her springing from her bed. What was Granny doing? Bonita lifted the windowsill and peered out, her heart pounding.

"Why are you shootin' at them birds? They ain't botherin' nobody."

"Them's ravens, and I don't like them." Granny waved her arms and shouted, "Get out of here now, you old Raven Mockers."

Pulling a blanket over her flannel night gown, Bonita walked out of her room and to the front porch. "What in the world is a Raven Mocker?"

"It's one of the Cherokee death birds. If a Raven Mocker comes to your house, someone nearby is goin' to die."

"I thought the death bird was an owl."

"Them, too. Well, I scared them all off, so we should be safe."

WHEN BONITA ARRIVED at school that morning, Ross Stone grabbed her before she could step onto the front steps. "Come on, Bonita, let's show them how it's done."

They started doing her favorite new dance, the jitterbug. Bonita's brown eyes sparkled as she danced with her favorite dance partner. Ross swung Bonita into a dip so low that her long, wavy chestnut hair touched the ground. He had just pulled her back in place and gave her a resounding kiss to the applause and hoots of their classmates seconds before Principal Maxwell began ringing the bell to call school to order for the day. If he wondered why the older students were clapping and cheering as he walked down the steps of Jubilee High School, he gave no indication. He stopped ringing the bell when he noticed Bonita standing enfolded in Ross's arms.

"Ross Stone, this is your last warning. If I see you touching Bonita McKindle one more time, you will have a meeting with my board. And I *don't* mean school board."

Moving away from Bonita, Ross flipped his ebony hair out of his dark eyes so he could look straight into Mr. Maxwell's eyes. "That's a good one, sir." Ross gave him an apologetic smile and said in his most sincere voice, "I'm awfully sorry, Mister Maxwell, Bonita is just so pretty that I forget that we are in school sometimes. I promise I won't do it again."

"It seems like I've heard those words before, yet here you are, once more breaking the rules."

Bonita tried to help. "Please forgive him, Mister Maxwell. I should have refused to dance with him. If you punish Ross, you should punish me, too."

"Will you see that it doesn't happen again?"

"Yes, sir. I promise I will see to it that Ross behaves himself."

"All right. I will hold you to that promise."

As Mr. Maxwell walked away, Ross glanced around to make sure no one was watching. Then his long, brown fingers gave Bonita's left buttock a light pinch. "You little liar, as if you really want me to keep my hands to myself."

A quick burst of anger flared up in Bonita, and she gave Ross a quick slap. "I *do* mean it. Kisses and hugs are fine, but you ain't got the right to touch my fanny."

Ross rubbed his cheek and chuckled. "Whatever you say, honey. Don't forget to come to my house to the party tonight."

"I'll try, but I don't know if I'll have a way or not."

"Find a way. Ask that worthless brother of yours to bring you. I invited him to come, too."

"Sid is in trouble with Pa right now. He kinda messed up Pa's car, and he ain't fixed it yet."

"From what you told me about Sid, he can get his way if he wants something bad enough."

"You're right about that, all right. I'll put Sid up to askin' Pa tonight."

AT FIRST, ANDERSON said that it was too far out for Bonita to attend. Turning stubborn, Sid declared he was going no matter what. With a heavy sigh, Anderson conceded the two could go together— if they could catch a ride.

"Come on, Pa, let us borrow your car."

"Oh, no, boy. Last time you drove it, you brought it home with the fender all dented in."

"Now, Pa, you know I can get that dent out as soon as I get time to do it. It only happened because I was halflit, and with Bonita around, I won't be drinkin'. Besides the Stones don't allow no liquor at their parties."

"That never kept you from drinkin' before. But, go along with you. 'Tis true that you're only young once. Just be careful."

Anderson smiled and patted Sid on the back, his hands shaking so much that he almost dropped the keys. Bonita's heart filled up with pity, mixed with a little love.

BONITA'S TOE STARTED tapping as soon as they drove up to the Stones' crowded yard. "Oh, Sid, listen to the music. It must be comin' from the new phonograph the Stones bought." As she opened the car door to join the party, she noticed Sid's immobility.

"Well, why are you just sittin' there? The party's inside."

He rolled down the driver's window and lit a cigarette. "You go on ahead. I'll be in directly."

The party was in full swing when Bonita finally opened the front door. She couldn't help herself. It had been several months since she had been in the house, and her curious nature forced her to look around the packed, two-story farm-house to check if anything had changed since she had last attended a party there. The walls were still covered with family pictures, featuring all kinds of faces, in all shades of brown, as well as some in much paler shades, dating back to the mid-1800s through the 1930s. There was a new picture of a smiling, taupe-colored baby boy. That must be the first grandbaby, born a few months ago to young Susan Stone and her new husband, Tommy Swimmer. Loud laughter caught her attention, and she pushed her way to the front of the crowd. Bonita loved to dance, and a stranger was demonstrating some dance moves she had never seen.

The instructor, a tall, rather homely girl, grinned at her. "Well, hello, dearie. What's your name?"

"Bonita McKindle."

"Oh, yes, I've heard of you."

Bonita wondered why the boys nearby broke-out into giggles. "What's your name?"

The strange girl grinned and fluttered her eyelashes flirtatiously.

"Why, I'm Laverne, Laverne Stone. Michael Stone is my uncle. Now come a little closer, Bonita, and do what I do."

Even with all of the good-natured fanny swats and cries of, "No, silly, like this." from the odd girl, it didn't take Bonita long to catch on to the new steps.

She had danced with nearly every boy at the party except for Ross, who was nowhere in sight. When she was scanning the room for him one more time, she heard someone whisper, "Let's all go pee."

At this, all of the girls departed for some bushes behind the house, including the new girl, who squatted some distance away. Not wanting to seem unfriendly, Bonita hunkered down a few feet away from her.

The strange girl sprang up like a jack-in-the-box. "All done. See you back at the party."

When they got back, Bonita had to push her way through the crowd once more to see what was going on. On display was a fast moving, jiving Amelia Stone, dancing with her young-looking husband, who struggled to keep up with her.

In an undertone, Bonita turned to Emily Stone, who was standing nearby, "Ain't she a little old to be jitter-buggin'?"

"Ma, too old to dance? You gotta be kiddin'. She can sing and dance circles around all of us."

"Really? I thought since she's a granny now, she would just sit around, holdin' Susan and Tommy's little boy, and just watch everybody else. Guess I was wrong."

As if she heard Bonita's words, Amelia stopped dancing with her husband Michael and held out her arms for her fretting grandson. She wrapped the small baby in a miniature quilt, embroidered with his initials. Bonita watched as Amelia sat down in a large wooden rocking chair and began to rock and pat the baby on his back. She kissed his chubby, brown cheeks and smoothed the wiry, black hair that was sticking up all over his head. A grinning Michael brought her a glass of iced tea and pulled over a dining room chair to sit close beside her. He placed his finger in the palm of a tiny hand and beamed at the baby when he curled his tiny fist around it.

Bonita tore her gaze away from Amelia when Bart Studie asked her to dance. She spent the rest of the evening dancing and sharing refreshments with the other partygoers. No one knew the whereabouts of Ross.

When it occurred to her that she hadn't seen Sid since she had left him at the car, she turned to asking about him. She finally found a boy who had an answer for her.

"Sid? He's out in the yard, drinkin' moonshine."

Bonita was about to leave to check on Sid's condition when a shrill whistle sounded from where the strange girl was standing. She turned to see a grinning Michael Stone, addressing the crowd.

"Before you leave, I think the boys have something to tell you, girls."

At this the new girl came forward, lifted off her long, black wig, and revealed herself to be Ross Stone.

Michael reached over and landed a light kiss on his son's cheek. "With all that makeup, you make a passable girl, son, but you might want to wash it off now."

"Gladly." Still speaking in a falsetto, Ross jerked the dress over his head and threw it and a bra filled with socks to Emily. "Here you go, sis. You owe me a dollar. No one suspected a thing."

The boys all laughed at the girls' red faces. They exploded when Bonita turned red and said, "Why, I peed next to him."

SID WAS WAITING for her in the car when Bonita left the party. Reaching under the front seat, her fingers found a quart of moonshine. She rolled down the window and poured it out.

"What did you do that for?"

"Maybe I want to get home alive tonight."

"Well, smarty, I wasn't goin' to drink it. I was takin' it home to Pa."

"Well, he sure don't need it neither."

Sid put the car in reverse, barely missing the Stones' big white panel truck, changed gears, and started driving home. He glared at her but didn't say anything as he negotiated the twists and turns of the bumpy road.

Bonita mused about her relationship with Ross Stone. Unlike his older, quieter brother, Clay, Ross would do anything for attention, especially if females were present. He loved all of the girls, and most of the girls loved him even more. Bonita suspected that Ross's declaration of only loving Bonita was just said in the hopes she would grant him more rights to her voluptuous body. The only thing he seemed to love more than dancing or petting with a pretty girl was drinking with his friends, and Bonita had heard him boast about being able to out drink any man in the county. This was the obstacle that kept her from making a real romantic commitment to Ross. She believed she could make him monogamous if she truly wanted him, but she had always sworn she would never become involved with a drunk. She would never have that problem with Clay. She knew Clay would be a safer choice, but he didn't stir her blood like Ross did, and he would force her to settle down. For now, she contented herself with being Ross Stone's favorite dancing partner and sometimes girlfriend.

A FEW MONTHS later Bonita found Emily Stone sitting on the front porch of the Stone store. Emily looked up and noticed her. "Hello, Bonita. Come and sit with me for a little while."

Bonita smiled and sat beside her. "All right. I wouldn't mind a little gossip. What are you doin' at your grandpa's store? I hardly ever see you here."

"I'm supposed to be helping Grandma in the store. Since Susan got married last year, I am the main hand here. I try, but you know how she is. Can't nobody please her."

"Was your ma mad when Susan dropped out of college and ran off to get married?"

"She sure was. Ma didn't speak to Susan for six months, and she said that she wasn't going to make any more of her kids attend college at Tahlequah since they would probably just drop out like Susan. "

"Where's that good-lookin' brother of yours?"

"Which one? Clay or Ross?"

"Ross. Clay is all right, but Ross looks like Clark Gable, only darker and better lookin' 'cause his ears don't stick out."

"Yeah, Ross is the one all the girls are after. I think him and Clay went to Sallisaw with Pa. They're looking at some horse over there."

A red-faced, angry Martha opened the front door and yelled, "Emily, I need your help in here. I can't do everything by myself."

"All right, Granny. Just a minute. I gotta go, Bonita, but, if you have time, stick around, and we'll talk when things get slow."

She was debating on buying a soda pop when she heard a familiar voice. "Well, who do we have here? Bonita McKindle, what are you doin' lollygaggin' around the store on a Saturday mornin'?"

Bonita grabbed the small woman and hugged her tight. "Granny. Did you walk all the way here?"

"'Course I did. Poor people have poor ways. Besides I don't mind a little walk on a pretty day. "

She peered over her wire rimmed glasses and studied Bonita. "What are you doin' here, all dressed-up? Shouldn't you be home takin' care of your pa's stock?"

"Oh, I forgot you don't know. We don't have stock no more. Our cow and calf disappeared in that last rainstorm, and since I was stayin' at Aunt Esther's, no one went out lookin' for them. Then Pa got mad at the rooster for wakin' him up with his crowin' and shot him. Sid ran over our best layin' hens when he was drivin' around the yard drunk a few days ago. The rest of the chickens was so scared that they scattered all over the countryside. I would have caught them, but I didn't want to miss school to chase them, and they was long gone by the time I got home."

Granny shook her head in disgust. "And that's the very reason why Anderson McKindle will never have nothin'. All him and Sid care about is stayin' drunk." She put her hand on Bonita's arm. "I'm glad that you took after your ma's side of the family. You don't like to drink, and you don't care for them that does, do you?"

Thoughts of Ross made her wince. "No, Granny, I don't. I seen too much of it."

Granny gave Bonita a hug. "Good girl. See that you keep to that way of thinkin', and you might just make somethin' of yourself someday."

Bonita glowed at the rare show of affection and returned the hug with vigor. "Don't worry, Granny. I won't never forget what you taught me."

Granny gently removed Bonita's arms from around her neck. "All right. Enough of that. If you have nothin' better to do, you could help me carry my groceries home and spend the night or maybe longer. You haven't paid me a good long visit in quite a while, and I know you get tired of livin' with them drunks."

"I would love that."

BONITA WENT TO bed with a full, satisfied stomach and fell asleep with nothing on her mind but happy thoughts of living in security with her grandmother. The next morning, she fought against the urge to stay, warm and comfortable, nestled under the warm quilts where she had spent a good night's sleep. Granny wasn't in the house when she got up, but she had left her some warm cream gravy and a small pan of flaky biscuits. Next to the biscuits was a saucer of fresh, homemade butter and a can of sorghum. Bonita was starving, so she ate most of the gravy and four biscuits, three with gravy and one with the sweet butter and sorghum. She took a quick sponge bath, brushed her teeth and hair, dressed, and set off for school.

Bonita wanted to stay in the comfort of Grandma's house forever, but she had only been there a few days when Sid came roaring up one evening. When Bonita watched Sid hurrying to the house, she noticed something was different about him. After studying his expression for a few minutes, she figured out what it was. Sid was completely sober, and the mocking look in his blue eyes had been replaced with a wide-eyed look of intense fear.

"Who is it, Bonita?"

"Sid."

Granny stopped churning butter long enough to speak. "Wonder what he wants? Let him in, so we can see."

Sid's skinny frame was shaking, and he started a nervous chatter before he stepped over the threshold. "Bonita, you gotta come home. Pa's real sick, and I don't know what to do."

"Nothin' unusual about that. Pa's sick most of the time from drinkin' so much."

Sid shook his head. "Not this time. All he does is cough so hard you'd swear he's dyin'. I don't know what to do for him. Won't you please come home with me and take a look?"

Bonita started to refuse, but she took a moment to study Sid's pale face and scared eyes and changed her mind. She was Anderson's daughter, and it was her duty to help him. "All right, but if he ain't really sick, I'm comin' right back to Granny's."

Granny, who had heard their conversation, came into the room, wiping her hands on the faded apron tied around her waist. "Go ahead and go, Nita. He's still your pa, and you would feel bad if somethin' happened to him, and you refused to go."

SID DROVE LIKE a maniac. "Hey, slow down. It won't do Pa no good if we get killed goin' back home."

"We need to get home fast. Pa looked half dead when I left."

A strangling sound assaulted her ears as soon as she opened the front door. She ran into the bedroom, and what she saw frightened her. Anderson was leaning over the bed, coughing his insides out, and in the sputum, Bonita could see splotches of red.

She had to act fast. "Quick, Sid, help me get him back in bed."

Anderson grimaced and moaned as they lifted him up and placed him back on his pillow. Bonita yelled out another order. "Hurry, go get some fresh water."

Sid grabbed the water bucket and ran out the back door to the well. Bonita stared at her father's still form. Finally, he opened his cloudy blue eyes and spoke. "So now you know."

Bonita's heart pounded. She dropped her eyes. "Know *what*, Pa?"

"I got TB."

It was as she suspected, a death sentence. Sid came back to her side carrying a dipper of cool water. He held it out to his father. "Here you go, Pa."

"You'll have to hold it for him, Sid."

"Oh, all right."

After Anderson fell asleep, Sid walked into the kitchen where Bonita was cleaning. He lit a cigarette with slender, shaky hands and sat down at the table. "What are we goin' to do?"

Bonita pitched some more dirty dishes into the sudsy tin dish pan. "We got to take care of him."

Sid turned even paler and shook his head. "But you see I ain't no good at takin' care of folks. If you hadn't come home with me today, I don't know what might have happened."

Bonita threw down her dish cloth and turned to frown at Sid. "Listen, I need you to help me. You can stay with him while I am at school, and when I get home, I'll cook supper. I will take care of him until he settles down for the night, and you'll be free to do whatever you want to do. Now that's the way it's goin' to be from now on."

Sid didn't answer for several minutes. He just looked at the floor and took several puffs of his cigarette. He scowled at her before he mumbled something.

"What was that? I couldn't hear you."

"Said I'll do the best I can, but don't blame me if it ain't good enough."

"That will have to do, then."

For several weeks Sid made an effort to do his share. He grumbled a little when she woke him up every morning before she set off for school, but he got up and saw to his father's needs. Sid patiently served the meals Bonita left on the stove. He kept the fire going in the wood stove so that Anderson wouldn't get chilled, helped him get dressed, and assisted him with trips to the outhouse, or on particularly bad days, with the bed pan. In short, he did everything she asked him to do to make their father's illness more bearable.

Bonita missed socializing with her friends before and after school, but she kept her sad feelings to herself and did what had to be done. Even if Sid didn't care for their father as competently as she did, she didn't complain. She was just happy there was someone around to share the burden.

Life rolled along until the warm spring morning when she walked into Sid's room to wake him and discovered he was gone. So, she stayed home from school that day to care for her father and the next day and the day after that.

Home evolved into prison in the days ahead, and she served a long hard labor sentence, caring for her bedridden father. At first the worst part was the nausea that gripped her every time she carried the foul-smelling bedpan across the room, to the back door, and out to the outhouse to be dumped. After a while she got used to it, but by then the bodydraining, mindeating exhaustion had set in, and it never left her.

When her friends saw she wasn't coming to school, they visited to keep her company, but that didn't last long. The stench and the despair of the dying soon drove them away. Part of Bonita was glad when they left. It was hard to be reminded of what other fifteen-year-olds were doing. They were learning, flirting, loving, dancing, and living while she was trapped with her dying father.

But the other part of Bonita howled when they stopped coming. She was desperate for any new thing to break up the stark monotony. Where was Sid? If he hadn't run out on her, she would still be in school and still have a life. If he ever came back, Bonita would make him rue the day he broke his promise to her.

One morning Bonita was sitting at the kitchen table, staring morosely into her cracked coffee cup. She hadn't even washed her face or brushed her hair that morning. It just didn't seem worth the effort since no one ever saw her except Pa. She jumped when she heard a loud knock at the door and a familiar voice.

"Bonita, are you in there? Let me in."

"Just a minute, Ross."

Bonita ran to her bed and searched through the tangled covers until she found her brush. She quickly brushed her hair out and poured some water from the drink bucket onto her hands. She splashed some water onto her face and rubbed it dry with a tea towel. Only then did she answer the door.

Ross rushed in and gave her a big hug. "Are you ever comin' back to school?"

"I want to, but Sid run off, and I don't have nobody to help me."

"Sounds like somethin' that good-for-nothin' would do. You go on to school today, and I will stay with your pa."

"Are you sure? He ain't easy to take care of."

"I helped take care of Grandpa Clay when he was sick, so I know what to do, and I would rather take care of your pa than go to school."

"All right then, but just for an hour or so. I need to talk to Mr. Maxwell and the teachers."

"Take as long as you want."

Bonita changed clothes and put on her scuffed black and white saddle oxfords. She called out her thanks to Ross as she closed the door behind her. Bonita took a deep breath of fresh air and looked around her. For the first time in several days, her heart glowed with light and hope.

BY THE TIME she got to school, Mr. Maxwell had rung the morning bell, and all of the students were in their classes. Bonita paused outside on the front steps, suddenly feeling shy and embarrassed, and wished she hadn't made the trip to school. She mumbled to herself, "I don't have to talk to Mister Maxwell. He'll probably fuss at me. Maybe I can just tell Miss Thirsty."

Miss Thirsty, her favorite teacher, had often praised her for her understanding of literature and her writing skills. Bonita could talk freely to her with no fear of condemnation. She knocked lightly on the door of her classroom. Miss Thirsty came to the door, dressed in a maroon floral shirtwaist, which set off her taupe colored skin and dark hair and eyes. She smiled when she saw Bonita and came out into the hall to speak to her. Bonita quickly explained her situation, but her teacher's response surprised her. "Don't quit school, Bonita. Get Sid to help you. He can take his turn in the day while you are at school. Then you can take over in the evening."

"I tried that, ma'am, but Sid left me high and dry. I can't depend upon him. No, I have to quit for a while, but I'll be back. Thanks for all of your help, Miss Thirsty. I'll bring back that poetry book that you loaned me in a few days."

Her teacher's eyes filled with tears. "Don't worry about that. Consider it a present to one of my favorite students."

"Thank you, then. Thanks for everything."

Before Bonita left through the front door, she watched Miss Thirsty walk over to Mr. Maxwell's office. She knew they were talking about her and didn't believe she would ever come back. But she would. She swore a vow as she touched the wooden door of the old rock school she had come to love, dabbing at her watering eyes with her only white lace handkerchief. Someday she would come back, finish high school, and make a good life for herself.

ANDERSON INSISTED THAT his bed be moved in the corner of the front room where he could be more part of any activity that happened in his house. He had lots of visitors, too, at first. But after his former drinking buddies had cleaned out his supply of liquor, they quit coming around. Now the only ones who came to visit were an occasional relative, like Granny, Aunt Hester, or Uncle Wade. The preacher came every week or two to talk and pray with her father, but most of the time, Anderson pretended to be asleep when he came. Then there was Ross.

Ross came over two or three times a week to "spell Bonita," but she suspected that it was mostly to give him a good excuse to play hooky and a chance to kiss and try to fondle her. She welcomed him for whatever reason he came, craving the company and needing a break from the heavy lifting that came with caring for her father.

One morning he brought a visitor with him, her favorite uncle, Arthur O'Dell. Arthur walked through the door, his blue eyes and wind-burned face, fairly beaming with joy. "Hello, Dutchman. How's my girl?"

"I haven't heard that name in a while. Maybe someday you'll explain it to me. I'm better now that you are here." Bonita ran to him, enveloping the slight, sandy-haired man in a gigantic hug. Unexpectedly, she embarrassed herself by bursting into tears.

Her uncle patted her awkwardly on the shoulder. "Easy, young'un. What's wrong?"

"I'm sorry, Uncle Arthur. Pa has just been so sick, and I have been mostly by myself, tryin' to take care of him."

"Well, not completely by yourself. This young man saw us with a flat on our truck a few miles from here. He helped me change it and rode with us over to your granny's house where I left Sadie and the kids. He seems real concerned about you and your pa. Told me all about it. Good man." Uncle Arthur slapped Ross on the back.

Ross grinned so broadly that his dimples popped. "Why, it's no trouble a'tall."

She took Ross by the hand and smiled into his dark, laughing eyes. "I don't know what I would do without Ross all right."

"Well, much as I appreciate young Ross, I think it might be time that your family stepped in to help. Sit down, and let's talk."

Uncle Arthur explained how good his wife Sadie was at taking care of sick folks. Since Anderson drew a good check, and they could use the money, Arthur, Sadie, and their two children would move in to live with him. Anderson surprised them by opening his eyes and joining in with the conversation.

"Arthur, it's good to see you, man. Did I hear you say that you and Sadie are willin' to live with me and take care of me until I am at myself again?"

Arthur laughed. "Why you old son-of-a-gun. Have you been playin' possum the whole time we been talkin'? Here let me get a good look at you."

Arthur spent some time studying Anderson's emaciated form. "You know I think my Sadie could do you some good. Bein' raised in the old Cherokee ways, she knows a lot about herbs and how to make them into medicine, and if nothin' else, she will fatten you up, and that will make you feel better."

Anderson nodded his head in agreement. "They's a lot to be said for them Cherokee potions and poultices. I'd be right glad to give them a try."

Abruptly, he started coughing his deep, wracking cough, and Arthur grabbed a dipper of water. Bonita rushed to her father's side to help, but her uncle waved her away. "That's all right, Dutchman. I can handle a little cough. You and your feller drive my truck on over to your granny's house and help Sadie move our stuff over so we can set up our household here."

As they were walking out the door, Arthur stopped them. "Here's an idea. It's going to be crowded here with me and my family. You might druther stay with your granny. You probably could use a rest anyway, so just take some of your clothes and such with you as you go."

Arthur suddenly stopped speaking and put his hand to his mouth. "Lord, I just thought how that sounded. I don't mean to run you off, Bonita. You can stay here if you so mind. It's your pa's house."

She turned back and kissed her uncle on the cheek. "Don't worry, Uncle Arthur. I am just thankful that you and Sadie are willin' to help me. Where I stay doesn't matter in the least. We'll be back soon with Sadie and the kids."

After she gathered a few things and tied them up in a blanket, they walked to the truck, and Ross put his arm across her shoulders. "Did you mean what you said about not carin' where you stay?"

"Yes, I'm just happy to get help. Why did you ask?"

"Oh, just somethin' I'm thinkin' on. I'll tell you later after I get it all thought out."

Granny frowned when she saw Bonita with Ross, but she didn't say anything. She was all smiles when Bonita told her she would be staying with her. When Paul, Arthur's ten-year-old son, said he wanted to help, Granny tousled his dark hair and pinched his plump cheeks. "Good for you. Here, carry this bucket of canned preserves that I am sendin' with you to Anderson's."

Next, she turned to the fair-haired, blue-eyed, eight-year-old girl and gave her a quick hug. "Betty Sue, if you ain't the spittin' image of your daddy. You come back and see Granny real soon, all right?"

As Bonita was preparing to go back with Ross, Sadie, and her children, Granny stopped her by putting her hand on her arm. "Bonita, since you are goin' to be stayin' with me, why don't you just let Ross take Sadie back to Anderson's? That way the truck won't be so crowded, and the kids can ride up front instead of freezin' in the back? You already brought your clothes here, so you won't need to go back for a while."

"All right, Granny."

She turned around and called, "Bye, Ross. See you at school in the mornin'."

His face had an expression she had never seen on it before. He looked downright sullen and angry.

THE NEXT MORNING, Bonita walked to school from Granny's house. She was a bird set free and caught herself skipping to school, like she did when she was much younger.

She had just rounded the corner and was less than a half mile from school when someone jumped out of the bushes near the road and startled her. "Boo."

Ross sprang upon her and tackled her to the ground.

"Ross, you fool. Let me up before I scratch your face."

He laughed and put out his hand to help her up. "Simmer down, honey. I was just playin' with you."

She slapped his hand away and got up from the ground. "Ross, look what you did. You got my dress all dirty."

He tried to make amends by brushing her off with his hands. "Here, I dusted you off. It's just dust, not dirt, came right off."

She wasn't ready to forgive him so quickly. "You better not do that again."

He looked at her with his big, dark eyes and reached for her hand. "I'm sorry if I made you mad, Bonita. I guess I just got a little carried away."

"Guess you did." But she let him hold her hand. As usual, she couldn't stay angry when he looked at her with those dark, glowing eyes.

"Come on, let me walk you to school. You know Miss Thirsty ain't there no more."

A little of the sunshine went out of Bonita's day. She had been looking forward to being in her favorite teacher's class. "Really? Where did she go?"

"Heard she got married over Christmas. Miss Chambliss is fillin' in for the rest of the year."

"Miss Chambliss. She used to be real mean to Ramona Freedle in fourth grade, always makin' fun of the way she looked and smelled. I was glad when I heard she quit."

"Well, she's back and meaner than ever. I even heard that some of the girls are talkin' about gettin' back at her."

"What are they goin' to do?"

"Don't know. Just heard they're plottin' somethin'."

HER FIRST MORNING back to school was every bit as good as she had imagined. All of her friends greeted her, and she breezed through her morning classes. Ross, Bonita, and their friends ate lunch together at the wooden picnic tables under the big oak trees. After lunch, it was time for English, which had once been her favorite class.

Within a few minutes in her first day in Miss Chambliss's class, she understood the feelings of the girls in the class. All dressed-up in a frilly pink and gray floral silk dress, her coal-black, dyed hair coiled into a tight bun on her head, bright blue eyes, snapping behind her wire-rimmed glasses, Miss Chambliss stood at her desk at the front of the room and lectured nonstop on American literature. If any student dared to raise a hand to ask a question, said hand was quickly lowered when Miss Chambliss gave the offending party a killing look.

Bonita, who had been sitting midway in the class, with her head down, pencil scribbling furiously on her brown, blue-lined tablet, paused for a minute and looked around the classroom. Of the eighteen students in the room, only the five on the front row and Bonita were taking notes. The other twelve were staring down at their tablets.

She looked at Ross and the other three males in the class. He grinned at her and winked.

Miss Chambliss glared at Bonita when she noticed their interaction. "I'm sorry, Miss McKindle, am I boring you? Are you so advanced that you already know everything I am attempting to teach you? Or, perhaps you're like many in this class, just too stupid to understand what you're being taught?"

She gasped, turned her blushing face toward Miss Chambliss, and started stammering out an apology.

Ross stood up in a fury, sweeping his books and school materials to the floor. "Don't you apologize to that old hag, Bonita. You ain't done nothin' wrong."

In a flash he was at her side, grabbed her hand, and began pulling her out of the classroom.

Miss Chambliss turned beet red and screamed. "Get out of my classroom, you deviants, and don't come back."

Miss Chambliss wrote Bonita's full name on the board but only wrote Ross's first name before the teacher sat down abruptly at her desk in dismay. Ross tugged on her hand and pulled her out, followed by eleven other students, walking out of the classroom and down the hall.

BONITA'S FELLOW STUDENTS hugged and consoled her as they stood underneath one of the large oak trees in the schoolyard. Fiery Athaliah Scott offered her praise as she patted her on the back. "Bonita, you just did what we have been talkin' about doin' for weeks. You put that heifer in her place. Maybe now she will either quit treatin' her students like dirt or go somewhere else to teach."

Bonita borrowed Ross's handkerchief to wipe her eyes and blow her nose. "I'm afraid I didn't do nothin'... nothin' but get us all kicked out of school."

Ross leaned over and gave her a quick peck on the cheek. "Don't you worry about a thing, sweetheart. My pa is on the school board, and so is Athaliah's. Maxwell wouldn't think about throwin' us out. Speak of the devil. Here he comes."

Wearing a big frown, Principal Maxwell rushed over to where they were sitting. "Miss Chambliss tells me that you students decided to take a break from her class. Miss McKindle and Mister Stone, I need to speak to you. The rest of you, go back to class."

Athaliah tossed her fire-red ponytail and stood her ground. "Sorry, Mister Maxwell, but we're comin' with them. What happened today concerns all of us."

"Indeed, Miss Scott. If you feel that strongly, you may all have your say, but I will call you all in a few at a time. Miss McKindle, Mister Stone, and Miss Scott may come back with me to my office. Others who wish to speak to me may come to my office and turn in your names to my secretary, and I promise to see you all before the day ends."

He turned abruptly toward the rest of the students and clapped his hands twice. "Now off with you. Go back to class and stop by my office afterwards if you wish to speak to me."

MOMENTS LATER BONITA, Ross, and Athaliah sat on a worn leather sofa in Mr. Maxwell's office, awaiting their turn to speak. Bonita looked around the room and saw a bookshelf, filled with books, and a picture of Mr. Maxwell's well-dressed, attractive wife, flanked by two curly-haired boys, looking down at the laughing baby girl in her lap.

He spoke first. "Miss McKindle, Miss Chambliss tells me that you were the first to disrupt her class."

"That's a lie. All Bonita did was stop writin' for a minute and look around."

"Mister Stone, I didn't ask you, and if you don't keep quiet, you will leave the room."

In a small, trembling voice, Bonita spoke up. "Sir, I just came back to school today, and I was trying my best to keep up, but I just couldn't do it. When I looked up, I noticed that almost nobody was even trying to take notes. I'm sorry, but I couldn't help it. I looked right at Ross, and he winked at me."

"Mister Stone, haven't we discussed this before? I have told you not to show your affection for Miss McKindle at school."

"Yeah, I know. But it was just a little wink. There was no call for Chambliss to be so mean to Bonita about it."

Athaliah tossed her ponytail and blurted out her feelings. "Sir, you don't know what has been goin' on in that classroom ever since Miss Chambliss came back here."

Resting his chin on his fist, Maxwell directed his attention toward her. "Please enlighten me, Miss Scott."

After a long recounting of harsh words that Miss Chambliss had spoken to her students, Athaliah ended her discourse. "And if you don't believe me, ask any of them kids, and they will tell you the same thing. Or if you don't believe them, go talk to Annie Nofire. She will tell you that Miss Chambliss called her a "dumb Indian," and that's why she quit school last month. I don't need to tell you how that made her and the rest of the Cherokee students feel, even those of us who have just a drop like me.

Mr. Maxwell frowned for a minute but quickly resumed his wooden expression. "It seems I will need to check into these matters further. But, Mister Stone, there is still no excuse for you making a scene in the classroom and inciting others to join you in leaving there."

Athaliah quickly offered a defense. "Ross didn't incite any of us. We have been talkin' about doin' somethin' for weeks. We all left on our own."

Mr. Maxwell showed his first sign of anger. He gritted his teeth and gave Athaliah a stern look. "*Doing* something? Are you saying that what happened today was part of a plot to disrupt the classroom? Because if you are, young lady, you may all find yourselves in serious trouble."

Athaliah turned so pale that her numerous freckles disappeared, and Ross took over the defense. "No, nothin' like that. What happened today was sorta an accident. Everybody was just gettin' tired of bein' treated so bad."

"How about your actions today, Mister Stone? What do you have to say about them?"

"Well, I guess I should have held my temper, but it's hard to stand by when a girl is bein' mistreated."

"Hmmm, yet you didn't get upset when Annie Nofire was allegedly called names."

Ross looked down at his hands for a long time and didn't speak. Finally, he spoke in a low, halting voice. "And I feel shame that I didn't, especially when she talked about dumb Indians. My family's Cherokee, and we been in this country since the Trail of Tears. So has the Nofires. I should have spoke up right then, and when I got home, I should have told Pa what was goin' on."

Mr. Maxwell looked away for a moment, cleared his throat, and dismissed them. "Go to your last class and offer your teachers your apologies for being late. If they ask you why, tell them you were with me. This is not over yet. You may be called back in later today or tomorrow."

As they walked away, Bonita heard him talking to his secretary. "Tell Miss Chambliss that I must speak to her before she leaves today."

Before they separated to go to their different classes, Bonita to algebra and Ross to American history, Ross whispered something in her ear. "Meet me at the front door after school. I got somethin' important I want to show you."

Bonita nodded her assent and went on to her last class. Mr. Strickland didn't ask Bonita why she was late, but he frowned at the students who clapped for her when she walked through the door. "No foolishness, class. We have a lot to cover before the bell rings."

As the dismissal bell rang, Bonita found herself surrounded by a dozen or more members of her class. She shook off their complimentary words with, "I really didn't do anything. It was all Ross and Athaliah."

Ross soon showed-up, took her arm, and ushered her away. "Come on, Bonita. Let's leave before Maxwell makes us talk to him some more."

WHEN THEY WERE out of sight of the school, Ross stepped off the dirt road that most of the students were taking to get home. He pulled her into the woods and clasped her to his chest, bending down to kiss her passionately.

When she finally was able to push him away, he put his thumb under her chin and tilted her head upward so she was looking into his dancing, black eyes. "Bonita, when Chambliss was bein' so mean to you today, it just made me realize how much I love you. That's why I knew it was time to trust you with my secret."

She knew what he expected her to say, but she couldn't. She really liked Ross, and she loved being protected by him. But she didn't love him, so she said nothing. She just smiled, brought his fingers to her mouth, and kissed them.

This seemed to satisfy him, and he gave her a quick hug. "You'll always be my girl, Bonita. Now follow me."

ROSS LED HER through the dark woods for some time until they came to the opening of a small cave. He brought out a flashlight, which he had hidden in a tree knothole that blocked the entrance. "Come on. We just need to walk a little ways in."

She held back. "I don't like the dark, Ross. You never know what might be waitin' for you in it."

"The only thing waitin' for you is somethin' good. Now, come on, just hold on tight to my hand."

"Promise you won't let go?"

"Never."

Bonita almost asked him if he still had feeling in his fingers after being in the dark cave for a few minutes. She was holding his hand in an iron grip, but he never complained.

After what seemed like an eternity, they stopped walking. "Sit over there on that ledge, and I'll show you my treasure."

The light moved away from her, and she shivered. "Hurry up, Ross."

Suddenly the light and Ross appeared at her side. "Here you go, sweetheart. A beautiful ring for a beautiful girl." He placed a shiny gold band on her finger.

"Is this what I think it is?"

"It is if you think it is a weddin' ring. You see me and you ain't goin' back to that school. We're goin over to Arkansas to get married."

"But I'm barely sixteen, and you're not seventeen yet. We ain't old enough to get married."

"We could pass for eighteen, and besides, I know a place in Arkansas where they don't ask to see proof of age."

He handed her a small, heavy wooden box. "Open it."

She complied and gazed at a box full of silver dollars. "Where did you get these?"

"Found them. I been savin' them."

"You didn't steal them, did you?"

Although she couldn't see him clearly, she knew he was frowning.

"I did not. When Grandpa Clay passed away a while back, Ma told me to move his clothes out of the room where he had been stayin'. When I did, I found a small trunk underneath some old blankets in the closet. When I went through the trunk, I found that box with the silver dollars in it. I have been hangin' on to the money all this time, except for the money I spent on your ring a few weeks ago. Now I'm goin' to spend the rest on a new life. If we hurry, me and you can walk to Stilwell and catch the last train to Hot Springs. When we get there, we'll rent us a room and get married tomorrow. Then we'll look for a little house to live in, find us some jobs, and live happily ever after, like them old stories say."

"So, you want to honeymoon before we get married?"

"Nothin' wrong with that. We'll be lawfully married before tomorrow ends."

She ran her fingers over his handsome, smiling face and almost lost herself in his bottomless dark eyes. She backed away a few inches to gather her thoughts before she spoke. "Ross, you mean the world to me, and I will always be grateful for the way you have helped me."

"And you mean the world to me, too, sweetheart, and I can't wait to marry you. If we had the time, we could act like man and wife right now, but we gotta go if we want to catch the train."

"Wait a minute. I haven't said that I would marry you yet."

"But you have to marry me. You don't have anyone else to take care of you. Don't you see this is your only chance? You're always talkin' about gettin' away from your pa. If you marry me, I will take you away from this little dung heap. We'll make good lives for ourselves in Hot Springs, and you'll never have to take care of a sick, old man again or put up with your useless brother. I'm offerin' you a way out and a way to be happy."

Bonita sighed and shook her head. "I might marry you someday, but not this way. I don't want to run off like we have somethin' to hide. I want to get married in church, proper like."

His velvet voice turned into a snarl. "Well, you're makin' a big mistake, turnin' me down. Don't expect me just to wait around for you, twiddlin' my thumbs."

"Here's your ring back, Ross. Please don't be mad. I still care a lot about you."

He snatched the ring from her palm, wrapped it in some brown paper, and put it in the box with the silver dollars. He grabbed her hand and rushed her out of the cave. He never said another word until they passed through the entrance.

When he finally spoke, she cringed at his harsh tone. "Go on then. Since you won't be my wife, I need to hide everythin' in different places. Can't trust you not to come back and steal it."

She cried as she walked to her granny's house. What had started out as a beautiful day had ended in despair. Maybe she should have run away with Ross. She may have missed her only chance for happiness, but she remembered his drinking and dried her tears.

ON THE FOLLOWING Monday, Bonita walked to school alone. She was soon joined by her crowd of friends. When Athaliah greeted her, she took her elbow and drew Bonita aside.

"What's wrong? Where's Ross?"

"I don't know. We had a big fight."

"Well, at least the fight didn't keep him from talkin' to his dad. Miss Chambliss is gone, and the secretary, Miss Hawkins, will teach her classes until the end of the year."

Bonita sighed and mumbled, "That's good."

Athaliah grabbed her shoulder and gave her a little shake. "It's more than good. It's absolutely wonderful. Come on, Bonita, don't let a fuss with your boyfriend get your goat. Did you know that Annie Nofire is back at school, and it's all because of you? Now, give me a smile."

She manufactured a quick, small smile that didn't quite reach her eyes. "I'm glad to hear that."

AS THE SCHOOL year went on, she developed a new routine. After getting ready for school each morning and eating breakfast, she fed the chickens and milked the cow for Granny. Following that, she walked through the woods and down the rough dirt road to Jubilee School, timing it so that she always arrived less than five minutes before school started. If she got there too early, there was a chance she would see Ross dancing with his new girlfriend, Belle Springwater, entertaining the other students just like she and Ross had done in the past. If he and Belle weren't dancing, they were kissing and hugging behind the building in a spot the teachers couldn't see them.

Bonita tried to ignore any place where Ross and Belle might be because if he noticed her, he stared at her until he caught her eye. His bright smile immediately turned into a mean smirk. As he had always done, Ross missed a lot of school but seldom got in trouble for being truant.

Despite her hope that she was free from Ross's interest, Bonita worried that he wouldn't let her go.

II
CLAY
& ROSS

CLAY STARTED AT the sound of Emily's voice invading his sleep. He disentangled himself from his covers, sat up on the bed, and motioned for Emily to sit beside him. "What are you doin' in here?"

Her hands were shaking as she struggled to control her voice. "Stay out of sight, guys. Ma's on the warpath again, and Lord knows what she will do."

Ross, who was nursing a hangover from the night before, just pulled the covers over his head.

Clay rubbed the sleep from his eyes. "What happened now?"

"Pa's in bad trouble."

Ross mumbled something.

Emily reached over and pulled the covers off of him. "I can't hear you under those covers. What are you sayin?"

He covered his eyes. "Ow. That light makes my head hurt. I was wonderin' what Pa has done to make her mad."

Clay grabbed his arm and pulled. "Quit bein' a baby and get up."

Ross cussed under his breath, sat up on the edge of his bed, and rubbed his eyes. "So, what has Pa done now? She seldom gets mad at him."

Emily's dark eyes were huge behind her glasses. "I think she caught him cheating on her."

Both boys sat motionless in shocked silence.

Clay shook his head. "I don't believe it. Pa would never do such a thing."

Ross chuckled. "It don't surprise me none. Ain't you ever wondered why Pa makes so many trips to Sallisaw?"

"He's goin' to the horse races. Me and you have been with him plenty of times."

Ross smirked. "Come on, Clay. He's been goin' by himself since Ma turned up pregnant again. Ain't you noticed?"

"Can't say I have, but what of it?"

"Well, I followed him last week, and he went into that café where we always eat when we are with him. This time, though, he didn't eat. He just met that blonde waitress that he always talks to, and they walked on over to her house. I hid in the bushes and drank while he visited her. When he came out, he was zippin' up his britches."

Emily made a gagging sound. "I would never've thought that of Pa."

Clay patted her on the shoulder. "Neither would I."

Ross huffed. "You two don't know nothin' about the way the world works. Ma's six months pregnant, and she ain't open for business right now, but his woman in Sallisaw is."

Emily shuddered and gagged again. "You can be so crude, Ross."

"Maybe so, but I don't cover my eyes when things happen like you do."

Their conversation was interrupted by a gunshot in the kitchen. Clay jumped up in alarm. "Come on, we gotta see what's goin' on."

When they came into the kitchen, his mother faced his father with a pistol pointed at his chest. A new hole above the stove testified that she had missed.

His father was cowering at her feet. "Don't shoot me, Amelia. I'm sorry. It won't happen again."

His mother's eyes were pitiless and as black as coal. "You're right. It won't happen again because you'll be dead."

Clay slipped up behind his mother and grabbed the pistol. Amelia fought him, but he was able to wrest it from her hands.

She beat on him with her fists. "Should have stayed out of it, Clay."

In tears, Emily ran to her mother. "Ma, Clay had to stop you. He couldn't let you kill Pa. You don't want to go to prison, do you?"

Amelia collapsed, sobbing, into a heap on the floor. Their pale father stood up and faced his three children. "I'll go live with my folks until things settle down. I'm sorry this happened."

Ross's eyes were as black as his mother's. "You should be."

Michael grabbed his coat from a hook on the wall and slunk out of the kitchen like a beaten dog.

Ross turned and spoke to Mary, Zack, and Abigail, who were crying, after watching the scene. "Come on, kids. I'll fix you somethin' to eat. Emily, maybe you better put Ma to bed."

Clay went back to his bedroom and hid the pistol behind some old quilts in the closet.

Emily joined him there in a few minutes. "Ma's in bed, but she's not asleep. She wouldn't let me stay and comfort her. I was wondering about something. How do you think Ma found out?"

"Ross probably told her."

"Why would he do that? He should've realized it'd break her heart."

"It probably slipped out when he came in half-drunk this mornin'."

"That makes sense. What are we goin to do now?"

"Just wait until Ma wakes up and see which way the wind blows."

ROSS VOLUNTEERED TO stay home with his mother and Abigail. Everyone else went to school.

Abigail, a quiet, dainty little girl, looked up at her big brother with tears in her amber eyes. "Is Ma sick?"

"No, just really tired. Just be extra quiet all right? I'll lay right here on this divan so I can hear Ma when she wakes up. Can you just play quiet by yourself?"

"That's what I always do." Abigail went back into the girls' bedroom likely to play with her dolls like usual.

Ross realized this was the longest conversation he had ever had with his youngest sister. She was a pretty little thing but a bit frail. Abigail would probably do well in school when she finally started next year and would be the smartest one in her class, just like Emily.

He closed his eyes for a minute, and the next thing he knew his mother was saying his name. "Ross, wake up. I fried up some sweet potatoes for you and Abby and warmed up some pinto beans and corn bread. "

"All right, Ma." Ross looked at his mother's swollen, red eyes. "How are you doin'?"

She turned away from him. "I'm fine. Sit at the table. I got some things I want to talk to you about while we're eating."

Ross's growling stomach reminded him he had slept for four hours and was starving. He gobbled down several spoonful. "This is sure good, Ma. I didn't know how hungry I was."

"Eat all you want. Abby and I never eat very much in the middle of the day. I am going to need your help to move us."

"Move? Why do you want to move?"

"This is your pa's house, and I want no part of it. We are going to move to your uncle John's old house."

"Will that be all right with Uncle John?"

"He shouldn't mind. He moved his family out of there last year. We will start packing tonight when the kids get home from school. Everybody will stay home from school tomorrow, and we'll finish up. With any luck, we'll be at our new place by tomorrow evening."

"All right if that's what you want to do."

Amelia leaned over and gently pushed his hair out of his eyes. "You need to let me trim that for you, son. Thank you. I knew I could count on you."

When Ross told Emily and Clay about their mother's plans, Emily sputtered out her indignation. "Why are we moving way out there? We'll have to get up at dawn to get to school on time."

Clay frowned as if perplexed. "Why is Ma set on movin'? This house is a lot bigger and in a lot better shape."

Ross shrugged his shoulders. "All I know is Ma says she don't want no part of Pa's house."

Emily fumed. "That's her foolish pride talking."

"Well, I don't think she'll take that from you or Clay."

Clay's eyes cut over to Ross. "Maybe you can talk sense into her."

"Nah. It don't matter nohow. I would just as soon live there as live here. Livin' a long ways from the school just gives me a better excuse for missin' it."

Amelia burst into their room like a whirlwind. "Time to get to work. Boys, go out to the shed and get those big boxes I have been keeping and bring them up into the house. "

"Emily, I need you to start going through the girls' room and separating everything into two piles, what we should keep and what we will throw away."

Clay gaped at Ma. "Ain't we goin to have supper first?"

His mother almost snarled at him. "I should have known all you would be thinking about is your own stomach. We will have a late supper tonight. I want to see what we can get done before it gets dark."

Clay's stomach was growling loudly, but Ross and Emily kept quiet.

Young Zack didn't know better. "I'm so hungry. When are we goin' to eat?"

Emily put a finger to her lips and quietly handed him and Abigail some cold, leftover biscuits. They stuffed them in their mouths and left to sort through their belongings.

When it was almost dark, their mother brought out a kerosene lamp and placed it on the kitchen table. "Come on, kids, wash your hands and come and eat." She placed a large platter of fried eggs, cold ham, and biscuits in the center of the table, along with a pitcher of fresh milk and a quart of apple preserves. Everyone fell in and filled their plates and glasses.

Ross looked over and saw that Amelia was slowly consuming some milk and one cold biscuit. "Ain't you hungry, Ma?"

"No, not really." She stood up and directed her attention to her oldest son.

"Clay, I'll need you to get up extra early in the morning and take care of the stock. We can't take them with us this trip, and I don't want them to suffer until we can get back over here to get them. We'll finish packing and load up the wagon with the necessities and the extras we can carry. I think if we work hard, we can get loaded up and out of here by noon. All right, kids, clean up the kitchen and make sure the little ones get to bed. That's where I'm going now. My feet are swollen, and I need some rest."

After she had walked away, Emily shook her head. "Poor Ma. She looks all worn out."

Clay smirked. "She'll wear us all out before tomorrow is over."

Ross stood up. "Well, I can't help leavin' good company, but I got a bottle of shine that's got to be finished before I go to sleep."

Emily gave him a sour look. "How about a little help?"

"Oh, you got plenty of help. Clay and Mary are good hands." Ross left the table and went outside.

A HALF-ASLEEP Clay heard his mother knocking at the door at daylight. "Get up, boys. We got a lot to do today."

Clay groaned and sat up in bed. He looked over at Ross's bed. It was empty.

Amelia knocked harder the second time. "Are you coming out, or do I need to come and wake you up?"

Still half-asleep, Clay got up and partially opened the door. "I'll be out in a minute."

"Where's Ross?"

"I don't know. Guess he never came to bed."

After most of the heavy work was done, Ross showed-up, smelling of whiskey and cigarettes.

Clay waited to hear harsh words from his mother, but she just gave a sigh of relief. "Thank goodness, you're here, Ross. I was getting worried about you."

When he was sure his mother was out of earshot, Clay rounded on Ross. "It's about time you got here. Me and the girls about dropped the cook stove tryin' to get it out to the wagon."

"All right. All right. I'm here now. What do you want me to do?"

A FEW HOURS later, Ross looked around the table at his exhausted looking siblings, "Well, there's nothin' left to eat, so I guess we better pack up this old table and get on our way."

When they arrived, they began unloading the wagon. Ross noted there were only two bedrooms in the dusty, little cabin. "It's so cramped in here, and we don't need all this furniture. What do you want me to do with it, Ma?"

"Just leave the extra in the wagon for now. Just set-up my bed and Emily's bed for the girls and the young ones to sleep on in the bigger bedroom. You can set up two beds for you boys in the second bedroom. Get the table and chairs out so we'll have a place to eat, and you can leave the rest for tomorrow. We'll finish unpacking and clean this place up tomorrow."

By the time they had obeyed her commands and had eaten some biscuits and cold ham, they all fell into bed, even Ross.

Ross had been asleep for only a few hours when a flashlight in his eyes woke him. A trembling Emily stood over him with the flashlight, and Mary cowered behind her, chin quivering and tears streaming down her cheeks. Clay slept on, oblivious to the girls' interruption.

Emily shook Ross's shoulder. "Wake-up. Can't you hear that?"

Ross cursed and grumbled. "Hear what? I don't hear nothin'."

"Hush. Be quiet and listen."

Clay sat up. "I hear a kid cryin'. Probably Abby."

"It's not Abby. That's the sound of a little baby, not a seven-year-old. Besides I checked on her, and she's sound asleep. So is Zack."

Mary finally stopped sobbing long enough to speak. "What is it, a ghost?"

Ross sighed. "Remember I told you there ain't no such thing? Give me that flashlight. Clay, grab that one on the dresser. We'll go check what's goin' on. Hurry up and get some clothes on."

THE SOFT CRYING continued as Ross went outside with Clay and searched the grounds. He shone his light under the house.

Ross yelled and jumped back, dropping his flashlight. Clay ran up to him, frantic. "What's wrong? What did you see?"

Ross's voice shook as he picked up his flashlight. "Swear to God, Clay. There's a little man under the house."

"A man? You wait here, and make sure he stays. I'll go get my gun."

After Clay left, the crying stopped. A masculine voice spoke in Cherokee. "I'm coming out now that I got your attention."

Ross gasped as a three-foot Cherokee man, dressed in a small hunting jacket and trousers that were made from some kind of animal hide, crawled out from under the house. "Why are you so afraid? You're Cherokee and should know about the Little People. I am one of them, and I was sent to give you a warning."

Ross closed his eyes and opened them again, surprised to see the little man was still there. "All right then. Grandpa Sam told me Granny Bluebird believed in Little People, but I thought they were just part of the old stories. What do you want to warn me about?"

"Well, I'm as real as you, but here is what I was sent to tell you. Your mother, Bluebird's great-granddaughter, has lost her baby, and she is going to die if you don't get her some help. Now, go, and tend to her, but don't tell anyone you have spoken to me."

Ross took a few steps and suddenly remembered his manners. He turned and said, "Wa-do," but the little man was gone.

He met Clay, pistol in hand, on the front porch. "You can put that away. My eyes was just playin' tricks on me. Let's go inside."

"Are you sure? I don't like the idea of a strange man hangin' around here, and what was makin' that racket?"

"Don't know, but it stopped, so let's forget about it."

"Well, I'm goin' to look around some more before I go in."

"Suit yourself."

ROSS FOUND MARY, trembling in his bed, while a tense Emily sat next to her, waiting for word. "Did the man get away? Clay came in here and got his gun."

"I think I just dreamed him up. Probably all the shine I've been drinkin' lately. Say, did you look at Ma when you checked on Abby and Zack?"

"No. Why do you ask?"

"I have a feelin' we need to see about her."

Emily shone the light first on Abby and then Zack, who were sleeping with their mother. When the light touched her mother, Emily stifled a small scream. "Ross, her side of the bed is covered with blood."

Ross knelt by his mother's side and touched her hands. "She's cold. Hurry, go tell Clay to ride to Uncle James's house and tell them to come and help with Ma. After that, he needs to ride to Doctor Jamison's house and tell him to get here—quick. Just hope he's not on a call somewhere. Mary, go find some towels and blankets. We gotta stop the bleedin'."

When Clay came back some three hours later, he had their father with him. Ross slumped in a corner of the front room, like the rest of the family, including Uncle James, who had arrived with Aunt Penelope not long after Clay had left. Emily fell into Michael's arms. "Pa, I'm so glad you came. Doctor Jamison says it's touch and go, and I'm scared to death."

The younger children ran to join her, all pressing their way to their father's arms. Clay stood close by but didn't touch Michael. Ross remained in his seat, too exhausted to get up, and watched the scene. Uncle James stayed in his chair as well, looking off into space.

An angry Aunt Penelope came from Amelia's bedside. "I don't know if Amelia wants to see you or not from what Ross told us."

Emily looked up from her father's embrace. "Well, I'm happy to see him, and I think Ma will be too when she comes out of this." She burst into tears. "If she comes out of this."

Michael handed her a handkerchief and hugged her. "Your mother is the strongest woman I know. She'll be all right."

Ross watched as Michael stumbled away to his mother's bedroom. He moved like a man who was in shock.

Penelope stood up and walked over to where Ross sat. "We're going home now, but you get us word if there's any change, all right?"

Ross stood up and hugged her. "Thanks, Aunt Penelope."

He turned to James. "Uncle James, could I catch a ride with you to the store? I need to stop by and tell Susan and Grandpa and Grandma about Ma."

James favored Ross with a rare smile. "Sure you can."

Ross turned to Clay. "I'll be back soon."

SOON AFTER THEY left, the sober-looking physician, carrying a small bundle, came out and spoke to Clay. "Here's the poor baby. It was a boy. Your pa said to bury him under the big oak tree. I believe your mother will live, mostly due to Penelope, who got the bleeding stopped before I got here. I gave your mother some medicine to fight infection and bring down the fever. What she really needs, though, is some blood to replace what she has lost and some good bed rest. Your father needs you to get a wagon ready so she can be taken to Hastings Hospital in Tahlequah."

After Clay took the baby outside, he couldn't resist looking at it. He pulled the blanket back and stared at his tiny, shriveled-up baby brother. Something was familiar about the high cheekbones and broad nose. It came to him that he was looking at his mother's face. If this child had been born, he would have looked just like her.

AMELIA WOKE UP to find herself in WW Hastings Indian Hospital in Tahlequah. By her side was her husband Michael, nodding off in sleep. How did she come to be in Hastings, and what was Michael doing here? The last thing she remembered was going to sleep with Zack and Abby in her brother John's old house. She ran her hands over her body, discovering her flat stomach. Feeling a moment of sadness for the loss of her baby, she looked over at the man who had helped her make another tiny life. A mixture of relief and guilt filled her soul. She hadn't wanted another baby, but she knew that she would have loved it like the others if she had carried it to term. Amelia was weak, and she needed to stay with Michael for now. But she resolved in her heart that things were going to be different in the future, and she would never be vulnerable and powerless again.

When she came home, she was much thinner and seemed to have lost a lot of her stamina. While she was gone, Michael and their children moved everything back into their old house, which greatly pleased their children. Sometimes when the talk turned to strange or scary stories, Emily or Mary would tell a story of a mysterious crying baby the night Amelia had miscarried.

One morning a couple of weeks later, Amelia caught Michael sitting in the front room by himself. As she walked into the room, he put out his hand to steady her. "Are you feelin' up to walkin' about?"

"I can manage. We need to talk." She sat down beside him on the sofa.

"Sure. What about?"

"We need to have a new understanding."

Michael frowned at her as if puzzled. "What do you mean?"

"I won't stand for being treated the way you've always treated me."

He blushed. "I—I promise I won't see any more women."

Amelia almost laughed when she saw his startled face. "Well, I hope you don't, but that's not really what I want to talk to you about."

"Then what?"

"I want to talk to you about the family business."

"You mean the store?"

"Yes. When your dad passes, the store will go to you, and I know you have no real interest in it."

"Susan and Tom can keep runnin' it as far as I'm concerned."

"That's fine with me too for now."

"What do you mean for now?"

"The time is fast approaching when country stores will have to close because everyone'll drive to town to buy their groceries. When the time is right, I want to sell it at a profit and open a store in Stilwell."

"In other words, you want to make the business decisions?"

"Yes, I do. If I lose money doing it, you're welcome to take the reins back."

Michael paused for a moment and then nodded. "Consider it done. 'Course I'll still need money to keep up the place and maybe buy a horse now and then."

Amelia took his hand and shook it. "Deal. And one other thing?"

"What's that, darlin'?"

"You'll never go to Sallisaw by yourself again."

He touched her cheek. "Done."

IT WAS LATE spring. The day was humid, and Bonita was feeling thirsty. She remembered her granny had given her some change from the last time they had sold eggs to the Stones. She stopped for a quick detour at the store to buy a soda pop.

When she approached the store, she noticed a haggard, middle-aged woman sitting on a bench on the front porch. When the woman raised her head, she recognized her. It was Amelia Stone, looking like a walking skeleton.

She recalled someone had requested prayer for Amelia Stone at church one Sunday. When she asked her granny about it, Della had said, "She lost a baby and a lot of blood. For a while, they didn't know if she wasn't going to make it or not, but they say she should be home from the hospital soon."

Bonita was shocked. "Isn't she a granny? Why would a granny want to have a baby?"

Grandma just shook her head and sighed. "You just don't understand, girl. Sometimes the babies come whether you want them or not. I had my last baby when I was forty-five-years-old. All of my kids were grown and out of the house, except for Ella, who was eight, and here comes another little one, your uncle Sean."

That's why Amelia looked so hollow-eyed and bony. "Hello, Mrs. Stone." Bonita started to open the screen door to the store.

Amelia put out her hand to stop her. "Wait a minute. You're Anderson McKindle's daughter, aren't you?"

"Yes, ma'am. I am Bonita McKindle."

"All right, girl. Come over to the picnic table. I need to have a talk with you."

Bonita hesitated, and Amelia grabbed her by her left elbow and pulled her down the steps in the direction of the old, weathered picnic table that Josh provided for his customers. Something started churning in her stomach. What did Ross's stern looking mother want to talk to her about?

"Sit down, girl, and listen. Now, let me say first that I don't have anything against your father. He has always been my friend, but I can't go on ignoring what your influence is doing to Ross."

"I'm sorry, ma'am, but I don't know what you're talkin' about."

Amelia frowned and bent down so that her glittering black eyes were peering directly into Bonita's frightened brown ones. "Don't lie to me, girl. I know you have been pulling Ross away from school almost every day. It might not matter to your father, but I want all of my children to finish school and get diplomas."

Bonita swallowed twice and finally spoke in a voice that was almost a whisper, "Ross used to stay at my house some to help me take care of Pa, but I never asked him to. He's not doin' that now, though, because he's mad at me."

Amelia shook her head and squeezed Bonita's elbow hard. "I don't believe you. The principal tells me that Ross only comes to school two days out of five, and he has been seen walking through the woods with his girlfriend."

She struggled to get away, but Amelia had an iron grip on her elbow. "Let me go. You're hurtin' me. I'm not Ross's girlfriend anymore. Belle Springwater is."

Amelia stared at her a few more minutes and suddenly released her hold. "You better be telling me the truth. Go on about your business. I need to find that Springwater girl."

She walked to the store's front porch and stood, watching Amelia, who, with some difficulty, climbed into the family's old Ford truck and drove away.

Her hands were shaking, and even though her thirst wasn't quenched, she walked home.

She thought about her encounter with Amelia on the way home. Ross has a scary ma. Sure, she missed having Ross by her side, but she was glad she wasn't Belle Springwater right now. Amelia Stone was bound to make someone else pay for Ross's bad behavior. Who needed a boyfriend who might get you beat up? She resolved to forget about boys and study hard so she could graduate from high school. If she got lonesome, she would just attend church more and go to every social event her community offered.

III
BONITA
& BOB

FOR SOME TIME, Bonita had been visiting her father on Saturdays and taking care of him all day to give Sophie, Arthur, and their kids a break. She planned on getting up early the next day, which was Saturday, and spending the day with her father. Most Saturdays she could count on seeing Bob.

Bob Smith, the son of a former drinking buddy of her father, was a frequent visitor. He came three or four days a week and often brought venison, skinned squirrels, or just a rabbit he had shot in the woods.

While Bonita busied herself with preparing the food in a way her father could tolerate, Bob would keep Anderson occupied by telling him all of the latest news. He would usually stay until Bonita had the meal cooked, eat with them, and go home. He treated Bonita with the utmost courtesy, always arriving sober and clean, and sometimes even carrying a small gift for her.

Anderson viewed these proceedings with unhidden glee. "It's about time you opened your eyes and seen what kind of man Bob is."

"I will admit he is a better man than I thought he was, Pa. He's the only one of your friends who has stuck by us, but he is nearly forty-years-old. Besides, I'm too young to get married."

"I was several years older than your mother, and we was happy."

"Well, I still don't want to get married. I like my life pretty much the way it is. I just want to finish school and get a good payin' job someday."

She finished her sophomore year feeling hopeful about her future until she found a letter addressed to Uncle Arthur in the mailbox.

Arthur nearly snatched the letter from her hand when he saw it. He skimmed over it, chuckled, and handed it to Sophie to read. Sophie read it and gave a big whoop, startling Anderson into a quick state of wakefulness.

He looked at Bonita with fearful eyes. "What's happened?"

Arthur laughed and patted Anderson on the arm. "Nothin' bad. Somethin' good for a change. Looks like me and my family will be travelin' back to California. My last boss, Mister Carter, wants to hire me as the new foreman of his place in Fresno. It will be good to have a steady livin' again."

Anderson's eyes didn't lose their scared look. "If you go back to California, who's gonna take care of me?"

"Now, sir, don't you worry. We'll figure things out before we go."

Bonita's heart sank. She knew who would take care of Anderson.

SOME THREE MONTHS later, on a chilly September morning, she was startled to wakefulness by the bright sunshine that pierced the frosted windows and danced across the bare, pine floor. She hadn't slept this late in over three months, ever since she had started taking care of Pa again. Oh, God. What did the awful stillness in the front room mean? She had become so accustomed to the heavy breathing and hacking cough that she instantly knew something was wrong. Could he have passed away, all alone?

She didn't even bother to put on the quilted housecoat Grandma had made her for her sixteenth birthday. She ran barefooted into the front room as fast as she could.

She blinked her eyes in disbelief. She must still be asleep and dreaming in her little iron bed. No, it was true. There was Pa, looking pale but ablebodied and clothed in his patched overalls and red flannel shirt, sitting on their old, faded brown sofa, smiling and staring dreamily into space.

"Pa, what are you doin' up? You go right back to bed this instant. You'll catch your death." She covered her mouth when she realized what she had said.

But he only laughed and made a joke. "No, darlin', I done that some time ago."

"I'm sorry, Pa. I didn't mean anything by it. But how did you get up and dressed?"

"It's easy to explain that. While you was lazin' in bed, I had some company to help me."

"Who? Bob? But he was only here yesterday. He seldom comes two days in a row."

"No, 'twasn't Bob."

"Sid, then?"

"No, I fear Sid has left the country, but we'll hear from him by and by but not today."

She let out a long, pent-up sigh. "Stop makin' me guess. Who's been to see you?"

He chuckled. "Oh, come now, gal, can't a father do a little foolin' on his daughter's birthday?"

She smiled and slowly shook her head. "Sometimes you can sure surprise me. I didn't think you even knew when my birthday was. You're right. It's September 13, my seventeenth birthday. I can't believe I completely forgot it. Tell you what. I'll fix us up a special dinner today. It might not be fancy, but since you're feelin' like eatin', I'm feelin' like cookin'."

"Don't you want to know who I seen?"

"Yes, but you won't tell me."

"All right. Guess it will just be my little secret. Make me some coffee, won't you?"

She placed her hands over her father's arms and squatted down until she was looking him directly in his twinkling, blue eyes. "First, tell me who."

"All right, all right. Your uncle Arthur's back from California to visit. He says that his wife, what's her name again?"

"Sadie."

"That's it, Sadie. Anyways, Sadie and your granny, them two women, commenced cookin' almost as soon as they got to Della's house yesterday. They're goin' to bring us your birthday dinner, here at the house about noon. Arthur told me all about it when he was helpin' me get my clothes on."

"What? You mean we're havin' real company and you let me sleep until nearly eight o'clock? My lands, Pa. How will I ever get this house ready for company? I gotta sweep and dust and scrub the floors. I better fix myself a sleepin' place off of the kitchen again so our company can sleep in my room."

His face fell. "I thought you would be happy."

"I am happy. I love to hear Uncle Arthur talk about how they've been doin' since they moved back to California, and I can't wait to see him and his family. It's just I got a lot to do. What kind of pies do you think I should make?"

"How about that fancy coconut pie you made for my last birthday?"

"Yeah, I could make a coconut and maybe a chocolate meringue pie, but I don't have coconut or cocoa."

He reached into the wallet in his overalls and pulled out a wad of bills. "Here, take some money and buy what you need at the store. See if you can buy some small presents for yourself and everyone. We'll call it a mix of birthday and early Christmas."

"Thanks, Pa. That's real generous of you." She leaned over and placed an uncustomary kiss on her father's cheek.

He turned bright red. "Go along with you, you silly girl. You got to hurry if you're goin' to be ready by noon."

She rushed over to the Stone store, at first fighting the brisk fall wind that pierced her thin cotton coat and brought new color to her sun-starved skin. But it had been so long since she had been away from her house that she eventually welcomed the wind as an ally to speed her on her way. She almost ran the last mile to the store out of sheer exhilaration.

When she opened the door, she set off a cheery sound of tinkling bells, and her ears caught the sound of a familiar voice. "Hey, Clay, here's another pretty girl that our mistletoe caught."

Ross took her breath away as he caught her in his arms and gave her a sound kissing. She stepped back and looked at him. "Ross, I thought you was mad at me and was fixin' to get married."

"Bonita, you was my first girl, and I could never stay mad at you. Anytime you want to take up where we left off, I'll welcome you back."

"What about Belle? She's tellin' ever'body you're gettin' married."

"Maybe we will, and maybe we won't. But if you'll come back to me, we can get married tomorrow." He grabbed her and attempted to kiss her again, but she pushed him away.

Josh came around the corner and saw what Ross was doing. "Ross, if you're going to manhandle all my customers like that, I'll soon be out of business. Now, let that girl go. Sorry, Bonita, these fools put that mistletoe up three months early."

"Ah, Grandpa, I don't bother all of your customers, just the pretty ones. You're not mad, are you, Bonita?"

"No, I guess not, but don't do it again. It's not fair to Belle."

A flash of anger crossed Ross's face. "Maybe you'd rather kiss Clay."

He quickly twirled her into his brother's arms, but Clay turned red and immediately released her. "Sorry, Bonita. Ross, I'm goin' to kill you."

"Now, why would you want to do that, Brother? You know you've been hankerin' after her for a long time. I just done you a favor."

Clay blushed even more and stammered. "Wait until I get my hands on you."

"You'll have to catch me first." He ran out the door with Clay close on his heels.

Bonita wasn't sure what had gotten into Ross, but she straightened her skirt and turned to Josh. "Do you think they'll hurt each other?"

When she didn't get a response, she looked over to where Josh sat on a stool behind the counter. The old man was nodding off. He suddenly jerked awake and looked at her. "Sorry. I didn't hear you. What did you say?"

"That's all right. Do you think they'll hurt each other?"

"Nah, they've been doin' this all their lives. They hardly ever do any real damage. Now what can I do for you, Miss Bonita?"

"I need some bakin' goods and other things. Do you have any coconut and cocoa? Oh, and I want to look around for a birthday present for myself and presents for our company that's comin' for dinner."

"Well, happy birthday, young lady, and yes, I have coconut and cocoa both, right there on the shelf in front of you. Look all you want. With more and more folks goin' in to Stilwell, or Tahlequah to buy groceries, I've got a lot to choose from right now."

She finally decided on a bean flip for Paul, a baby doll for Betty Sue, some chocolate drops for both kids, some red gingham material for Sadie, a fancy, rose-colored hairbrush for Grandma, some cherry-smelling tobacco for Arthur's pipe, and an imitation leather Bible for her father, who had been wishing for a smaller Bible to lay beside him because he said, "that family Bible takes up too much room."

She didn't think her father could read well enough to really understand what the Bible passages meant, but he seemed to get a sense of security by just having it by him. Her final selection was a bottle of nice perfume for herself. Now time to look at the baking supplies.

By the time she had finished with her shopping, the two rowdy youths were back.

"Happy birthday." Josh called out as she was leaving.

Clay opened the door for her. "Happy birthday, Bonita. Do you want me to carry your groceries home for you?"

"No, thanks, Clay. I can manage."

Ross followed her out the door and whispered in her ear. "Happy birthday, Bonita. You know I meant what I said about I would take you back in a minute, but I won't stand in your way if you would rather have Clay. I wanted to let you know before he leaves."

"Well, that's my decision, not yours. Where is Clay goin'? Ain't he graduatin' next May?"

"Don't you know? Clay's ridin' off to Texas. We got kinfolks down there, some of Ma's family. Some cousin's got a big ranch down there, not far from the Palo Duro Canyon, and he said he would hire Clay on to work there. Though to tell the truth, I think he'll enlist in the army first chance he gets."

"I'm surprised your mother would allow him to do that."

"Oh, she threw a hissy fit about it, but Pa said that Clay is already eighteen, so there's nothin' she can do about it. 'Course Ma's not speakin' to Pa right now, but she'll get over it like she always does."

"Please tell him I wish him the best."

"I will sure do that. Goodbye, pretty lady."

"Goodbye, Ross."

As she walked home, she pondered what Ross had said. She knew Clay was attracted to her, but she never paid him much attention since she had been so mesmerized by Ross. But with Clay going so far away, there wasn't much chance of a romance anyway.

When she got home, she almost tripped over Anderson trying to sweep the floor. He had already tried to dust because her few what-nots seemed rearranged.

"What do you think you're doin'?"

"Just tryin' to help."

'You won't be any help to me if you make yourself sick before the company comes. If you want to help, why don't you sit down and try to wrap these presents up for me? She handed him all of the gifts, except his own, and some scissors, twine, and tissue paper that she had purchased.

While he clumsily wrapped the packages, Bonita scurried around, putting the house in order and baking her pies. By noon, the two lightlybrowned pies were cooling on the counter, the small house was reasonably clean, and after helping her father with shaving, she took a sponge bath and quickly dressed. She looked at herself critically in the mirror and added a little rosecolored lipstick and a small amount of the new perfume behind both ears. Not bad, but she shouldn't have wasted her money on rouge. The bottle was still almost full since she never used it. All the rushing around had given her more than enough color in her face.

She had just tied her long, chestnut mane back with a red ribbon when she heard, "Come in, come in. Hey, Bonita, they're here."

She drew back the sheet that provided a door for her room and ran smack into her uncle's embrace.

"Well, Dutchman, let me look at you." He turned her around so that she was facing her father. "Anderson, how do you manage to keep the young bucks away?"

"She keeps them away herself. Won't take up with nobody. The only one she ain't run off is Bob Smith."

Granny rolled her eyes. "And speak of the Devil."

Bonita looked up to see Bob coming in with his arms full of wood.

"Hello, ever'body. I seen the car, but I didn't know who it was. Sorry to bother you when you're havin' company. I'll just put this wood in the wood box and go on home."

Anderson waved him into the room. "Now, Bob, you know you're always welcome here. Come eat dinner with us. You know Arthur and Sadie, don't you?"

Bob hurriedly put the wood away, brushed his hands off, and vigorously pumped Arthur's hand. "It's been a long time, Arthur. Good to see you, and this is your wife?" He energetically shook Sadie's hand, as well.

"Yeah, this is my old lady, Sadie. And these are our kids, Paul and Betty Sue. We got two more older kids, but they have moved out on their own."

"Glad to meet all of you."

Sadie called out, "Pleased to meet you, too," as she hurried away to help Della in the kitchen.

"If you don't mind me askin', Arthur, why would you call a young girl, Dutchman?"

"You know, I really don't know myself. I just started callin' her that when she was a little thing. Maybe 'cause she is Black Dutch on her pa's side, along with the Irish, the French, and the Cherokee."

"Now, sir, that brings up another question I've always wondered about, what kind of people is Black Dutch?

Granny jumped into the conversation. "Bob, I think they's German, least that's what I always heard."

"Granny, Mister Strickland says that Black Dutch are really Basque." Bonita loved talking about her favorite teachers and their opinions.

Granny smirked. "Well, I know Mister Strickland can't never be wrong, but just in case, I wouldn't be so foolhardy as to call myself Black Dutch in public, leastways not now, with all the trouble overseas. Now, come on, women, we got to get this dinner on the table 'afore it's cold."

"Let me help you carry it, Mrs. O'Dell." Bob helped the women unload the heavy pots and pans of food. "My, oh, my, do I smell chicken and dumplin's?"

"You do at that. Here hand me that so I can put it on the table. You go back and get another load."

Bonita leaned over to Sadie and whispered, "Granny must really be feelin' spry as bossy as she's actin'."

"You think she's bossy now. You should've seen her yesterday and this mornin'. She had me runnin' around that kitchen like a chicken with its head cutoff."

Granny stopped her scurrying and looked at them. "What's that?"

"Nothin', Granny."

"Then quit that whisperin' and get back to work."

She giggled and gave Granny a mock salute. "Yes, sir."

"Now don't you get smart."

"Sorry, Granny."

With Della driving them on, the women had the meal on the table in a matter of minutes. It looked so mouth-watering that Bonita, along with everyone else at the table, grabbed the nearest bowl and began filling her plate. She looked over at her father, noticed his hesitation, and set the bowl back down.

"No, today we are goin' to bless our dinner first."

Bonita sat still with her mouth wide open and listened to something she had never heard before, her father praying.

"Lord, I'm sorry we don't thank ya the way we oughta. Today I just want to say thanks for all the good things you have gave us, our family and friends, and good food to eat. Forgive us sinners. Amen."

Arthur echoed his words. "Yes, forgive us sinners and amen. Why, Anderson, I never knowed you was a religious man."

"Never was 'till here lately. Seems like life is different now since I been sick. I know thangs now that I never knowed before. I use'ta think God was mad at me all the time, and that's why he took my Ella. That's why I drank all the time... to get back at him somehow. Now I know He didn't have nothin' to do with it. It just happened. Just like this TB that's killin' me. And pretty soon I'll get to see my sweet Ella, and that lets me know that He loved me all the time, but I was just too blamed blind to know it."

Granny passed the hot biscuits to Arthur, who was sitting on her right. "That's right pretty talkin', Anderson, and I'm glad you feel that way, but this food's turnin' colder by the minute. Let's eat."

They heaped their plates full of the hot, hearty food, and when they had emptied those, they filled them up again. When the men began talking about third helpings, Bonita protested. "Lord-a- mercy. How can you have room? I'm goin' to have to wait a while before I can eat any sweets."

Bob leaned over and pecked her on the cheek. "Just don't wait too long, or there won't be no sweets left."

Bonita blushed and choked on her water.

Granny leaned over and patted her on the back. "No carryin' on at the dinner table. It's bad luck."

Having recovered, Bonita defended Bob. "Oh, Granny, you think ever'thing is bad luck. Did you all know that this woman had me huntin' all day for one of our best layin' hens once, so she could chop her head off for tryin' to crow like a rooster?"

Bob asked, "Did you find her?"

"Yeah, finally."

Bob nodded his head in approval. "And it's a good thing you did, too. If you hadn't of, you would have had a death in your family."

Uncle Arthur looked up from buttering his biscuit. "Ma's right, Dutch. You don't mess around with things like that."

Bonita scoffed. "Like what?"

"You know, supernat'chral things. Why, Ab can tell you some tales that would scare the wax out of you."

"Well, I'm a bit big for Uncle Ab's booger tales. 'Sides, he just makes them up to scare little kids."

Della folded her arms and glared at Bonita. "Some of them tales come from real life, like that story about the old house where you can hear dishes rattlin'. Onc't they found bodies in that house where folks really did starve to death. So, don't be too sure, missy. Ab Seaward is a mighty strange man. Ain't nobody ever told you about him?"

"No, what's so strange about Ab? I know he's never married, but I figured that was because he is so bashful."

Della lowered her voice. "He has the sight."

Bonita frowned. "What does that mean?"

She stopped eating and looked down at her plate. "I don't like talkin' about such things. You never know what might be listenin', but I will this one time for you. When Ab was borned, his daddy was already dead. Little folks who never see their daddies sometimes are give the gift of second sight. It was 'specially strong in Ab 'cause he was born with a caul on his head."

"What's a caul?"

She gave Bonita an exasperated look and whispered, "I can't tell you that in mixed company."

Bonita knew that begging wouldn't budge Della, so she changed her question. "Oh, all right then. What's second sight?"

"That means that Ab sees things and knows things in his spirit the rest of us don't. Sometimes he knows things before they even happen."

"Like what?"

"Tell her, Anderson."

He swallowed hard, rubbed his chin, and began. "Ab could never stand to be in the same room with Ella. Whenever he seen her, he would get this real sad look in his eyes and would leave wherever she was. I kinda thought maybe he was just sweet on her himself and couldn't stand to see her with me. The mornin' you was born I was drunk and out of my head with worry over Ella. I went to the store for some tobaccy, and I saw Ab with that same skeery look on his face. I grabbed him 'afore he could leave and said, 'Lis'en, little man. I wanna know why you act so wild around me and my Ella.'"

She focused all of her attention on her father. "What did he say?"

"He begged me to let him go, of course. Said that knowin' would just make it worse. But I held on to his shirt collar until he almost lost his wind.

"Finally, he spoke. 'I could always see Death on Ella from the first time I seen her with you.'"

"What did you do then?"

"I got fightin' mad, and I asked him if he meant I was to blame for Ella bein' sick."

"What did he say?"

"He said any man who married Ella was goin' to be her death 'cause she weren't strong enough to have babies."

Anderson put his head in his hands and sobbed. Everyone looked at him and each other, but no one moved to comfort him.

Finally, Granny put a trembling, bony hand on his shoulder. "Let it be, Anderson. My girl would have never been happy if she couldn't have a husband and babies, and she was happy with you. I know 'cause she told me more than onc't. I just didn't want to hear it. That was my sin."

Bonita's words came out sad and low. "That's why you was cold toward me for so long. It was me bein' born that brought on her death."

Anderson raised his head and wiped his eyes on the white handkerchief Arthur offered. "And that's a lot of water under the bridge, and I'm right sorry I done you so wrong."

"That's all right, Pa." She walked over to Anderson's chair, threw her arms around him, and gave him a strong hug.

Della shook her head. "I swan, child. What did I just tell you about carryin' on at the dinner table?"

After dessert, consisting of coconut and chocolate pie, as well as a two-layer chocolate cake baked by Sophie, was consumed with as much appetite as the main course, the family gathered around the old potbelly stove. As Bonita sat on the divan between Bob and Arthur, she looked around at her family's happy faces. Her heart was full of love and comfort, feelings she seldom experienced. She sat close to Bob and listened as the men talked about the opportunities which awaited hardworking "Okies" in California.

Anderson looked over at Bonita and Bob. "You know this will likely be the last birthday I celebrate with you."

She had to swallow a lump in her throat before she could speak. "Hush, Pa. That ain't true."

"Now, you hush, and let me speak my piece. Sometimes a man just knows thangs. Anyways, while I'm at myself, I want ever'body to know what I want. Bob, do you want to marry Bonita?"

Bob's eyes danced. "Yes, sir, you know I do."

"Would you take good care of her?"

"The best I know how."

"That's good. Here's what I want to do. If you two marry and take care of me till I die, I'll see to it that you get the place and what little I got. It'll stake you till you get to California."

Bonita frowned at the conversational shift. "What's all this talk of dyin'?"

Della patted Bonita's hand. "Death is part of life, child. Your pa's just seein' to it that you're taken care of after he's gone."

Uncle Arthur murmured his agreement. "That's right, and I know I can get Bob on at Carter's Ranch. Maybe if I have my own kin to talk to, I won't be missin' this old place so much."

Granny huffed. "Won't be missin' your old ma, neither, I suppose."

Arthur gave Granny a reassuring pat. "Now, Ma. I'll still come by and see you when I can, and Sadie will write and let you know how we're doin'."

Bonita sat stunned, taking in every word. She realized she better say something quick, or they would have her married off without her consent.

"Hey, don't I have a say in all of this marriage business?"

Bob's face fell. "Don't you want to marry me, darlin'?"

"I don't know. Give me a little time to think about it."

Arthur laughed. "Who does she remind you of, Ma?"

Della sniffed. "Why, I'm sure I don't know what you're talkin' about."

Bob stood up and stretched. "Well, folks. I gotta get up early in the mornin' and help a feller with his plowin'. Thanks for the mighty fine meal." He drew Bonita aside and whispered in her ear. "You think on what was said here tonight, darlin', and I'll see you again soon."

"I will, Bob. Good night."

THE NEXT MORNING Bonita walked into the kitchen where Della was stirring a pan of white gravy. Sadie took some fluffy, golden biscuits out of the oven. "Good mornin'. Can I help?"

"We about got it done, but you can wake the kids up for breakfast."

"All right. Granny, maybe after breakfast we could have a talk?"

"How's about we talk while we're doin' the dishes?"

"Okay. That sure looks good. It seems like a long time since I had your good biscuits. Mine are all right, but they can't compare to yours."

Granny didn't say anything, but she grinned like she was pleased with the compliment. "Enough talk. Let's eat."

After breakfast Sadie said, "All right, kids. Come and help me tidy up the house."

While Anderson and Arthur talked, Bonita dried the plates, saucers, cups, and silverware and put them away. As Della moved on to the pots and pans, Bonita asked, "Do you really think I should get married? I'm not sure if I love Bob or not."

"Well, girl, you gotta get married sometime. A single woman can't hardly make it on her own unless she's a teacher or somethin'. At least

Bob is willin' to help you with your pa. Not every man would do that." Della paused in washing dishes and looked her in the face. "I only got one question. Does he still drink?"

"No, I haven't seen him drink in a long time."

"Well, maybe you oughta take a chance on him. Besides, your pa says he will give you all he has after he passes to help you on your way to California."

"What makes you think I want to go to California?"

"Do you think I don't see how those Cherokee eyes of yours shine ever' time someone mentions California?"

"Do I really have Cherokee eyes?"

"Yep, just like mine. You're one of the few in the family that took that after me. You took the eyes after me, but that wanderin' spirit is like Arthur. You won't be satisfied until you see new land."

"Can you blame me, Granny? The only other state I've ever been in is Arkansas, and that don't count since it's just a few miles away."

"It's a big decision, so take your time makin' it."

"Guess I'll go walkin' and do some thinkin'."

SHE PUT ON her coat and whistled for her granny's dog Buttons to accompany her. No Buttons appeared. She was just setting off when she felt a cold nose on the back of her leg. "Hey, girl. I didn't hear you come up." She stroked the collie's silky ears and laughed when the dog almost knocked her over with her wildly wagging tail.

"I'm glad to see you too. Do you want to take a walk with me?"

She looked around at the leaves of the trees that were just beginning to change and inhaled a big lungful of fresh air. She took off running with Buttons at her heels, like she did when she was a few years younger. She ran on and on until she came to her favorite place by the little branch that snaked its way through her granny's land.

She arranged herself on the big rock that she sat on every time she visited her special place. Resting her chin on her hand, she stared into the clear spring water and studied on her problems. Uncle Arthur won't be here but another few days, and then I will be on my own again, taking care of Pa. She groaned, and tears filled her eyes. I can't go back to that.

Buttons licked her hand, and she looked into the dog's warm, brown eyes. "What should I do, Buttons? If I marry Bob, I will have someone to help me, and maybe someday I can do what I always wanted to do, see all kinds of beautiful places. But, on the other hand, if I marry Bob, I will be tied to him. What if I decide I don't really love him and don't want to be married anymore? If only there was some way to get help and still get to finish school. Then maybe someday I could get a good job far away from here. Maybe I could even travel. But that's not goin' to happen unless I can figure out a way to make it happen."

The dog whined, and she stood up. "Sorry, girl. I promised you a walk, and all I'm doin' is sittin' here, worryin'. Come on. Another good run may be just what I need."

She sped off with Buttons at her heels, barking joyously. They ran on together for several minutes until she had to stop and catch her breath. "All right. That's all the runnin' I can do. Let's get back home and help Granny with the chores."

AT THE END of the day, she didn't join the others in the usual nighttime conversation in front of the wood stove. "I'm extra tired tonight. I think I'll turn in early."

Sadie snickered. "That's a good idea. When you get married, you won't have time for rest. Sleep while you can."

She tried to sleep but woke up every hour or two to ponder the decision she had to make. Finally, when the first ribbon of daylight began peeking through the kitchen window and her temporary bedroom, she gave up all notion of sleep. She threw back the warm flannel sheets and patchwork quilts and sprang from the bed. She dressed, made the bed, and sat for a while, slowly brushing the tangles out of her thick, long hair. When she heard Granny rattling pots and pans in preparation for making breakfast, she threw back the curtains and walked into the kitchen.

Granny almost dropped the cast iron skillet she was carrying to the cook stove. "Lord a mercy, girl. You liked to have scared me to death. What are you doin' up so early?"

"Couldn't sleep."

"Guess you was worried about what to do. Did you make up your mind?"

"I did."

"Well, don't keep me guessin'. What did you decide?"

She hesitated. "Sorry, but I think Bob should be the first to know."

Granny scowled and huffed. "Well, if that's the case, make yourself useful. Go check the henhouse and see if the hens laid us some eggs for breakfast."

"Sure." She walked to the henhouse with her granny's cane basket over her arm. One question kept burning through her brain and heart. Did she make the right decision?

THAT AFTERNOON, SHE heard a knock at the door. She opened the door to be greeted by Bob, standing on the front porch, with a big grin on his face and a bundle of drooping gold chrysanthemums in his arms. He leaned over and kissed her on the cheek, "Good afternoon, darlin'. Here's you some flowers that almost look as pretty as you."

"Good afternoon, Bob. Thanks for the flowers. I'll put them in a vase with water in a little bit. Won't you come in and have dinner with us?"

"I really wish't I could, but I told Moe Feathers I would help him kill hogs this evenin'. Thought we might need the extra money when we get married."

She closed the front door and motioned for Bob to sit beside her on the porch swing. "If we get married, Bob."

Like the flowers, he had brought her, Bob seemed to droop in front of her. "You mean you're thinkin' about turnin' me down?"

His heart-broken eyes touched her tender heart. "Oh, Bob, quit lookin' so sad. I'll marry you, but under my own terms."

His face shone. "Oh, Bonita, you've made me so happy. I promise you, honey, that you will never regret marryin' Bob Smith."

"Even if it may not be exactly the way that you thought it would be?"

His broad, rough hands encircled her slim waist, and he hugged her close. "All I care about is that we are getting married, honey. Go ahead and tell me what hoops you want me to jump through. I'm more than willin'."

"All right then. Quit huggin' me so I can talk."

He chuckled as he released her. "Go ahead, boss. Tell me what you want me to do."

"I'll marry you at the Baptist Church the evenin' before Uncle Arthur and his family leave for California. That way they can all be at the weddin'. You need to come up with enough money for us to spend our weddin' night at the Stilwell Hotel."

"That all sounds fine."

"Well, here's the part you might not like. I want to go back to school again. I've already missed some of my junior year, but if I work extra hard, I can catch up. You're goin' to take care of Pa all day while I'm at school. You'll cook for him, help him get dressed, and just do what he needs for you to do for him. When I get home, I'll take over."

"For how long?"

"Until I finish school. Then maybe I can get a job, and we can save up money for goin' to California."

"How about your pa? We can't very well leave him here by hisself."

"Maybe we can take him with us. We'll just have to see how things are goin' in two years. Oh, two more things."

"What's that?"

"You gotta promise you'll never get drunk again, and I want you to teach me how to drive."

He rolled his laughing, blue eyes. "I can easily keep from gettin' drunk, but that last thing might be the hardest thing you asked me to do."

"Oh, you. No, it won't. I watched Sid drive for a long time, and I'm a fast learner."

"Well, watchin' and doin' is two different things, but we'll see what we can do. Now is that all?"

"Yes, I think so."

He grabbed her hand and shook it. "All right. You got a deal. Now I better get over to Feathers's house so I can start earnin' that hotel money."

IV
THE
MARRIAGE

BONITA AND BOB were married two weeks later. Clever Della had made over Sadie's best white silk dress into a wedding gown, trimmed with lace, for Bonita. Her father, supported by Uncle Arthur, walked her down the aisle of the Jubilee Baptist Church. Their only guests were Granny, Arthur and his family, and Bob's quiet older brother, Herman, who barely said five words to Bonita.

After the short service, Anderson gave her a rare hug and stood with his hands on her shoulders, looking into her face. "You look real pretty. I only wish your ma was here to see you today."

He blinked the tears away, and she fought to keep control over her own emotions. She took a deep breath, let it out, and said, "So do I, Pa."

He wiped his eyes with the back of his hand and handed her an object wrapped in newspaper. "Here I found this the other day when I was lookin' through your mother's things. It was a weddin' gift that Amelia Stone gave us. Your ma always really liked it."

"Amelia Stone gave you a present? Now that does surprise me."

"Oh, you don't know Amelia like I do. We used to be good friends when we was both younger. Now go ahead and open it."

She unwrapped the Blue Willow sugar bowl that had once been his bank. "It's beautiful, Pa. I have always liked it, and now I will love it since I know it belonged to my ma. It's heavy too."

"Yeah, I been savin' up my change and extra bills for a while. Thought you and Bob might need it."

"Thanks, Pa." She kissed him on a blushing cheek.

"I got somethin' for you, too." Della handed Bonita a starched handkerchief with knots tied on both ends. She quickly untied the knots and unwrapped a small silver ring with an opal setting.

"That ring has been in the family for a long time. The story goes that my grandma Tooka Glory got that ring from a Scottish trader. He gave it to her to thank her for savin' the life of his little son with her Cherokee medicine."

She quickly put it on her bare ring finger. "Thanks, Granny. It just fits. But why didn't you give it to me so I could be married in it? You knew Bob couldn't afford to buy me a weddin' ring."

Granny clucked her tongue. "Girl, will you never learn? You can't wear an opal to get married in. Opals would bring bad luck to the marriage. You should put it on another finger to be safe."

"Well, bad luck or not, I'm wearin' it on my weddin' ring finger, and I won't never take it off either."

She leaned over and gave Della a big smack on the cheek. Della grabbed the handkerchief out of Bonita's hand and began rubbing it off. "Now look what you did. You got red lipstick all over my face."

"Dutchman, I feel real bad because I don't have nothin' to give you but a wish for your happiness."

"That's all I need, Uncle Arthur. That and your love."

"You'll always have that. Now let me hug you one more time because we won't be here when you get home tomorrow."

A few hours later Bonita pushed a snoring Bob off of her and climbed out of the small featherbed they had put to hard use a few minutes before. She wrapped herself up in the patchwork quilt that her grandma had sent "because hotel rooms are always cold." Granny was right again as she was about a lot of things.

Last night Granny took her aside for a talk. "Don't you be thinkin' that your weddin' night will be all happy and romantic. Just try to relax. It helps with the pain because, yes, you will be hurtin', my girl. The man enjoys the act, but a woman has to just endure it, at least at first. "

She was right about the pain, and she prayed Bob would sleep for the rest of the night. Meanwhile she could curl up like a cat on the shabby, overstuffed armchair by the bed, under Granny's comforting quilt.

TWO DAYS LATER, Bonita was back in school where she was warmly welcomed back by Athaliah and the rest of her friends. She looked around the schoolyard for her former boyfriend.

Athaliah noticed. "Are you lookin' for Ross? I thought you was a married woman."

"I was just wonderin' where he was."

"Some people say that him and Belle run off and got married."

Bonita's eyes doubled in size. "Lord, I bet Amelia Stone will snatch Belle bald-headed when she finds them."

Athaliah shook her head. "Nah, she'll just give her a tongue lashin'. She won't do nothin' physical because she could accidentally hurt her grandbaby."

"Really? You mean Ross is goin' to be a daddy?"

"That's what I heard. Bet you're glad you ain't his girlfriend now."

"You would win that bet. There's Mister Maxwell. Time to go in."

She still liked school, but shuffling school with marriage was a harder business than she thought it would be. She dealt daily with the usual tedious chores of waiting on a bedridden patient because Anderson had a relapse right after Thanksgiving and seldom left his bed. In addition, she had to face the new urgent demands of her husband. Gone were his courteous deeds of the past. She brought in all the wood now, and sometimes even had to split her own kindling. Bob mostly lay around the house, talked to Anderson, and waited on his meals and for her to come to bed.

She kept telling herself, "At least he keeps Pa company, so I can go to school and get out of the house now and then."

He helped her with the heavier chores like turning Anderson in the bed to prevent bedsores, raising him to a sitting position on the days Anderson felt like it, and giving him baths. He also continued to hunt from time to time and brought home fresh meat. She was tolerating things fairly well until the day Sid came home.

At first she didn't know the tall, thin, bearded man who knocked on the front door. Then he yelled, "Ain't you gonna let me in?"

The man who walked through the door looked older and harder. She wouldn't have known him if she hadn't recognized Sid's voice.

"What are you doin' here?"

Bob scolded her. "Now, honey, that's no way to talk to my new brother-in-law."

Sid shook Bob's offered hand and smirked. "Brother-in-law, huh? No kiddin'?"

"Yeah, your sweet sister finally talked me into marryin' her."

"I talked you into marryin' me. What do you mean by that?"

"Settle down, sis. You know she never could take a joke."

"So I found out."

Bonita's sigh came from the bottom of her soul, but she kept her worries to herself. She had no idea what she was going to do if Pa started drinking again?

Sid just stared when Anderson explained to him he was leaving the place to Bonita and Bob when he passed away.

After the explanation was over, he gave a short laugh and said, "Well, if the cat hadn't stopped to take a leak, the dog wouldn't have caught him. Do y'uns want to play poker?"

He handed Bonita a ten-dollar bill. "Here, why don't you use this to fix us up a special dinner, kinda my homecoming dinner? And take your time, us men have things to do."

THANKING GOD THAT she could drive to escape, Bonita drove Anderson's car to the Stones' store and rushed through her shopping. She wanted to get home before Sid had time to do mischief. Her arms were full of groceries, and she didn't want to put them down, so she kicked on the door until a red-faced Sid came to open the door.

"Guess what? I just won back my half of the place."

She slammed the groceries down and walked over to her father. "What? Pa, you promised."

He regarded her through bleary, drunken eyes. "I should never have promised you such a thang. How could I cut off my only son? "

She walked over to Bob who was busy gulping down the moonshine Sid had given him. "Bob, how could you have gambled away our future?"

He tried to draw her down on his lap, but she avoided his clumsy hands. "Relax, honey, I'll win it back for us."

"No, you won't. You'll lose the other half if I let you." She grabbed up the cards from the table and threw them in the wood stove.

Bob backhanded her. "You got no right to do that."

She ran out of the house and jumped in the car. She looked back once, but no one followed her.

SHE DROVE AROUND aimlessly on the dirt roads for a while. It was quite late when she finally got to her grandma's house, and the little log cabin was completely dark. Granny must already be in bed, and she hoped she wouldn't scare her to death.

Buttons barked a warning.

"Who's there?"

"Just me, Granny. Sorry I woke you up."

"Lands sakes, child. What are you doin' here at this time of night? Don't just stand there, come on in. The fire's almost gone out, but I can stoke it up in no time."

"Here, let me help you."

"No, you just sit. Now tell me what's wrong that you come runnin' to my house in the middle of the night?"

She burst into tears. "Bob slapped me."

Della stood still and stared at her. "He did, did he? What did he do that for?"

"He was mad because I burnt his cards."

"And why did you burn his cards? Don't you know menfolks don't take kindly to you burnin' their play pretties?"

"Well, Sid used them to steal half of Pa's place, which he had promised me was mine, and I was afraid Bob would lose it all 'cause he was so drunk. I hate him. He's nothin' but a weak, slobberin' drunk, just like Pa."

"Now I'm sorry to hear that, honey, but sit down here. I need to tell you somethin'."

Della waited until Bonita had sat down at the kitchen table to resume her speech. "I had hoped he might stay sober for you like Anderson did for your ma. 'Course he's weak. Just about all men is weak. That's why us women have to be so strong. All the women in this family is 'specially strong, and no man's gonna run us off unless we want to go. Now I'll grant you, some men is weaker than others, and your man and Pa is some of the weakest, but they're all weak, 'specially when they get liquored up."

"Then why do they do it? Why do they drink 'till they ain't got no sense?"

"Because around here, men have always drunk, and they learn their sons to drink and then their sons after 'em."

"Oh, Granny, not ever' body drinks. I never heard of Clay Stone or his Pa or his Grandpa bein' drunk. Then there's the preacher and his family."

"And that's why the Stones have somethin' right now because they're not drinkers. But how about that Ross Stone? He's goin' to deal his folks some misery someday because of his drinkin'. And that Michael has always been one to womanize, but his wife holds her head high like nothin's wrong. 'Course the Preacher and his have religion, and that's been the savin' of them, and I was hopin' it might save Anderson, too, but I guess he's just too weak to hold out when the temptation comes. But back to Amelia Stone. That's the way you gotta be. You've made your bed, and now you gotta lay in it. We all marry for better or worser, and it always gets worser one way or the other, but a woman's gotta be strong and make the best of it. And one day the little ones start to come, and then it all seems worthwhile somehow. Though, they can be troublesome too at times. Now let's go to bed, and, in the mornin' I'll fix you breakfast, and you can drive back home."

All at once she was twelve again and having to leave her beloved grandma. "Can't I stay with you? I don't want to ever go back there."

"Sorry, but no, you can't. I would never come between a man and his wife. No, you'll go back in the mornin', and everybody will be sobered up and sorry for what they done."

IT HAPPENED JUST as Granny had said. Bob met her with open arms and an apology on his lips. Anderson didn't acknowledge her presence and looked at her vaguely when she spoke to him. He showed no interest when she offered him some warm biscuits and fresh churned butter Grandma had sent. Sid was still in bed, sleeping it off. A contrite Bob had washed the dishes and tidied up the kitchen, but she slipped from his arms when he tried to embrace her and busied herself with gathering up the soiled bed linens for laundering. Time for that later. He needed to know that all wasn't forgiven—yet.

Sid finally came into the kitchen, redeyed and pale. "Sis, just give me a cup of coffee. Don't feel like eatin' somehow."

Bonita wouldn't look at him. "There's some coffee on the stove. Get it yourself. What are you goin' to do with your half of the place?"

Sid shrugged his thin shoulders. "Don't know. Sell it, I guess."

She spotted her chance. "Why don't you let me sell it for you, Sid? I'll sell the place for a good price and give you half the money."

"I don't really feel like talkin' about it right now. My head feels like it's about to bust. I will say one thing, though, how can you get a good price around here? Nobody's got no money."

"Aunt Lucinda and Uncle Matt have more than most, and she has always wanted this place."

"What does she want this old shack for?"

"She don't care about the house. She wants the land for her cows to run on."

"Maybe so. We can talk later. My head's a-poundin'. Any liquor left, Bob?"

"'Fraid not. Bonita's done poured what little was left outside."

"Sis, you're a coldhearted and wasteful woman."

"Maybe, but at least my head's not ahurtin'."

"Well, I can see I won't get no sympathy here. Think I'll go over to Kate's and see if I can scare up a pint. Comin,' Bob?"

He looked at her stony face and shook his head. "No, guess not."

"All right then. Go ahead and stay home. I'll try not to tell the fellers how henpecked you are."

"Now, Sid, you know that ain't true—" began Bob, but Bonita interrupted.

"Get on out of here. Who cares about your opinion anyway?"

"Glad to. I know when I'm not welcome." Sid slammed the door on his way to the front porch and walked out to his father's car but soon returned.

"Do y'uns know where Pa's keys are?"

"Somewhere you don't need to know. Take the horse."

Bob frowned at her. "Ain't that a bit hard, honey?"

"That car is part of the place, and I don't want it wrecked when we got to have somethin' to drive."

"We'll see what Pa says about that. I'll be home for supper after he wakes up." He slammed the door even harder and walked to the ramshackle shed that served as a barn.

"I better help him saddle Trooper. Nobody's rode him a while, and Sid is in poor shape to ride."

"Suit yourself. I got things to do."

She worked out her frustrations by cleaning house all day. She washed, dusted, and scrubbed until the whole house was shiny clean. Although she checked on him several times, Anderson lay quietly in his bed, sleeping soundly.

"I better start cookin' supper before he wakes up," she told herself as she peeled some potatoes for frying. But he still wasn't awake when she was ready to fry the potatoes.

After she had set the table, Bonita stood above her father's bed and began gently shaking him to wakefulness. "Pa, it's time to eat. Pa."

Getting no response, she shouted at Bob, "Bob, come here. Somethin's wrong with Pa."

Bob touched Anderson's face, neck, and hands. "Oh, Lordy, Bonita. He's cold as ice. Give me the car keys, and I'll fetch the doctor."

"All right. But hurry."

Although it seemed much longer, Bob was back with Doctor Jamison in less than an hour. She had not left Anderson's side but continued to rub his hands and feet to warm them. She could barely feel a slight pulse in his neck.

The doctor immediately began to examine Anderson. When he had finished, he sighed deeply and shook his head.

"What is it, doctor?"

"Sorry, Bonita. He's in a coma, and it doesn't look good. You're going to have to take him to the Tahlequah Hospital."

"But Pa hates hospitals."

"I know he does, but we have no choice. Bob, help me load him."

She looked down at her father's face as she touched his wrinkled brow. We look a lot alike, but my eyes are different. It would be nice to be tall like him, too. He was probably a handsome man in his prime. Poor Pa.

When they got to the hospital, she said, "You better go home and try to find Sid. I'll stay with Pa."

Bob came back three hours later. "I done looked ever'where for Sid but looks like he left the country. But I did find Trooper out in the field. Guess he was smart enough to come home on his own."

"No great loss."

Although the doctor never expected it, Anderson came out of the coma by the next evening and gradually began to improve. It wasn't long before he was clamoring to be dismissed. "Come on, Doc, I'm feelin' good now. Let me go home."

Bonita, who had been helping her father with his breakfast, scolded him. "Now, Pa, you're goin' to have to be patient and quit pesterin' the doctor."

"Oh? Is that right? Are you my ma now, gal?"

"Of course not."

"Then quit tryin' to boss me."

He brushed aside the oatmeal she had been trying to spoon into his mouth and addressed the doctor, who was standing at the door. "Come on, Doc, when can I go home?"

"Soon, Anderson, soon. Let me talk to this bossy daughter of yours for a minute."

Doctor Jamison drew her into the waiting room. "Bonita, do you want to take your father home?"

"Well, sure, if he's well enough."

"That's the problem, you see. He will never be well enough. The tuberculosis will still kill him, and I think it will be fairly soon. Are you prepared to watch him die?"

"But, he's better." Bonita's voice sounded small in her ears.

"Only for the time being, and a lot of that is for my benefit."

"You mean Pa's only pretending to be well?"

"Something like that. He's probably halfway convinced himself that he's feeling good, and, psychologically, that's helped bring about an improvement."

"Oh, kinda like Granny says, 'If you tell yourself you feel good, you will.'"

"Exactly."

"Is he any better at all?"

"Yes, somewhat. The codeine, the rest, and a healthy diet have all helped, and, of course, he can't get liquor here. That's what brought him here in the first place. His weakened body can't survive being placed in another drunken stupor. Now can you give him the same kind of care at home?"

"I think so. Now that Sid is gone."

"Then I'll release him to your care in the morning. You may go give him the good news."

"I will. Thank you, doctor."

As she turned away, her head spun with dizziness, and she had to grab the doctor's arm to keep from falling. He steadied her and asked, "And how long has this been going on?"

"This is the first time. I don't know what's got into me. Probably a touch of the flu. I been sick at my stomach a lot lately."

"Mostly in the morning?"

"Why, yes. How did you know that?"

"When was your last period?"

Bonita colored instantly and stammered. "I'll have to think on that for a minute. I kinda lost track with all the trouble we've had lately." She gasped as she realized his implications. "You don't think I'm expectin'?"

"I wouldn't be surprised. You'll know for sure after I examine you."

A few minutes later, sitting on an examination table, she heard the news. "Congratulations, Mrs. Smith. It looks like your baby will arrive sometime in November."

Bonita pushed down the panic and maintained a calm exterior. "All right. Thank you, doctor."

"Do you want me to tell Mr. Smith?"

"No, I will tell him myself."

"All right. Now don't get nervous. You are a healthy young woman, and everything will be fine."

"I'm sure it will be. Thanks, Doctor Greene."

"You're welcome. Try to get some rest. You need it more now.

When your husband comes by in the morning, I will sign your father's dismissal papers."

She lay in the little cot beside Anderson's hospital bed and stewed all night. What was she going to do? If she was going to have a baby, she couldn't finish high school. If she didn't finish high school, she would have no future. She thought about going to one of the Cherokee medicine women and asking her to get rid of it. She had heard stories of girls who had done that very thing, but she couldn't bear to see an animal suffer, much less an innocent baby. No, she would have it, and her plans would just be delayed. But she would finish her junior year. School would be out at the end of April, less than one month. She could hide it from everybody until then.

The next morning when Bob came to see Anderson, Bonita met him with a wheelchair. "Bob, help me get Pa loaded. He's goin' to go home today."

His smile stretched from ear to ear. "Well, now that's fine. I'e missed your pa, but I have really missed you, honey. It's been real lonesome." He reached over and patted her bottom before he wheeled Anderson out the door.

AT THE END of the day, she fixed herself a bed on the floor beside Anderson. Bob frowned. "Ain't you comin' to bed?"

"No, I think I better sleep by Pa. He might need somethin' during the night, and I need to be where I can hear him."

He scowled. "Well, all right then, but don't make a habit of it."

"Okay. I will wake you up in the mornin' when I'm ready to walk to school. I'll leave you the car in case you have an emergency."

He sounded annoyed. "You're already goin' back to school?"

"Uh-huh. I don't want to get any further behind. There's only one month left, and I gotta get busy if I'm going to pass my junior year."

He knelt beside her and took her in his burly arms. "I'll help you all I can, honey, as long as you keep your promise to me."

"What promise?"

"To act like my wife." He thrust his tongue into her mouth and raised the hem of her grown.

She jerked it back down and pushed him away. "Bob, don't. Pa might see what you're doin'."

"Not much chance of that. He's out like a light. All right, you can have your way tonight. But, remember, tomorrow night it's my turn, and you have no say in the matter."

Bonita sighed. She would have to put up with his pawing again. "All right. See you in the mornin'."

The taste of vomit woke her up. She ran as fast as she could to the kitchen sink where she quickly emptied the contents of her stomach. The vomit burned her nose and left a sour taste in her mouth. After rinsing her mouth with water from the bucket sitting on the sink, she used the rest to wash the sink out. Even though she was weak and faint, she went outside and drew two buckets of fresh water, one for drinking and one for cleaning herself. She hastily got ready and went to the bedroom to wake Bob.

"I'm leavin'. I checked on Pa, and he's still asleep. You can fix you and him somethin' to eat after while."

"I thought you would at least cook me some breakfast."

Her stomach turned at the thought of food. "Sorry, I don't have time. I'll fix you a good supper."

He squeezed her bottom. "I'll count on it, and I'll count on other things, too."

She closed her eyes to keep from getting sick again. "See you later."

She ran out the door before he tried anything else. Once outside, she gulped a big breath of fresh air. That's better. Her stomach settled down, and it would be good to get away.

She worked hard all morning to try to catch up. When it was lunch time, Athaliah noticed that Bonita hadn't brought anything to eat. "Here, you go. I packed myself two boiled eggs today and two biscuits. I'll share."

All at once she was ravenous. "Thanks, Athaliah."

By the end of the month, Bonita's morning sickness was nearly gone, and she received a report card, promoting her to the twelfth grade. Now she had to figure out a way to tell Bob about her pregnancy.

ANDERSON PROVIDED THE solution to her problem a few days later. He coughed until he was gasping for breath, and she hurried to give him a drink of water.

"You know, as bad as I feel, you could show me a little mercy by givin' me a real drink now and then."

"If I start givin' you drinks, you won't be feelin' anything pretty soon because you will be dead."

He groaned and lowered his head. When he raised up, he had tears in his eyes. "And what would be so bad about that? There ain't nothin' for me to live for nohow."

Bob patted his shoulder sympathetically. "You know your pa has a point, Bonita. A little liquor could sure ease his sufferin'."

"Is that so, Bob? Pa, what if I was to tell you both that I know a big reason for you to look forward to livin'?" She offered her father a clean handkerchief to wipe his eyes.

He brushed her hand away and glared at her. "So, it's not enough for you to watch me suffer without offerin' a bit of comfort. Now you want to confuse my poor mind with riddles."

"Not at all, Pa. I just think a baby around here might change your way of thinkin'."

Bob whooped and swung Bonita off the floor. "Did you hear what she said, Anderson? I'm goin' to be a pa."

Anderson chuckled and clapped his hands. "And I'm going to be a grandpa. That is good news. Bob, put her down. You got to be gentle with womenfolk when they are in the family way."

"Oh, Lordy, you're right. I'm awfully sorry, Bonita. Here sit down in this chair and put your feet up. I'll wash the supper dishes tonight. You need to rest and take care of yourself."

She leaned back in the worn armchair and allowed Bob to position her feet on a hassock. She smiled and patted his cheek. "I could get used to this real fast."

THE REMAINDER OF her pregnancy was almost pleasant. Bob reverted to his considerate pre-marriage self.

Anderson took an interest in the world again and quit talking about his suffering. He told all visitors that he was going to hold on until his first grandchild was born.

Bobby Joe Smith came into the world on Friday, November 13, 1942. All of his close kin welcomed him, except for his great-grandmother Della.

"You should have held off until November 14th to have him. Babies born on Friday the 13th are prone to bad luck."

"Granny, if I had to carry him another day, I would have popped."

Della gasped. "Well, there's no call for talk like that. Remember we're in mixed company. Let me get a look at him."

She gently unwrapped the baby's blankets and peered at his tiny fingers and toes. Stretching out her hand, she touched one little palm and smiled when the baby wrapped his fist around her finger. "He's a healthy, strong boy who looks just like his mama."

Bob leaned over and covered the baby back up. "Maybe so, but I believe he has my nose and chin. Anyway, he's a handsome feller."

Della patted Bob on the back. "I won't quarrel with you about that."

ANDERSON NEVER ASKED for another drink, even when Sid came back home for a visit with a bottle of whiskey in his suitcase. Sid surprised Bonita by paying lots of attention to Bobby Joe. As he was bent over, staring at the baby one day, she asked him, "Do you ever think of havin' a wife and child someday?"

Sid raised up and grinned at her. "Sure I do. I'm goin' to settle down someday, quit the drinkin', and have a family. Just not ready to do it right away."

Seeing he was sober and in an agreeable mood, she decided to talk business with him. "Well, don't wait too long. You're not getting any younger. Say, I been meanin' to talk to you about somethin'."

"What's that?"

"I talked to Aunt Lucinda the other day about buyin' the place."

He sat down at the table and lit a Pall Mall. "What did she say?"

"She'll give us six thousand dollars cash money. Three thousand for you, and three thousand for me."

He took a long drag and let it out slowly. "Could be better, but not bad. I could use the money. I been thinkin' about tryin' my luck up north. Heard they got good payin' jobs in Detroit, and I've always been handy at fixin' cars, but I need a vehicle to make the trip. Three thousand would buy me a good used car, meet my needs on the way up there, and see me through until I get my first paycheck. I say, accept her offer."

She stuck out her hand. "All right. Let's shake on it. I'll let her know first chance I get. I just got to ask her to let us stay on the place until we can find a new one. She shouldn't mind since she's just after the land."

Sid took her offered hand and gave it a soft squeeze. "All right, sis. When do you think we can get the money? I'd like to get started before the first of the year."

"I can probably go see her tomorrow mornin' if you promise to behave yourself while I'm gone."

"Don't worry. I already finished off the whiskey, and I ain't got money for no more."

The following morning she drove to Aunt Lucinda's house with Bobby Joe lying in the back seat. After exclaiming over the baby's beauty, Lucinda asked, "Besides showing off this little man, what brought you to see me today?"

"Are you still interested in buyin' our place?"

"I am."

They made the deal and Bonita drove home. As soon as she placed the money in his hand, Sid said, "Bob, can you take me to Tahlequah to look for a car?"

"What's the matter, Sid? Is that money burnin' a hole in your pocket? I don't mind Bob takin' you if you behave yourselves."

Sid smirked. "What, don't you trust your own husband?"

"No, I don't trust you."

Bob put his hand on Bonita's arm. "I'll see to it that we both come home with no harm done."

She sat up, reading a book by a kerosene lamp until her eyes got too heavy to stay open. She threw the book down and went to bed, disgusted with Bob and Sid.

Early in the morning she was awakened by Bob's hands, fumbling at her gown. She slapped them away. "Leave me alone, you drunk."

"I ain't drunk, just a little lit. Come on, honey. I ain't had a drink since before Bobby was born. Can't you find it in your heart to forgive me?"

"No. You promised you would come home with no harm done."

As she started to get up from the bed, Bob grabbed her arm. "Well, there ain't no harm done. We both just drank a little before we come home. Won't you lay down and let me love on you?"

"I'll lay down, but keep your distance. You smell like the inside of a whiskey bottle."

"Suit yourself." He turned over and immediately started snoring.

Bonita sighed and put a pillow over her head.

When Sid got up at noon, he came to the table where they were all eating lunch. "Somethin' sure smells good."

Bonita frowned and ignored him.

"Can I get somethin to eat?"

Anderson stared into her face. "Ain't you goin' to fix Sid a plate?"

"He knows where I keep the dishes."

Sid shrugged his shoulders, got his dinnerware, and joined them at the table. "No call to get mad. We just celebrated a little after I bought me a car. Pa, you gotta see it. It's a beaut. Hardly any miles on it, runs like a top, and I only had to pay nine hundred dollars for it. I'll take you out to see it after we're finished eatin'."

After the meal was finished, Bonita cleared the table as Sid and Bob helped Anderson into his wheelchair.

"Ain't you comin' out to see the car, sis?"

"I can see it from the window just fine."

Sid's face fell, but he turned away and helped Anderson out the front door.

She watched the men from the kitchen window as she was washing dishes. The usually languid Sid was gesturing animatedly as he propped open the car's hood, pointing out the car's features to his father. Anderson and Bob were nodding in agreement to everything he said.

Men and their toys.

The next morning, Anderson stretched out his arms to Sid as he prepared to leave. Sid grabbed him in a fierce hug and said, "Goodbye, Pa. I'll come back for a visit as soon as I can."

Bonita, who was holding Bobby Joe, saw tears in her father's eyes, and her heart melted. "Come here, Sid. You need to hug Bobby Joe and me, too."

He grinned, hugged her, and kissed the baby on the cheek. "Take care of this little man, sis."

He offered his hand to Bob. "Take care of my family, Bob."

Bob shook his hand and patted Sid on the back. "I'll do my best."

BONITA WATCHED AS Anderson spent his last days, sitting in his bed, holding his grandson, marveling and smiling at every expression on the tiny face.

Anderson McKindle, husband of Ella O'Dell and father of Sidney and Bonita McKindle, died on January 12th, less than a month after his son left. Bonita held his hand as he breathed his last word, "Ella."

THE FUNERAL WAS a small affair. Most of Anderson's family members had already passed or were unable to make the long trip back home. His widowed sister Lucinda came, dressed in a black silk dress, accompanied by the sullen adolescent Matt and her youngest daughter who had never married. Uncle Wade, Aunt Esther, and Blythe sat beside Bonita, Bob, and Della. When Bobby Joe began fussing, Wade said, "Give him to me. I'll take him outside and play with him."

Della sniffed. "That Wade has always been a fool for kids."

Bonita smiled and turned to Blythe. "We kinda like him that way, don't we, Blythe?"

"I wouldn't want Pa to be any different from what he is."

Della rolled her eyes and shushed them. "Quiet now. I can't hear the preacher."

SHE LINGERED AFTER the others had left to go to her house for a funeral meal. "I'll be along in a little while, Granny. Just want to stay here with Pa for a bit."

Della offered her a handkerchief and patted her shoulder. "All right. Just don't be too long. You know how our menfolk like to eat."

"I won't be too long."

Bob, who was jostling Bobby Joe, put his arm around her. "Want me to stay with you?"

"No, you go on and help tend to Bobby Joe. I'll be home real soon."

AFTER THEY HAD left, Bonita knelt down beside her father's grave. "Goodbye, Pa. Wish things had been different between us but guess you can't have ever'thing." She dabbed at her tearing eyes.

"Wish you could see Bobby Joe grow up, and maybe you can. Anyway, I love you, Pa, and I will always miss you." She placed a red rose on Anderson's grave and walked home.

V
CALIFORNIA
DREAMS

LATER THAT SAME month Bonita, Bob, and Bobby Joe loaded themselves and their belongings in her father's battered, blue 1932 Ford. The car sunk low, burdened with their earthly possessions. Their destination and purpose, California, to work with her Uncle Arthur.

Never having been more than fifty miles from home, Bonita was awestruck by California at first, drinking in its desert, mountains, and ocean like a thirsty puppy. The ocean especially overwhelmed her when she first viewed it. "Why, there's no end to it." She sat staring childlike out the car window for several minutes until Bobby Joe's petulant crying pulled her away from her contemplation.

She liked the migrant workers' camp where they stayed, especially the modern indoor plumbing that she had seldom experienced. She even liked the white concrete barracklike structure that became their home for the next year. She wrote to Granny.

Our place is warmer and easier to clean than back home, and this new gas stove beats our old wood stoves by a heap. I'm never the least bit lonesome because there's so many Okies here to talk to, and we all feel like kinfolk since we're all so far from home. The only one I miss from home is you, Granny, and I miss the hills and trees. But Bob is making real good money, and Mister Carter says he's one of his best hands. It looks like we might get our own house in a few weeks. I guess moving here was for the best, but I wouldn't want to live here permanent."

Outgoing Bonita soon made friends with some of the other wives. One of them, Jenny, who was a pretty, plump thirty-year-old, had an old, battered station wagon that she drove around, usually crammed full of the workers' wives and their children. One morning, after the men had left, Jenny showed up at Bonita's front door. "Bonita, put on your swimsuit. Me and Trixie promised our kids we would take them to the beach, and you and Bobby Joe are comin' with us."

She first offered excuses. "That's real nice of you, Jenny, but I'm not much of a swimmer, and I don't even own a bathin' suit."

Trixie, who was only three years older than Bonita, giggled and handed her a brown paper sack. "I told Jenny that's what you would say, so I brought along an old suit of mine. I wore it when we first moved out here before I had Peggy Sue, and it should fit you. You can change at the bathrooms near the beach."

Margaret Ann, Jenny's smart, bossy, five-year-old, folded her arms and frowned. "But, Mama, Bobby Joe don't have a swimsuit like me and Peggy Sue. How can he go swimmin' without a swimsuit?"

Jenny reached in the back seat and tweaked her daughter's nose. "He's a baby so he can wear his birthday suit, silly."

"What's a birthday suit?"

"It's what you was wearin' when you was born."

"But babies don't have clothes on when they are born, do they?"

"Nope, and neither will Bobby Joe. Now, hush, and mind your own business."

Margaret Ann scowled for a minute, sighed as if she couldn't understand grownups, and turned to Peggy Sue to ask if she could play with her dolly. Peggy Sue agreed, and soon the little girls were chatting happily while Bobby Joe took a nap on Bonita's lap.

Later on, when Bonita came out of the bathroom in the modest, black one piece, Jenny whistled and Trixie complimented her. "You sure fill that suit out better than I ever did."

She, self-consciously, covered her abundant bosom. "You don't think it's too revealin', do you?"

Jenny rolled her eyes. "Who is here to see you, girl? Just some housewives and a few old folks enjoyin' a day at the beach."

"I guess you're right." Bonita held out her arms for Bobby Joe, and Jenny handed him to her. She laughed at the baby's hesitation to move on the wet sand.

"He just started crawling around the house last week, and he's not sure about that strange, new stuff touchin' his toes." She seated herself, with her feet dangling in the water, and pulled the baby into her lap. "Feel the ocean, Bobby Joe. Don't it feel nice and cool?"

In a few minutes, he was laughing and splashing in the surf.

While their mothers waded near the water's edge, the two girls ran in and out of the surf, laughing and splashing water on each other. Jenny emerged from the water and held out her arms. "Here, I'll hold Bobby Joe while you swim awhile."

Bonita hesitated. "I don't know. I only swum in the shallow water of a creek or river."

"Oh, come on, girl. Let me have the baby, and you take a little swim. How can you come to the beach without swimmin' in the ocean?"

"All right. I'll try it, but I'm not goin' very deep." After handing her baby over, she waded out and tried an awkward dog paddle. She panicked when the tide rushed in and sent her sprawling, but she stood up for a minute and tried it again.

Trixie swam beside her and offered advice. "Just relax and enjoy it, Bonita. Watch me."

Trixie showed Bonita how to propel herself through the water. "Now you try it."

Although she was still a little awkward, Bonita soon got the hang of it. She and Bobby Joe accompanied Jenny, Trixie, and their children several more times to the beach that spring, summer, and early fall. Bonita's new friends sometimes included their husbands in their social gatherings and invited Bonita and Bob to join them at their Saturday night cookouts.

No matter how she begged, Bob would never agree to go. "I'm with those fellers all day. Why do I want to spend my spare time with them?"

Hands on hips, she fired back. "That makes no sense. You aren't around me and Bobby all day, but half the time, you act like you don't want to be around us either."

"I don't know what you're talkin' about."

"During the week, you eat supper and go right to bed. On Saturday nights, you go drinkin' with your buddies, and you usually spend Sundays in bed, nursing a hangover."

Bob's face turned red and ugly, and he waved his fist in her face. "As long as I make the livin' around here, you can keep your mouth shut, or I will shut it for you."

Bobby wailed, she picked him up and went outside. She hugged her baby close and whispered to him. "I love you, Bobby Joe, but sometimes I wish I had never met your daddy. I should have stayed home and finished school somehow."

After they had both stopped crying, she went back into the house. Bob's loud snores shook the small house.

A FEW WEEKS later, a strange, warm Christmas Day greeted Bonita, along with the realization that Bob hadn't come home from his Christmas Eve revels. "Now, where is your daddy? He promised that he wouldn't get into any meanness. He just wanted to play cards and maybe drink a beer or two with the boys on Christmas Eve. Well, he'll be home directly I expect. Come on, little man, let's have some breakfast and a bath."

She filled the large stainless-steel kitchen sink with warm water. Bobby Joe crowed and waved his chubby arms as she lowered his plump little bottom into the soothing water. "You like that, don't you little man? Hold still now while Mama shampoos your hair. Ten little fingers, ten little toes. He's Mama's baby, and his name's Bobby Joe." She spontaneously broke into song as she often did.

"I've gotta think of another verse to this song someday, Bobby, but you don't mind, do you?" The baby responded in baby talk. "Know what, Bobby Joe? You are the most beautiful baby in the world. Yes, you are, my precious, and Mama wouldn't take a million dollars for you."

She kissed the baby's rosy cheeks, and he rewarded her with a mouthful of water. "You quit that splashin' Mama in the face, you naughty boy."

The baby laughed and began to splash harder. "You, stinker. Let's get this bath over before Daddy gets home."

AFTER SHE HAD Christmas dinner in the oven to cook, Bonita grabbed her purse and carried the baby over to the O'Cleary's house. She knocked on the front door. Gladys O'Cleary was different from the other worker wives, quiet and sad and hard to approach.

The red-eyed, pale, haggard woman opened the door. "Is anything the matter, Gladys? You don't look like you feel so good."

"Just the same old thing that's always the matter. Drunk men who drink themselves out of good jobs."

"I sure hope not. Do you happen to know where Bob is?"

"The same place as my old man. The county jail. And Mister Carter won't be likin' it a'tall, 'specially where your man is concerned, him bein' new and all."

Bonita chewed on her lower lip and silently cursed Bob for putting them in a bad spot. "Can you take me there? I got a little money to bail him out."

"Why bother? It might do the louts good to spend a little time in jail."

"But it's Christmas, and families should be together on Christmas."

"It's your family that you should be turnin' to. I'll drive you and the baby over to your uncle's place, and he can take you to the jail. I don't want to see my man today."

"Thank you, Gladys. Can we stop by the house first, so I can turn my dinner off?"

"Sure. Let me get the car started, and we'll be off."

On the way to Arthur's, Bonita learned that this was not the first time that Sean O'Cleary had been in jail for drinking and that he had lost two other jobs for it. Gladys was close to tears. "I just hope Mister Carter will be soft on him, but he is dead set against any kind of drinkin', so I don't know."

TWO HOURS LATER, Bonita was sitting at Uncle Arthur's house, listening to a repentant Bob, pleading on the phone with Mr. Carter not to fire him. "I'm real sorry, Mr. Carter. I swear to God I'm not a drinkin' man. It was just Christmas Eve, and O'Cleary talked me into takin' him to the beer joint for a couple before I went home. Some fellers from Preston's ranch came in and started cussin' you and yours. Well, we couldn't stand that, seeing's you been so good to us, so we took up for you. It got a little out of hand, and the barkeep called the law on us. You can take the damages out of our next month's checks, only please don't let us go. I got a family to feed, and I got to have this job."

Mr. Carter, who was hard of hearing, talked loud enough for them all to hear. "You should have thought of your family before you started tearin' up the joint. But you are a good worker, Smith, and I guess everybody's entitled to one mistake. Just don't hang around O'Cleary and his kind again. 'Course I guess you won't have to worry about it because he's gone. This is his second mistake."

Uncle Arthur took the phone from Bob's hand. "Thanks, sir, for givin' my kin another chance. I'll do my best to keep my eye on him."

"See that you do."

As Arthur drove them to get Bob's car, Bonita thought about sad Gladys and wondered if she would share her fate someday.

BOB WAS TRUE to his word for the next several weeks. He worked hard, and they were able to buy a better car and a crib for little Bobby. He balked, however, when Bonita asked him for extra money for a new dress or a good pair of shoes.

"Why do you need something new all the time? You don't do nothin' except stay around the house or gossip with them old hens."

"Well, maybe if I had some decent clothes and shoes, I could look for a job. Then I wouldn't be havin' to ask you for money."

"Oh, no. No wife of *mine* will ever work. You stay here and take care of Little Bobby. Maybe we'll get him a brother real soon."

"Lord, I hope not. I just now got my figure back. But what's wrong with me workin'? Trixie's been workin' at the lemon plant for half a year, and her and Dave's got all kinds of money. She leaves Peggy Sue with Jenny, and she don't even cry for her. I could do the same with Bobby Joe."

"You're not workin', and that's all I'm gonna say about it."

Bonita mumbled under her breath. "We'll see about that."

IN MARCH, BOB lost his job for drinking again, and they were forced to sell their old car to buy groceries and pay the deposits, rent, and utilities for a new place. Bonita began working at the nearby lemon plant. Bob ranted at first, but Bonita said, "Somebody's gotta buy the groceries, and I don't mind helpin' out for a while."

She enjoyed getting out, but Bob sat around the tiny house in a dejected state and made promises. "This is only temporary, honey. As soon as Preston begins hirin' for the new crop, I'll have a new job, and you can quit and stay home again."

But when Tom Preston was asked, he said, "I already heard about you, and I don't need a drinkin' man when I can get ten Okies for every open slot."

So she continued working and meeting new people. She soon learned the Californians turned frosty when they heard she was from

Oklahoma, so she learned not to tell them. By the time they knew where she was from, they usually liked her for her cheerfulness and ready acceptance of hard work and long hours.

Some of the men tried to flirt with her, but she could usually fend them off with talk of her husband and little boy. The women liked her because she always did her share and more of the work, and she seemed genuinely interested when they told her of their joys and problems.

THINGS WENT ALONG pretty smoothly until the middle of August. Bonita had learned she could pacify Bob by turning over most of her paycheck to him. She always took out enough for food, rent, an occasional luxury, such as tiny overalls for the baby, as well as a small amount that she squirreled away each week in a secret hiding place. Each pay day Bob would glower and say the same thing. "You should give me all of it. I'm the man around here."

She smiled and offered sweet words. "But, honey, you know where it's all goin', so why worry about it? Why don't we all walk to the new picture show in town tonight?"

BOB AND BONITA'S quarrels were always lost in the dark of the theater. Their petty arguments were washed aside in the rushing tide of the drama and fantasy that was depicted there. Bob always behaved better after viewing a movie, so she didn't begrudge the precious change it took to pay for it.

This particular night, though, even a trip to the picture show didn't solve their problems. Bob insisted he would walk Bonita and Bobby home and go back to the local joint for a few quick ones.

Sometime early in the morning, she was awakened by a pair of shoes, smacking her head. "Bob, what are you doin'?"

She dodged dresses, skirts, and shoes that were sailing through the air.

"What I should have done a long time ago. I'm fixin' it so my wife won't leave me and go out to work no more. If you don't have nothin' to wear, you can't work, can you?"

Bob giggled hysterically as he threw all of her clothes into the yard.

He slapped her as she tried to retrieve her clothes. "No, you don't, you hussy. You ain't goin around those men anymore, all dressed up. I seen how they look at you. They want what I'm goin' to get right now."

She was relieved when Bob passed out on top of her a few minutes later. She dragged herself from under him, picked up her screaming toddler, packed a suitcase, and started walking to Uncle Arthur's house.

A FRIENDLY TRUCK driver picked her up after asking, "How old are you, girlie?"

"Nineteen."

"And already with a kid? You're no older than my Connie. She's still in school. Where are you headin'?"

"To Carter's Ranch. I can pay you if you'll take me there."

"Keep your money. It ain't much out of my way."

That night Uncle Arthur put Bonita back on a bus to Aiden.

WHEN BONITA FIRST arrived at her grandmother's house, she was surprised to see tears in the old stoic's eyes when she embraced her. "'Nita, I never thought to see you again."

"Why, Granny? You should've known I'd turn up sometime."

"I just been feelin' poorly lately, and I weren't sure I'd last before you come back. Now, though, since you and this little man are here, I'm feelin' much better. Hey, little man, let me look at you."

She lifted the child's chin and stared into his large, luminous brown eyes. "I'm glad he's got your eyes. You and poor Eva, the boy, and me all got the same dark eyes. Cherokee eyes, though I never claimed it."

"I always wondered about that. Why didn't you claim your Indian blood? You might have got some land for it."

"Your grandpa was dead set against it. Maybe it was just as well. I might have got a guardian, too, and I never wanted no blamed man, white or dark, tellin' me how to handle my affairs. Remember Sally Shoatshooter? The government gave her some land all right, but that no-account guardian they appointed for her sold most of it off for his gamblin' debts. No, sir, I know what I am, and it's nobody else's business."

Della stood up and looked out the front door. "But where's Bob? You shouldn't never travel 'cross the country without a man. No tellin' what might happen."

"I've left him for good. And there's no sense in you tryin' to talk me out of it. I'm gettin' a divorce."

"Humph. There's no accountin' for this younger generation of womenfolk, but we'll talk later. Now sit down and rest your bones."

VI
WAR

AFTER A FEW days, Clay told his cousin he had changed his mind about working for him. There was a war brewing across the seas and talk that the United States would be joining in soon. Clay had heard the old men talk about fighting in World War I, and he wanted to know what it was like. Just had to make up his mind which branch of the military he wanted to join. He had never flown in an airplane and had no desire to do so, so that did away with the air force. Although he was a strong swimmer, he didn't like the idea of being at sea for weeks at a time. His talents ran toward horses and marksmanship, but he doubted if there was much call for horse riding during this war. A good shot, though, would likely be in demand, and the army needed plenty of those.

SOME THREE MONTHS later, he was sitting in the barracks of Camp Bowie in Texas, daydreaming about a dark-haired girl that had recently captured his heart. The music on the radio switched to the background when the announcer broke into the program, jarring him from his thoughts of Rosita. *"The Japanese have bombed Pearl Harbor. I repeat, The Japanese have bombed Pearl Harbor."*

The laughter and the horseplay abruptly ceased. One tall, lanky Texan stood up and addressed the crowd. "Well, boys, the Japs just brought a hornet's nest down on their ignorant heads and looks like we'll be marchin' off to war sooner rather than later."

Clay wondered if his liberty pass for the next weekend had been canceled. If that happened, he might never get to meet Rosita's parents. He might never get to hear that low, melodic voice, patiently trying to teach him Spanish or kiss those warm, sweet lips again. Even worse he might never get another chance to press himself against her lush, full body. Rosita had pulled away from him the last time he had held their embrace a little too long.

He remembered how her dark eyes flashed as she murmured something in Spanish and followed with English. "No, Clay. I know what you are trying to do, and I can't allow it. First, you must meet my father and mother. Then we will see."

He gave her a peck on the cheek. "Okay, honey. I will gladly meet your parents. I have some leave comin' so I'll plan on comin' to your place next Saturday morning."

Now he might never get to meet her parents.

All thoughts of Rosita were driven out of his mind five minutes later when Sergeant Simms showed up. "All right, ladies. Listen close. I got some news for you. No more passes. We gotta train harder if you poor nimrods are goin' to have a snowball's chance in hell to survive the war."

CLAY CUSSED THE sergeant, along with the other men, when he realized he might never have another chance to see Rosita. It grew harder and harder to keep his feelings to himself as the sergeant drove them unmercifully. On Christmas morning, he lined-up to the hated voice.

"Good mornin', ladies. It's Christmas mornin'. Time to celebrate." Sergeant Simms feigned surprise when his words were met with frowns and eye rolls. "Come on, you nimrods, didn't you hear me say it was Christmas? It's Christmas? And I'm your Santa Claus."

Simms turned to walk away. "Guess if you don't want your mail and presents, I can find some other guys who will appreciate them."

"No, Sarge. We're sorry."

"Yeah, we want them."

He turned and threw the mail bag. "Boone, you pass out the mail. "

"Stone, come here. I need to talk to you."

Clay's heart rate sped up, and he broke out into a sweat. "Yes sir."

Simms lit a cigarette, took a puff, and looked him over. "Don't look so scared, Stone. This is your lucky day. Do you want to know why?"

He pushed the fear down. "Yes, sir."

"The higher-ups say your marksmanship is the best in the camp, and you make me look good. So, I figure I owe you a little present, this bein' Christmas and all." Simms handed him a tin of homemade cookies. "My wife makes extra every year for me to share with my army buddies. This year that buddy is you."

When he saw Clay's hesitation, he thrust the cookies into his hands. "Go ahead, nimrod, before I change my mind."

"Thank you, sir." Clay walked away a few steps, opened the tin, and inhaled the delectable aroma of fresh baked oatmeal cookies. He wanted to gobble them down immediately but restricted himself to take out only two, one for now, and one for later.

"Anyone want a homemade oatmeal cookie?" His offer earned him more points for being "a nice guy."

Clay was playing poker with friends when the conversation turned to the 2nd Battalion. Private Palmer, a short bulldog of a man, mumbled an obscenity and threw down his cards. "I fold. You know what I don't get? I don't get why we ain't bein' sent to Africa. Why the Second?"

Sarge, who was walking by, overheard him. "That's easy enough to answer. Because they said so, and they always know what's best.

Besides, some of you guys are scheduled for extra training, like Stone. Since he's such a hotshot on the rifle range, we're goin' to see how good he is with bigger toys."

AS A RESULT of his intensive training, Clay found himself in charge of a Browning M1919 machine gun when he sailed from the States in 1943. His destination was Algiers, and his goal was to run the Axis forces out of Africa.

Once he got over a bout of seasickness, Clay, like most of the men in his outfit, was itching to fight. As he stood at the ship's railing, wide eyes were taking in the new sights and sounds of a different continent. His ears detected the hum of discontent.

One of the younger soldiers was holding court. "I thought when we was assigned to "Old Blood and Guts," our days of waitin' was over. Looks like just more of the same old, same old."

An older man named Ben reached over and gave him a rough head rub. "Boy, how many times do I have to tell you? Patton prefers more experienced troops fightin' in Africa, so we gotta train some more. It don't matter much who your commander is. It's the army what decides how they best can use you, and all you can do is like it and go along."

"Well, I might have to go along, but they can't make me like it. More trainin'? By the time the army gets through trainin' us, the war will be over."

After spending a few weeks training in Arzew and Rabat, some of the men were pulled to guard a group of POWs. Clay's division, sent to Italy in September of 1943, soon learned to regret their impatience for combat. They fought hard in Salerno, Italy, and Clay soon lost track of how many men he had killed. It was easier to count how many of his companions were wounded and killed, far too many. Clay pushed down the sorrow and fear and kept firing. He was glad when the word came to retreat.

The tent was quiet that night. No one laughed. No one moved to play cards or shoot craps. Exhausted men lay motionless in their cots, dreading the day ahead.

Clay and his battalion went on to fight at the Battle of San Pietro, which was brutal. The heavily armed Germans greeted them with strong opposition, and they suffered more than 4,000 causalities. Somehow, with the help of the 504th Parachute Infantry Regiment, they were able to repulse the Germans and were awarded six weeks of rest to recuperate and receive replacements. It was tough to go back into battle after their respite was over.

They fought on throughout Italy, and at each battle, Clay killed more men and lost more friends. He had been lucky in Italy, and when they were greeted with cheers at the gates of Rome on June 5, 1944, he breathed a sigh of relief.

One pretty Italian girl named Angelina was especially glad to see Clay and his money. Business had been slow. He finally got to finish what he had started with Rosita. He got up the next morning, lit a cigarette, and surveyed Rome from Angelina's bedroom window. He had a day of leave to spend with her, and he wanted to see the sights of Rome.

That night he drank wine with Angelina at the Roman Forum and kissed her goodbye. He pressed a fifty-dollar bill into her hand, and she covered his face with kisses and thanked him profusely. He was grinning big when he arrived back at headquarters.

OLD BEN LAUGHED when he saw him. "Looks like somebody had a good time. Ain't seen you grin like that in a coon's age. Too bad it won't last."

"What do you mean?"

"Just get some rest. We're goin' to France next, and Colonel Pike says he wants to see you. Pronto."

Clay had a bad feeling when he saw who was waiting outside to see their commander. John Reece, called Big John because of his size, was sitting outside the door, chain smoking. John threw down his cigarette and stomped it out on the pavement. "Well, glad you're finally here. Now maybe I can find out what the captain has in mind for me and you."

"Probably somethin' to do with shootin', since we're the best shots in the company."

"Yeah, that's what I'm afraid of."

A few minutes later the colonel's assistant ushered them into his new office. "Come in, gentlemen. I have something I want to discuss with you. Sit down and make yourselves at home."

After a bit of chitchat, he addressed the reason for their summons. "I am sending you and a few other select men into the French countryside a few days early on a reconnaissance mission before the main force lands. Any questions?"

Big John raised his hand. "Yeah, why us?"

"Some people need protection, and I'm trusting the two of you to provide it. "

The colonel noticed Clay's frown. "Come on, Stone. You got a question. Out with it."

He looked into the colonel's slate blue eyes. "How are we goin' to keep from gettin' caught? Neither one of us speaks French or German, and Big John will stick out like a sore thumb."

"Gee, thanks, Stone."

"No, he's right. You two would be sitting ducks in France if you tried it on your own. But, you see, one of the men who is going with you speaks French and German, so that will help. But what will help even more is our French allies will be monitoring your every move and will send some of their people to accompany you."

He opened a desk drawer, took out two thin paperback books, and handed them each one. "Study these phrase books every chance you get. Now good luck, men. You'll receive more information on a need to know basis, and I don't need to tell you to keep this conversation to yourselves. Dismissed."

As they returned his salute and started to walk away, the colonel snapped his fingers. "Wait a minute. I almost forgot."

They turned around to face him again. "I'm sending two of my men with you, Sergeant O'Neal and Captain Braun. Braun will be in charge. All right, you can go now."

John waited until they were out of earshot to speak. "Stone, I believe we just jumped from the fryin' pan into the fire."

Clay nodded his agreement.

TWO WEEKS LATER, they met their translator, Smythe, a short, bearded man with a receding hairline, Sergeant O'Neal, a stocky, freckled Irishman, and Captain Braun, a muscular, broad-shouldered man of medium stature.

After introducing them to each other, the colonel explained the procedures they would follow.

"You will be taken to a spot close to the French coast where you'll disembark on a dinghy. Once you get to shore, you'll hide the dinghy and make your way up the bank through the woods. Once you're in the woods, you'll be contacted by the French group, who will inform you of your next step. Now I'll turn you over to the officer in charge, Captain Braun. Good luck."

They followed the impassive Braun to the front of the building. He motioned for them to stop and silently studied each man before saying, "Meet back here at dusk."

After he walked away, O'Neal chuckled. "Braun ain't much of a talker, but he's a good soldier. I would advise you to eat all you can today. There's precious little food where the Frenchies live. See you at dusk." He strode away, whistling as he went.

Smythe shook hands with each of them. "Glad to meet you. Most people call me Smitty, 'cept for Braun, but then I don't call him captain, neither. O'Neal's all right, but Braun's hard to take, if you know what I mean. You guys are from Texas, right?"

"Texas born and bred." He punched Clay in the arm. "Stone here ain't so lucky. He's from Oklahoma."

Smitty grinned. "Well, I'm not from here, neither. I'm from Louisiana. They brought me here because my mama was a Cajun who taught me to speak French, and they needed a translator."

Clay was curious. "Where did you learn to speak German?"

"That I learned in high school. I always had a knack for languages. I can speak Spanish, too. Well, guess I better get back to my barracks. I promised to teach some of the guys how to play chess. See you later."

John waited a few minutes and said, "Egg head."

"Nothin' wrong with bein' smart."

"Won't be much good in a fight."

"Hope it don't come to that."

"It likely will. Why else would they have four tough guys along?"

LATER THAT NIGHT, as they made their way quietly up a steep embankment and through the woods, O'Neal whispered, "Thought the Frenchies were supposed to meet us somewhere close by. Wonder where they are?" Rifle extended, he scanned their surroundings.

A few seconds later a soft feminine voice, with a slight French accent, startled them. "We are right here." Clay jumped at her voice. If she had been a German, he would have been dead. A small woman, whose big bright eyes and quick mannerisms reminded Clay of a bird, appeared out of the darkness.

By her side was a stocky Frenchman, only a few inches taller than she. "This is Francoise. I am Heloise. Follow me, but don't talk. We saw Germans on the beach earlier today."

She led them deeper into the woods, where a makeshift camp was set up, and motioned for them to stop. "Sit down. Francoise will tell you the plan."

Francois talked quietly in heavily accented English, reverting now and then to French. Clay was glad he had memorized the French phrase book. He thought he understood most of what Francois said, but Big John and O'Neal looked confused.

When he had finished talking, Smitty spoke up. "Don't worry, guys. I can fill you in on anything you didn't understand. Just know we will eat and sleep here tonight, and in the morning, Heloise and Francoise will take us into town."

After gobbling some thin stew, a hunk of thick, brown bread, and a cup of weak tea, Clay stretched out on a thick blanket under a big oak tree and soon fell asleep. The bright morning sun woke him as soon as it rose, and, for a minute, he didn't know where he was.

As soon as they finished their coffee and bread, Heloise said, "Francois has some French clothes for you to wear. Put them on, follow me, and for God's sake, be quiet."

A few minutes later a seemingly different group of men stood in front of Heloise, except for John, who had been given nothing to wear.

O'Neal pointed at him. "How about John?"

She frowned. *"Monsieur* John is more of a challenge. Francoise, please show him how he must act."

Francois mimed the walk of a cripple, dragging one leg behind him. He opened his mouth slightly, and his face assumed a vacant look.

They all laughed, except for Braun, but John protested. "Why do I have to be the village idiot?"

Heloise patted his arm sympathetically. "Because no one suspects an idiot. Here put on this jacket and hat. Our seamstress worked all night, sewing two coats together for you, and we stretched out the beret so that it can fit your large head."

After he was dressed, she said, "Now, *Monsieur* John, let me see your act."

Half-heartedly, John went through the motions. "You must do better than that. Show him again, Francois."

Braun's voice was as steely as his gray eyes. "Shape up, soldier."

O'Neal gripped John's shoulder. "Come on, John. I know you're embarrassed, but we ain't got all day."

JOHN PASSED INSPECTION the next time, and they set out. Heloise whispered a warning, "Keep your heads down and don't talk. Remember the Germans aren't your only enemies. There are several German partisans among the local French."

They walked into the town with no one giving them a second look.

Clay wondered what they were going to do if they ran into some Germans who asked to see their papers, but they only encountered a handful of Frenchmen. Heloise kept to the backroads, and they soon arrived in the courtyard of a Catholic church.

"*Monsieur* Smitty, you, *Monsieur* Clay, and *Monsieur* Braun, go inside and get the package. I will go with you to show you the way. Francois, *Monsieur* John, and *Monsieur* O'Neal will wait in the courtyard for you."

Clay took a deep breath and steeled himself for what lay ahead. No one had mentioned retrieving a package, and he still wasn't sure what he was expected to do. They went through the backdoor and walked down the hallway. Heloise led them to an office door. Before they could step inside, they were stopped by two Germans.

Clay thought their luck had run out, but whatever Smitty told them seemed to satisfy their curiosity. They were waved inside. Two priests, one old, bearded, and fair and one young, thin, and dark, looked up and stared intently at them.

The younger priest broke into a smile and said in English, "Thank, God, you have come. I am saved."

Heloise hushed him. "Not so fast, my friend. We still have to get you out of this building."

The older priest nodded his head. "Yes, Simeon. Heloise is correct. Keep your English to yourself and keep your head down."

He made the sign of the Cross. "May God go with you all."

Heloise placed Simeon between Clay and Braun. "Guard this package with your life, monsieurs."

The two Germans met them again at the back door. This time Clay understood them. "Halt. Where are you going with the priest? He is under arrest until the commandant arrives to question him."

Seeing the one on the right raise his weapon, Braun pushed Simeon behind him and said, "Shoot."

In an instant, Clay pulled out his firearm and shot the German on the right and then the one on the left. Both slumped to the floor, dead from head wounds.

Heloise yelled, "Hurry. The shots will be heard. We must go now."

They ran out of the building, Braun keeping a tight grip on Simeon. On the outskirts of the courtyard, they were joined by Francois, John, and O'Neal. John had dropped his idiot act and had taken up a rearguard position. Some townspeople had heard the shots and were gathering near the church.

Heloise said, "Wave your guns, and they will scatter."

They all did as she said, except for one brutish partisan. As soon as their backs were turned, and they were running away, he fired.

One bullet struck Big John in the back of the head, and he fell.

Clay turned and shot the partisan. Braun yelled, "Don't stop. O'Neal, check John out and catch up with us at the boat."

AS THEY RAN into the safety of the woods, they surprised a young German soldier taking a smoke break. Seeing his predicament, he threw down his weapon, and put up his hands in surrender.

Clay stopped running and stared at him. Scared blue eyes searched his face for a sign of mercy. The young German took a worn wallet from his pocket and showed him pictures of a pretty, young woman and a smiling infant.

Braun took command. "The rest of you keep runnin'. Come on, Stone. We don't have room for prisoners. Shoot him."

Clay shook his head. "Captain, I can't shoot someone who's beggin' me to let him live."

Braun took out his gun and aimed it at Clay's head. "Shoot him. That's an order."

Clay turned and stared down the barrel of his commander's pistol. Braun wouldn't back down. It was his life or the German's. He had killed men during the war, but not like this. Not in cold blood when a man had surrendered and was pleading for his life. But an order was an order, no matter how much he hated it.

Clay fired once, striking the German in the head, killing him instantly. He sensed something rise up from his spirit and leave, as if a part of his soul had died along with the man. Then he turned and knocked Braun's gun away from his head and glared at him. He stood like a statue, fighting an intense desire to shoot Braun.

He finally moved when Braun barked an order. "Let's go."

They scrambled down the embankment and found their party and the boat they had hid in the bushes. Braun said, "All right, get in."

Clay stood stock-still with his arms folded across his chest. "No."

Braun got in Clay's face. "You don't tell me no, soldier."

"We gotta wait on O'Neal and John. You told O'Neal to catch up with us."

"*Monsieur*, I know you want to save your friends, but *Monsieur* John is dead, and the Germans will be here any minute."

Smitty took a stance beside Clay. "We're going to wait."

Braun swore. "You're gonna get us all killed." Looking at his watch, Braun clenched his jaw and spit out his words. "We'll wait just three minutes and no more."

As soon as he finished speaking, Clay looked up to see O'Neal sliding down the embankment. He fell at their feet and said, "John's dead, and the Krauts are in the woods lookin' for us."

Heloise said, "Our friends will cause a diversion to give you time to slip away."

Francois shook their hands, and Heloise kissed each of them on the cheek. "*Merci*, my friends. May you all find your way back home soon."

O'Neal looked at the priest as they helped him into the boat. "I hope you're worth it, man. We lost a good soldier today."

Simeon shook his head. "No, I'm not worth it, but the information I have about the death camps is worth everything."

Braun ignored Simeon and turned his wrath on Clay and Smitty. "If I wanted to, I could bring charges against both of you."

Smitty smirked. "But you won't. You need me in case the colonel comes up with any more schemes that require my talents. And I advise you to leave Clay alone, too, because the colonel is going to be very pleased with the work he did today."

That night Clay waited until everyone was asleep. He arose from his cot and quietly slipped away. He found a quiet spot away from the camp lights, lowered himself to the ground, and cried for his friend and the family man he had killed that day.

The rest of the war went by in a blur. He took some bullets in his back in a skirmish with a German patrol two weeks later. He spent several days in the field hospital recuperating from the surgery performed to remove the slugs. Smitty, O'Neal, Ben, and others from his company came to visit.

While in the hospital, he developed a raging fever and a bad infection. The surgeon operated again and discovered a bullet he'd overlooked lodged close to Clay's tailbone. Clay's stay was extended two more weeks while he was treated for the infection. Meanwhile, his company was sent to another location.

The day before he was dismissed from the hospital, Colonel Pike came to see him. After seating himself at Clay's bedside, he handed Clay a carton of Pall Malls. "Smitty said you like these. I never got to properly thank you for the good job you did in rescuing our Jewish friend from the Nazis."

Clay gave him a nod of thanks. "Just following orders, sir. The other guys all did their part too."

"I know they did, but you are a lot younger, and you lost a buddy, so it was harder on you."

Clay looked away. "Yeah, I miss Big John."

"Well, besides thanking you, I came to bring some news. When you're dismissed in the morning, you'll be sent on a transport truck, along with some replacements, to southern France. You'll rejoin your company, and you'll get to be part of an important battle, Operation Dragoon."

Clay fought in several battles before the war ended, and he killed a multitude of enemy soldiers. He only regretted one death. The only death that haunted him in the years to come was the young German who had begged for his life that day in the French woods.

VII

LOSS

BONITA WAS SITTING on the front porch, enjoying a rare summer breeze as she trimmed Bobby Joe's curly, blond hair. "Be still, Bobby Joe. Mama might cut your ear if you keep on wigglin' around."

Bobby Joe stopped abruptly in mid-wiggle, and Bonita looked up to see what had caught his attention. An old red pickup was driving up the lane to her grandmother's house.

She put down her scissors, untied the towel that was around his neck, and lifted him from the chair on which he had been sitting. "Go inside and play. We can finish your haircut later."

"Good mornin', Bonita. I just moved back to Jubilee. Been workin' in Tulsa in the oil fields. Just heard you was back, too." Grinning broadly, Ross Stone walked up the steps of the porch and sat down in an empty chair.

"Hello, yourself. How's the family?"

"Well, Depends on what family you're askin' about. The last we heard from Clay he was fighting somewhere in France. He was in a hospital for a while, but he got all right."

Bonita's hand flew to her mouth. "Oh, no. Was he hurt bad?"

"Yeah, had to be operated on a couple of times from the bullets he caught. But you know Clay, tough as a boot. He's fine now. I guess you know Grandma Martha passed away last spring, and Grandpa seems a little lost without her. He's still workin' at the store, though. Susan and Tommy and their kids have moved in with him, and they're helpin' him with everything."

"Yes, I heard about that. It must be hard on him to lose someone he's been with almost his whole life."

"Well, I probably won't never know what that's like, because I'm a divorced man."

She sighed. "That's too bad, Ross. I was hopin' you and Belle would be happy with you havin' a little girl and all."

Ross took her hand. "You want to know what our biggest problem was?"

She tried to extract her hand, but he held on. "That's really none of my business. Now can I have my hand back?"

He gently kissed her hand. "Oh, but it is your business. Because *you* was our biggest problem."

She jerked her hand out of his grasp and frowned at him. "That can't be right. How could I be a problem when I wasn't even here?"

Something stirred inside when she heard Ross's low, rumbling chuckle. "I think you know exactly what I mean. Our problem was Belle wasn't you. I only married her because she was pregnant."

Pushing away a growing desire, she stood up. "I think you better leave right now. I'm not goin' to sit here to be accused of breakin' up your marriage when I wasn't even here."

Another chuckle stirred her feelings again, but she ignored them.

As Ross stood up, he stretched himself out like a lithe, well-muscled tom cat. "All right, Bonita. I'll go, but I'll be back. Promise me you'll think about somethin', will you?"

"What's that?"

"Both of us are divorced now, and we got nothin' to lose. We're still young, and we might as well have a little fun. Think about it, all right?"

He leaned over and kissed her on the cheek. "See you again in a day or two, honey."

He blew her a kiss as he walked to his truck.

Della came out as soon as he drove away. "What did Ross want?"

"To have a little fun."

"Humph. You know what he's talkin' about, don't you? Just remember, you ain't divorced yet. You and Bob's just separated, and you might want to get back together for your little boy's sake."

Bonita shook her head and grimaced. "Like I told you before, Granny. We're never gettin' back together. I'm not goin' to live my life with another drunk."

"Well, remember that the next time Ross Stone wants to take you somewhere. Because that's what he is, just another drunk."

STANDING WITH HER arms folded, fighting not to give in, Bonita grimaced as she faced Ross the next morning. "Ross, how many times do I have to tell you? I'm not goin' fishin'—or anywhere else—with you today."

"Give me one good reason why you can't, and I'll leave."

"I already gave you three." Bonita used her fingers to count off.

"I need to help Granny with the chores. Bobby Joe is too much for her to handle all day. And, most of all, it wouldn't be respectable for me, as a married woman, to go fishin' with a divorced man."

Ross put her fingers to his lips and kissed them. As she pulled them away, he used his own fingers to count off.

"I said I would do the chores for you. Bobby Joe can come with us. And, as for the least important reason, why do we care what people think of us? Besides, we're just two old friends, spendin' a little time together to catch up, and Bob here wants to go fishin', don't you, boy?"

Ross bent down and swooped Bobby Joe from his feet while he giggled and said, "Fish."

Ross laughed and hugged him. "Smart boy. He already knows what he wants. And we shouldn't disappoint him."

Seeing she was outnumbered, Bonita agreed. "Oh, all right. I'll take you up on that offer to do the chores first. We'll go with you as long as we're back in a couple of hours. Bobby Joe needs his afternoon nap."

Ross set Bobby Joe down. "You bet. Just tell me what to do first."

"You can start by milkin' the cow."

As Ross turned away, Bonita grabbed his arm. "One more thing."

"What's that?"

"No funny business."

Ross held up his right hand. "I swear I will be as solemn as a judge."

When Bonita told Della where they were going, her face turned to stone. "You're makin' a big mistake, missy. And don't say I didn't warn you."

She walked away and left by the back door.

AS SOON AS they arrived at the creek, Bobby Joe was beside himself with excitement, jumping up and down at the edge of the water. Bonita laughed at him. "He's played by the ocean and loved it, but he's never been on a creek bank before."

"Well, we're goin' to fix that right now." Ross scooped Bobby up in his arms and sat down in the shallow water.

Giggling as Ross dangled his chubby toes in the water, Bobby looked up into his face. "Fish."

"Yep. Those are fish, all right. Little minnows nibblin' on your toes."

She smiled as she saw how naturally Ross and her son interacted. If she had married Ross when he asked her, Bobby Joe could be his son.

Ross pulled out a cane pole from the back of his truck and a coffee can full of worms and handed them to her. "Ain't you goin' to fish?"

"You first. I'll tend to Bob while you fish. When you get tired of it, we'll trade off."

She got several bites, but each time she jerked the pole out of the water, the fish and her bait were gone. Feeling frustrated, she walked over to where Ross and Bobby were playing in the water. "Your turn. I can't catch nothin'."

He took the pole from her hands and examined it. "Maybe your hook's not big enough. I'll change it out and find you a new spot."

She watched as Ross skillfully cast the line some distance away. His attention was so focused on landing a fish that she could admire him without attracting notice. He had grown from a good-looking boy into a strikingly handsome man, and she ached to have his strong arms around her.

Suddenly, he jerked the pole, and silver scales glistened in the sun. "Ha. He's a big sand bass. No wonder you couldn't catch him."

Bobby Joe clapped his hands and yelled, "Fish. Fish."

"That's right, boy. It's a *big* fish. Bring me that minnow bucket, would you, honey?"

He caught two more sand bass, and Bobby applauded each time. After the third fish, Bonita noticed his eyes were getting heavy, and she laid him down on a quilt she had placed in the soft grass above the creek bank.

She walked over to where Ross was fishing.

"Boy asleep?"

"Uh-huh."

"Come here and fish a bit."

As he handed her the pole, he put his arms around her. "Here. I'll help you cast."

He stepped back but stayed close behind her. She felt his breath on the back of her neck. Her heart sped up, and she squelched the desire to put down the pole and throw herself into his arms.

"You feel it, too, don't you?"

She took a deep breath to calm herself. "I don't know what you're talkin' about. I'm just standin' here fishin'."

Another chuckle. "Sure, you are, honey. And you just missed a bite. Let me help you bring him in."

His arms came back around her, and she forgot to breathe.

After the fourth bass was caught and strung, she started to walk away. "Guess you better take us home now. I need to get Bobby Joe in bed."

He put his arms around her and turned her toward him. "What's the hurry? He looks like he's sleepin' fine."

"We need to get home. He's goin' to be wantin' his dinner when he wakes up."

"We got fish. I can build a fire and cook them right here."

"He's too little to eat fish. He might choke on the bones."

"I didn't think about that. All right, I'll take you home... but on one condition."

"What's that?"

"You'll let me give you a goodbye kiss."

She opened her mouth to protest, but the next second Ross invaded her mouth with a thrusting tongue. Her bones melted, and her flesh fell away as she was consumed by his lust and her need. If it hadn't been for the rough rocks that he attempted to lay her on, she would have never come to her senses.

When she felt their sharpness digging into her calves, she pushed back and yelled, "Stop."

He sighed and let her back up but kept his arms around her. "Are you sure?"

"Of course, I am. What do you take me for, Ross Stone?" She pulled herself out of his arms.

"Darlin', I would take you anyway I could get you."

Bonita smacked him in the face.

Ross rubbed his cheek and gaped at her. "Why'd you do that for?"

"You had it comin'. Now take us home."

"I'm sorry, Bonita. I guess I just got carried away a little."

"More than a little."

SHE DIDN'T TALK to him all the way home. When they parked in front of her grandma's house, he pleaded with her. "Please, Bonita. Please forgive me. I have just loved you for such a long time that I forgot myself. It won't happen again."

She struggled to open the door and carry Bobby out. "You're right. It *won't* happen again. Because there won't be another time."

"Here, let me carry him."

She allowed it, and they walked up to the front door. As he handed Bobby over to her, she saw tears in his eyes.

"Please, won't you at least think about forgivin' me?"

As she looked into his large, dark, wet eyes, her resolve shattered. "I'll think about it."

His smile lit up his face. "That's all I ask."

TWO DAYS LATER Bonita saw Ross, but he didn't see her. She was shopping at the back of the Stones' store when she heard the front door open. Amelia Stone, who was helping out that day, had barely spoke when she came in, but she had a lot to say to the newcomer.

"Ross, what are you doing here? I thought you were working today."

"I was, but I asked the boss if I could leave early, and he said I could."

"Why did you want off early?"

"I needed time to get ready. Thought I might go by Della O'Dell's house and see if Bonita will go out with me this evenin'."

Amelia's volume and tone reflected her anger. "How many times do I have to tell you? You shouldn't get involved with a loose woman like Bonita Smith."

Ross chuckled, and Bonita could picture his grin as he made a joke. "How many times do I have to tell you, Ma? Bonita ain't a loose woman, and I should know because I tried to loosen her up more than once."

Amelia didn't laugh, and Bonita knew the harsh words she spoke were for her benefit. "Ross, you've already made three big mistakes in your life. You quit school, you got a girl pregnant, and you abandoned your daughter. If you get involved with Bonita Smith, you'll be makin' a fourth mistake."

Ross's tone was just as cold. "And I don't see that as bein' any of your business."

When he slammed the door, the whole store shook.

"YOU CAN COME out now, Bonita. I know you have been listening."

Bonita's cheeks were red, and her heart was hammering. She stepped out and faced Amelia. "I don't know what I ever done to you to make you hate me so much."

Amelia's puzzled gaze surprised her. "I don't hate you, child. I just don't think you're the right woman for my son."

"Not good enough, you mean."

"Not *strong* enough. You're just like your father, lovely to look at, but weak at your core. Ross needs a woman who's stronger than he is, someone who can help him fight his destructive impulses."

Bonita put the items she had chosen on the counter. "I won't be needin' these after all." She slammed the door almost as hard as Ross and walked home, crying.

LATE THAT NIGHT she was awakened by strange sounds coming from the front porch. As she ran into the living room, she heard Della's loud whispers. "It's that fool Ross Stone, drunk as a skunk and whooping like a wild Indian. See if you can get rid of him, or he'll wake the baby up."

Ross grabbed her as soon as she opened the front door. "There you are, darlin'. What took you so long?"

"Hush, Ross. You're goin' to wake Bobby Joe up."

"So, what's wrong with that? We can take him to the lake with us. Bet he ain't never seen a big lake like Tenkiller." He let her go and gave her a little push. "Go on and get him. We'll all go to the lake."

"Ross, it's the middle of the night. We need to wait until mornin'."

His smile faded, his eyes turned black, and his tone grew belligerent. "No, we gotta go now. Nighttime is the best time to fish. Everybody knows that. We'll fish until daylight, and then we'll jump in the lake and go swimmin'."

He shoved her, and she almost fell. "Go on now. Go get the boy. Don't make me tell you again."

Bonita went back in and locked the door behind her. "I'm scared, Granny. He's gettin' rough."

"He's a mean drunk then, and somebody could get hurt. Don't mess with him. You go on back to your baby. I'll take care of Ross Stone."

Della brought out a shotgun she had been hiding behind her back.

"Where did you get that?"

"From the back of the closet. I got it out when I heard him carryin' on."

Bonita put her arm on Della's shoulder. "You won't shoot him, will you?"

"Not unless I have to. Go on now and see to your baby."

Bobby Joe was whimpering, and Bonita picked him up. She could hear Ross banging on the door and Della yelling, "I told you to get away from my door, and you better listen."

When she heard gunfire, she ran into the front room with Bobby in her arms. "Don't shoot him, Granny. "

"I didn't shoot him, just shot near him to run him off. Look out the window and see for yourself."

Bonita watched as Ross stumbled back to his truck, started it up, and roared away.

SHE FRETTED ABOUT him all day. Once she went outside to drive over to the Stones' Store, remembered her latest confrontation with Amelia Stone, and came back inside.

But still she worried.

Della noticed her worry and scolded her. "You need to forget all about that Ross Stone. He's a mean drunk, and you're better off without him. Lord knows what might have happened if you and Bobby had gone off with him to that lake."

A dark feeling of dread swept over her when she saw the sheriff's car pull up that evening. When she opened the door, he wasted no time in small talk. "Miss Bonita, I need to talk to you."

"Sure, Sheriff. Come in."

He sat on the edge of the sofa, with his straw cowboy hat resting on his knees. "Did Ross Stone come by here last night?"

"Yes sir."

"What did he want?"

"He wanted to take me and my little boy to the lake with him."

"Was he drunk?"

"Yes sir."

Della came in from the kitchen and interrupted. "He was crazy drunk. Yellin' and whoopin' and pushin' Bonita around."

He turned his attention and his eyes to Della. "Was you women afraid of him?"

"We sure was."

"Scared enough to shoot him?"

Bonita gasped, and he turned back toward her. "I seen them shell cases on your yard. You got somethin' you need to tell me, Miss Bonita?"

Bonita wrung her hands. "Granny only shot close to him to scare him, and she only did it because she was afraid he might hurt us."

"Is that right, Della?"

"That's right." Granny's dark eyes glittered. "If I'd wanted to shoot him, I could have, and that's probably what he deserved. But if someone killed him, it weren't me."

Bonita sobbed. "Did somethin' happen to Ross?"

"That's what I'm tryin' to find out. His ma said he caused a ruckus at their house, hollerin' he was goin' to the lake with you, and she couldn't stop him. He never come home. Likely he's just passed out somewhere, but she's carryin' on that she knows somethin' happened to him. Michael asked me to see if I could track him down to put her mind at ease. You both say he was alive when he left your place late last night, right?"

After they had both agreed, Bonita accompanied him to the front porch. "Could I ask you to let me know what you find out about Ross?"

"Sure, Miss Bonita. Now don't worry yourself. Like I said before, I'll likely find him, sleepin' it off under a tree or somewhere."

DESPITE THE SHERIFF'S assurance, Bonita slept very little that night. The next morning Della asked her to go to the store for groceries. "I really hate to go back, Granny. Amelia Stone talked awful mean to me the last time I was there."

"Well, I would go myself, but my arthritis is acting up somethin' awful. We're all out of salt pork and beans, and our lard and baking soda is gettin' low. Can't you just go in, buy your groceries, and leave?"

She sighed. "All right. I guess I can try."

The store was packed. It reminded Bonita of the day the Pettibone girl disappeared. None of the Stone family was there, and Tom Swimmer, Susan's husband, was running the store with the help of his sister, Berniece. All around her, she could hear people exchanging gossip.

One heavyset, middle-aged woman was telling everyone, "I heard tell Ross Stone's gone off to live like a hermit in a cave in the woods. Got mad at his family and said he never wanted to see them again."

A sneering bootlegger was whispering to anyone near enough to hear him, "Nah, Ross got in trouble with the big boys for tryin' to steal their profits. He's on the scout, but they're hot on his trail. If they find him, they'll knock him in the head and drown him in the lake."

A young housewife entertained the crowd with a romantic story. "That good-lookin' Ross probably seduced the new Methodist preacher's wife and run off with her to Arkansas. She left her husband yesterday, you know."

The scariest and most believable story was related by the old Cherokee Moe Sanders. "Went by the Stone house this mornin' 'cause I heard they had trouble. We're kinfolks, you know, on the Wolf side. Amelia heard two birds close to her house yesterday morning, a screech owl and a raven. Last night she heard somethin' howlin' in the woods. Then she started howlin' herself and screamin', 'My boy is dead.' They tied her to the bed to keep her from hurtin' herself, and now she's layin' there, not movin' a muscle, just like a dead woman.'"

Moe abruptly stopped talking when he noticed Bonita, standing nearby. He pointed her out with his chin. "That girl there could tell us more about what happened. She was the last one to see Ross alive."

Bonita gasped as every eye turned toward her, and she ran from the store, sobbing. She almost fainted when the sheriff's deputy met her at the bottom of the steps. "Sheriff said to tell you what happened to Ross Stone. Said he knew you'd want to know. He's at the Stone house right now, tellin' them they found Ross's body in Lake Tenkiller a couple of hours ago."

For a second, she felt her surroundings fade away. The deputy kept her from falling by grabbing her arm. "Are you all right, Miss Bonita?"

She shook her head to clear it and brushed away his hand from her arm. "I'm fine. Thank you." She stumbled home in a daze.

Later, lying on her bed with a cool, wet cloth on her throbbing forehead, she heard Bobby Joe ask, "Why Mama cry?"

She was thankful when Grandma distracted him with an offer to take him for a walk, but she jumped when the backdoor banged as they left. Her nerves were on edge, her head hurt, and her soul was crushed and flat. She closed her eyes and sensed herself sinking into a dark oblivion. Her eyes opened in semi-darkness to the sound of a whining child.

"Come on, my boy. You need to eat if you want to grow up big and strong."

The whining stopped, and chubby arms reached out when Bobby saw her standing by the kitchen door. "Mama."

She made herself smile for him. "Well, hello, sweet boy. Let's eat some supper."

Della handed Bobby over. "What do you think we should take to the Stones tomorrow?"

Bonita closed her eyes in pain. "Do we have to see them tomorrow?"

Della put down her silverware and gave her a hard look. "Well, of course, we do. I knowed the Stones for nigh to thirty years, and your pa knew them before I did. Why, Amelia came to your ma and pa's weddin', bought them a present and ever'thing. It's our Christian duty to offer them a little food and comfort to help them through their hard time."

"I don't think they'll want to see me. Besides, how are we goin' to get our food to them? I can't very well walk, carryin' pots and pans, all the way to their house."

"Just walk over to the preacher's house in the mornin' and ask when they are takin' food. They probably won't mind if we hitch a ride."

"All right. I'll check the cabinets and see what we got to work with. I didn't get the groceries I went after today."

Numbly, she searched the kitchen until she found the ingredients for a big peach cobbler. Early in the morning, she would check the garden for green beans. She could cook a big pot of them with some bacon grease. Probably fix a pan of cornbread to go with them. That ought to be enough.

Even when Bobby Joe fell into a sound sleep beside her, she stayed awake, thinking. Would Ross be alive if she and Bobby had gone to the lake with him?

After she had snapped the beans, put them on to cook, and asked Della to tend to them, she walked to Preacher McGinnis's house. A flushed Polly McGinnis welcomed her. "I told the mister you would probably be over this mornin'. We won't be goin' until around noon. I been bustlin' around all mornin', tryin' to get somethin' cooked. Just bring your food over by then, and you can ride with us."

"Are you sure you have room? The Potters might need a ride too, and there's a bunch of them."

"Well, bring your food over, and we will see."

All the way home she prayed that the Potters would all go, and she wouldn't have to face Amelia Stone. In case they didn't, she would work on Grandma.

"Grandma, there's a good chance that the preacher won't have room for all of us to ride with them today. Why don't me and Bobby carry your pans over, and you can ride with them? You ain't been away from the house in quite a while."

"I'll consider it, but you really should go, too."

But Bonita shivered at the thought of facing Amelia Stone and her family.

When they arrived at the McGinnis house at a few minutes before twelve, Bonita was glad to see that all four members of the Potter family had already claimed the back seat. When Mr. Potter saw them approach the car, he said, "You kids climb on our laps, and let these ladies sit."

She smiled at him. "That's all right, Mister Potter. If you'll just make room for Grandma, Bobby Joe and I can walk back home. He's been known to get car sick if he gets too crowded in the back seat."

About five hours later, Mr. McGinnis delivered Grandma back home with her empty pots and pans. She bustled into the house, bursting with excitement. "Oh, you should have saw all the folks that were there. I saw almost everybody I know and plenty that I don't. The family is all takin' it pretty good, except for Amelia. She's not talkin' or eatin', just sits in her rockin' chair, rockin' and starin' off into space. "

"Are all of the kids there? "

Grandma smirked. "You are really askin' me if Clay Stone was there, ain't you?"

"Well, maybe."

"He's not home yet, but they're pickin' him up in the mornin' at the depot in Stilwell. The funeral'll be day after tomorrow at the Baptist Church. Close enough that we can walk."

When the day of the funeral arrived, Bonita dressed Bobby and herself in their best clothes. Della wore her good black dress and pinned a black pillbox hat atop her braided bun.

She frowned at her grandaughter's blue floral dress. "You need to buy you a nice black dress for funerals."

"Maybe I will someday when I get some money ahead, but this is the best I can do today. At least it's not bright"

When they got to the church, Bonita went to sit in the back row, but Della resisted. "You can sit back here if you want to, but I can't hear or see anything from here. Let's sit closer to the front."

"You go ahead, Granny. I need to sit close to the back in case Bobby fusses. "

As if he were taking a cue from his mother, Bobby began to whine. "See what I mean?"

"Humph. Suit yourself." Granny seated herself on the third row.

She picked Bobby up and took him to the small foyer where a large, metal drinking cannister, with small paper cups, was kept. "Hush, Bobby, and I'll get you a drink of water."

As she was guiding the cup to his little mouth, the church door opened, and the Clay family filed in. She hurriedly moved aside to allow them room to enter the sanctuary.

Most of the family spoke or nodded to her. The last ones to enter were Amelia Stone, being supported by her husband Michael and her daughter, Emily. Right behind them was Belle Springwater and Ross's little girl, Rose. Amelia and Belle stared straight ahead, but Michael and Emily spoke to her.

A tall, handsome soldier brought up the rear. Clay's eyes met hers, and he smiled. The smile disappeared when he saw Bobby Joe by her side. His green eyes widened with shock, but he gave her a quick nod.

The casket at the front of the church was closed. Granny had told her this was done because of the damage the water had done to Ross's body. Bonita cried when she realized she would never see Ross's beautiful face again.

When Bobby looked at her in alarm, she forced a smile. "Time to sit down, son. You be a good boy now."

The service was short and relatively quiet. The only signs of mourning were wet handkerchiefs and stifled sobs. Bonita was glad that Bobby Joe fell asleep so she could listen to the preaching and the songs sung in Cherokee.

She was able to dissuade Grandma from joining the procession to the Clay Family Cemetery by saying, "It's too far to walk and carry Bobby, and if I put him down, he will wake up and cry."

"All right. Truth be told, I don't feel up to a long walk myself."

BONITA CRIED ON and off for days after the funeral. She couldn't stop asking herself if she were to blame for Ross's death.

VIII
A NEW
LIFE

SEVERAL WEEKS LATER, Bonita drove her old white Studebaker to the Stones' Store to buy groceries. Over the last couple of months, she had learned to only shop on Saturdays to avoid seeing Amelia Stone. Amelia never worked on Saturdays, leaving the store in the hands of her oldest daughter Susan and Susan's husband, Tom Swimmer.

Once Susan drew her aside on the pretense of showing her some new merchandise. When they were in a quiet corner where no one could hear, she put her hands on her hips. "Why do you only come here on Saturdays?"

She blushed and stammered a bit. Regaining her composure, she got out, "I think you know why."

Susan smiled reassuringly. "If you're talkin' about Ma, she never mentions you or even Ross anymore. I think she wants to forget about it, and I don't think she would say a word if you shopped while she was here."

She returned the smile. "I'd rather not take the chance."

Susan stifled a giggle with her hand. "Yeah, I know what you mean. By the way, I see you're drivin' now. I like your car."

"Thanks. It's all I could afford on my salary as a bank teller."

"I heard you got a job workin' in a bank in Tahlequah. Do you like it?"

"Yes, I do. I was so long finishin' high school, I wasn't sure I could find a job, so I was glad when they hired me at Cherokee National."

"Well, good luck to you. Guess I better get back to work."

As Bonita walked around the store, she heard someone crying. She peered up into where the big feed sacks were stacked and saw an old man, sitting on a stack, head bowed, rocking and sobbing. "What's wrong? Can I help you?"

He stopped rocking, raised his head, and met her gaze. "I'm lookin' for Martha and Ross. Do you know where they are?"

Tears of pity filled Bonita's eyes. "No, I don't, Josh, but I will get someone to help you."

She went to the counter where Susan was working on some accounts. "Susan, your grandpa is sittin' on the feed sacks, cryin'. He says he's lookin' for Martha and Ross."

Susan closed the big book and sighed, "Not again. Tom, he's up on the feed stacks again. You better get him down before he falls."

She heard someone talking under his breath in Cherokee, and Tom came around the corner. "I'll get him down, but I think you better take him to stay with your ma. I can't get nothin' done for having to fetch him down a dozen times a day."

Susan sighed. "All right. Just get him down, and I'll take him to Ma to watch." She turned to Bonita. "He's been this way ever since Ross died. Half the time he don't know where he is or who we are. His mind's gettin' worse all the time. Go ahead, finish your shoppin', and pay Tom when you're done."

Bonita put her hand on Susan's. "I'm so sorry this happened to Josh. Pa always thought the world of him."

The other woman wiped away a tear. "We all did and still do, but in some ways, it's like we already lost him."

A WEEK LATER, Bonita and Grandma were sitting on the porch talking, watching Bobby play at their feet with a small toy truck, when a shiny black Chevrolet pulled up in front of the house.

"Good mornin', ladies." Clay Stone, trim and elegant in his Army uniform, walked up the front steps. "Who's this good lookin' little man?"

"This is my little boy, Bobby Joe. I saw you at the funeral." She blinked her eyes to keep from crying. "I'm so sorry about Ross."

Clay looked down at the floor, and when he raised his eyes to meet her gaze, she saw tears glistening in them. "We all are. "

He took out a white handkerchief from his back pocket, wiped his eyes, and handed it to her to use. "They let me come home for the funeral, and when I went back, they made me wait another month before they signed my discharge papers."

"That's a nice car you have there."

"Yeah, I bought that in Dallas and drove it home." He looked around the yard. "Where's your old man?"

Grandma glared up at him. "They's separated, but she's still a married woman."

"Not for long. The divorce will be final in a few weeks. It would have been done long ago if I hadn't listened to Granny and put it off."

Clay's green eyes danced. "Is that right? In that case, would you like to come to a party at my house tonight?"

Bonita's heart gave a lurch at the thought of dancing in the arms of the tall, handsome soldier standing before her. Then she remembered Amelia would be there, judging her. "I don't know. Grandma would have to mind Bobby for me."

Clay's hopeful green eyes dazzled her. "I'm sure your grandma wouldn't mind."

"You're probably right. Let me talk to her in private for a little while, please."

"All right. I'll wait at the car. You can come and tell me when you make up your mind."

At first Grandma balked, but when she looked at Bonita's hopeful face, she gave in. "Oh, go ahead, girl. It's been a long time since you got to kick up your heels. If you're set on carryin' on, I'd rather it be with a decent sort than with a no-account."

Clay grinned from ear to ear when she gave him the news. "Good. I'll come back in a couple of hours and give you time to get ready. Bye, boy."

Bobby Joe gave a saucy wave. "Who's that man, Mama?"

"Just an old friend of Mama's. Granny, what am I goin' to wear? I don't have nothin' fit to wear to a party."

"Wear one of your church frocks. That lilac shirtwaist looks nice on you, and I can sew a little lace around the collar and sleeves to make it dressier."

Bonita stooped to give her a hug and a kiss. "Thanks, Granny."

"All right. Better let me go so I can get to work. Now remember I don't approve of this, but you're young enough that you think you gotta have a man, and Clay Stone's a better man than most. Just think on this. War does something to men. He ain't the same boy you remember."

WHEN CLAY TOLD Amelia the news, she showed her first flash of temper since Clay's arrival. "You said you're bringing that McKindle girl? She's a married woman, and I won't have any harlots in this house."

Clay spoke in slow, measured tones. "She's separated from Bob, and they're almost divorced."

"With all the pretty girls chasing you, why you want to get mixed-up with a woman like that is beyond me. Especially when she might have had something to do with your brother's death."

Clay sensed the old hurt and anger rising, and he looked down to see his hands balled into fists. "Now, Ma. I don't want to get mad at you, but you know what happened to Ross was his own fault. If you won't let me bring Bonita here, then I'll take her somewhere else, and I'll be movin' to the hotel in town. Your choice."

Emily put her hand on her mother's shoulder. "Ma, since this is a welcome home party for Clay, don't you think he should be able to bring who he wants?"

Amelia shut her eyes for a minute, sighed loudly, and looked at Clay. "All right. Go ahead and bring her, but don't blame me when she breaks your heart."

THAT NIGHT, BONITA had the best time she had experienced in months. She danced with a few of the men at the party, enjoying their admiring looks and ignoring the women's scowls. Then Clay took over and scowled at anyone who dared to approach her for a dance. She spent the rest of the evening in his arms or close to his side.

Once she caught Clay's younger sisters, Mary and Abigail, whispering while they gave her dirty looks, but the older sisters were very friendly. Zack, who was a younger version of Clay, turned beet red whenever Bonita or any girl looked at him. Michael welcomed her with a big smile, but Amelia barely looked at her all evening.

The best part of the night came at the last dance of the evening. A lovestruck cowboy was crooning "You are My Sunshine" from the wind-up phonograph, and Clay's arms were holding her close to his lean, muscular body. He whispered to her, "I never stopped lovin' you, you know. All the time I was away I thought about you. It about killed me when they told me you was married, but when I came back from the war, I just had to see you." He pressed his lips to the back of her neck, and shivers ran down her spine.

When they parked in front of her grandmother's house, it was well after midnight. Clay clutched her to himself so tightly that she could barely breathe, but she didn't mind. She remembered this feeling from when Ross had caressed her on the riverbank. Bonita shook her head to send that memory away. Clay kissed her passionately on her eyes, her lips, her shoulders, but she came to herself as his mouth began traveling downward. "Clay, you mustn't. It's too soon."

"Too soon? I've been waitin' most my life for this."

"Not here and not now. I've got to go check on my little boy."

He settled for one long, deep kiss and walked her to the front door. "When can I see you again?"

"We better stick to Friday and Saturday nights. I have to get up early and drive to work during the week. We can see each other as long as Grandma will watch Bobby Joe."

THOUGH AMELIA RAILED against it, Clay continued to see Bonita every weekend. He had a fever that only her presence could cool. But although she allowed him liberties, she didn't grant him complete satisfaction, and the fever grew until he thought he would die from it.

When he first got home, he couldn't get enough of Amelia's home cooking, but after he started dating Bonita, his appetite fell off so much that even his father noticed. "Clay, are you sick or somethin'? You barely finish one plate of food these days."

Emily dug her elbow into Clay's ribs and grinned. "He's sick all right, *love* sick."

Michael chuckled. "I should have known. That pretty, little McKindle girl is keepin' your head so occupied that you don't know whether you're hungry or full."

Amelia huffed. "She's not a girl anymore, and her name's not Mc-Kindle. It's Smith. She's been married, and she has a child. Clay could do a lot better than Bonita Smith."

Clay got up from the table. "Did you ever think that maybe I don't *want* to do better than Bonita? She's the woman I want, and that's all there is to it."

Michael pushed his plate aside and grabbed Clay's shoulder. "I'm not losin' another son." He gave a sideways glance at Amelia who just scowled. "Come on. Let's get some air."

Clay's eyes warmed, and he grinned at his father and nodded.

LATER THAT NIGHT, parked in front of Della's house, Clay cried out, "Bonita, when can we get married? I can't wait any longer."

These were the words Bonita had been yearning for. She was burning for Clay as much as he burned for her, but she was no fool to risk an unwanted pregnancy when no words of marriage had been spoken. "It won't be long, sweetheart."

"That's what you keep sayin', but Bob keeps sittin' on them divorce papers. Maybe I need to have a little talk with him."

Bonita put her hand on his clenched fists. "That won't be necessary. He finally signed them, and I got them in the mail yesterday. The divorce will be final next week. Then we can get married, and we won't have to wait any longer."

"When next week?"

"Thursday."

"Good. Next Friday we'll drive over to Arkansas and get married. There's no waiting for tests and things there. Ask your boss for the day off and give him your notice."

"Why do I have to quit my job? I like workin' at the bank."

"We'll be movin' to Tulsa. There's lots of good payin' jobs there, and it will be good to get away from this place."

Bonita thought about protesting but didn't want to start their marriage with a fuss. Clay knew best, and she would find a new job in Tulsa.

They were married by the Fayetteville Justice of Peace the next Friday. She wore a pink satin dress that Clay had asked Emily to choose for him from a dress shop in Tahlequah. When he had handed her the dress on a hanger, he handed her a white paper bag. "You need somethin' pretty to sleep in, too."

That night Clay rented a room for them in the Cherokee Hotel in Tahlequah, and she allowed him to quench his fever in her welcoming body.

MARRIED LIFE WAS sheer bliss those first months. She kissed Clay goodbye every morning as she watched him stride down the street, his black lunchbox swinging in rhythm to the pumping of his long arms and legs.

Once, she noticed a painted-up blonde giving him the eye, but he didn't seem to notice. She couldn't really blame the hussy. With his dark looks and muscular 6'2" frame, Clay was a dead ringer for Clint Walker. The army had done away with the slight pudginess and the clumsiness that had plagued his boyhood. At 23 he was as near an ideal specimen of manhood as Bonita had seen off the movie screen, and she was incredibly lucky that he came home to her each night. Came home cold sober, eager to share the warm meal and exciting marriage bed that waited for him.

Her marriage would have been perfect except for two minor details. She had thought she would get another job when they moved to Tulsa, but Clay soon squashed her hopes. "You don't need to work. I make enough money in construction to support all of us, and you don't need that Studebaker if you're not drivin' anywhere. I'll sell it. The money will come in handy."

She meekly accepted that he knew best.

But the worse thing was Clay's jealousy. Once he had jerked her through the door of their house when one of their neighbors had called out a friendly greeting. "Why's old Jordan being so chummy all of a sudden? You been keepin' him company while I been workin'?"

Shocked and frightened, she begged him to believe she barely knew Hank Jordan, and he was just a neighborly person. He finally seemed to accept her explanation, but she caught him staring at her every time they were around men. She soon learned to keep her head down whenever she and Clay met a man. That way he couldn't accuse her of trying to attract attention to herself.

Bonita also worried about Clay's change in attitude toward Bobby

Joe. Although he had never been overly affectionate with her little boy, he had talked to him and occasionally patted him on the head. After they were married, Clay mostly ignored Bobby unless he thought Bobby was misbehaving, then he was quick to scold him harshly. When she looked at Bobby's stricken face, she wondered about the man she had married. Maybe Granny was right about war changing men.

But Bonita tried not to dwell on their problems and tried to focus on the good things. She loved living in a modern home. For the first time in her life, she lived in a house with a telephone, and she loved it. Unfortunately, none of her family had telephones, except for Uncle Arthur, and since that would be an expensive, long-distance charge, she seldom got to call him.

They did hear from Emily every Sunday afternoon. When she called, after asking how everyone at home was, Clay turned the phone over to Bonita, and went outside to smoke. Emily told her all the gossip and made a point of mentioning any news she had heard about Bonita's family. They talked for several minutes usually until Clay came back in and sat down to read the newspaper. One Sunday, Emily called with exciting news about herself.

"*Guess what, Bonita? I'm getting married.*"

"That's wonderful. Who's the lucky man?"

"*I don't think you ever met him. He took Mister Strickland's place as history teacher. His name is Thaddeus Donovan.*"

"What does Amelia think of him?"

"*Oh, you know Ma. First, she claimed he was too old for me. He's eight years older, but you would think it was twenty. Next, somehow, she learned he divorced his first wife, and that really set her off. Pa had to promise he would talk to Thaddeus and see if he was 'worthy' of me.*"

"Oh, no. How did that go?"

"*I guess it went all right because we're getting married as soon as school's out. And guess what? We're going up to Niagara Falls for our honeymoon.*"

"How exciting. Well, I think he's perfect for you. He teaches history, and you teach science. I bet you have really smart babies, too."

Bonita could hear the longing in Emily's voice. *"Oh, I hope so. We both really want kids. Thaddeus's first wife was so selfish that all she wanted to do was spend all his money on fancy clothes and run around with other men. He says he's glad to find a wife who loves him and wants the same things he does, a home and children."*

"I'm so happy for you. Now you let us know when you set the date. Maybe I can talk Clay into coming to your wedding."

"Well, he should be willing to come. He hasn't come home for a visit since Christmas."

"I know, but you know how stubborn he is. And here he comes now. Guess I better go keep him company. Goodbye, Emily. Tell everybody hello for me."

"I will. Goodbye."

WHEN SHE TOLD Clay Emily was getting married, he said, "Well, that's good. I was afraid she was goin' to end up as an old maid. There's no reason to go all the way back to Jubilee just to go to a weddin', though."

Emily called the next Sunday, and Bonita gave her the bad news. She wasn't concerned. *"Don't worry. I'll have Pa ask Clay, and he'll come."*

The next Sunday Michael called, and she heard Clay say, "All right, Pa. When is it again?"

She grinned when he said, "Well, I guess we'll be going to a weddin' in a couple of weeks."

He handed her a twenty-dollar bill. "Buy yourself something new to wear."

Bonita picked up Bobby, who had his arms up, wanting to be held. "How about some new clothes for Bobby? He doesn't have anything fit to wear to a weddin'."

Clay sighed, pulled out his billfold, and handed her a ten-dollar bill. "Always somethin' for the kid. Just bought him some new shoes last week. Didn't know kids was so expensive."

"Well, they're worth it."

"Yeah, if you say so."

The wedding was a big affair for Jubilee. They arrived the evening before at the Stone house to a regular hullabaloo. Emily greeted them at the door. "Ma is having a fit because Susan didn't make a new dress for Lydia. I gotta drive her to the store so she can find some material there. Guess she'll be up all night sewing. It really doesn't matter to me whether or not I have a flower girl at my wedding, but Ma wants everything to be perfect."

Amelia appeared at her side. "I don't know where your father disappeared to, but we better get to going. Clay, we left supper on the table, so help yourselves, and you can all sleep in your old room."

Amelia didn't speak to Bonita but surprised her by bending down to speak to Bobby. "Well, hello, little man. I am glad you came to see us. I made you a chocolate cake today. You can have some after you finish your supper."

"Thank you, Grandma Amelia."

"You're very welcome, Bobby Joe. Goodbye now."

Bonita's stomach growled at the big spread of food on the table. "Do you know where your mother keeps the silverware? I see plates and lots of food but nothin' to eat with."

Clay cut himself a piece of warm cornbread. "In the drawer closest to the sink. She probably got in such a tizzy about the wedding that she forgot."

Bonita laid forks, spoons, and butter knives beside their plates. They were still eating when Michael came in.

"When did ya'll get here?"

"Just a few minutes ago. Ma was lookin' for you."

Michael located some silverware and sat down beside Clay. "Yeah, that's what I figured, and that's why I made myself scarce."

Clay chuckled. "What's wrong, Pa? Ain't you enjoyin' the weddin'?"

"I'm goin' to enjoy it a lot more when it's done. Your ma has been like a mad, wet hen for days now, fussin' about the big weddin'."

For some reason, Bonita found herself defending Amelia. "I

guess it's important to her since Emily is the first of your kids to have a real wedding."

Michael looked up from buttering his cornbread. "You're probably right, but I would just as soon give them some money to get their house set up."

The small church was filled with the family and friends the next morning. A beaming little Lydia, dressed in the frilly, pink dress Amelia had made for her during the night, strewed pink rose petals down the aisle. She was followed by her mother and her aunts, all dressed in pink satin dresses.

Emily, her dark hair streaming down her back, dressed in a full, white satin dress, came down the aisle on her father's arm. Bonita nudged Clay. "Doesn't Emily look beautiful? I haven't seen her with her hair down like that since we were kids."

Clay smiled at his favorite sister. "She does look real nice at that."

Bonita looked over at Amelia. Her tired eyes shone bright with pride and joy for her second born. As her eyes scanned the crowd, she saw nothing but happiness in the faces around her. Emily had earned a place of honor in the community, as a dutiful daughter and a respected teacher.

CLAY'S GOOD MOOD from the wedding didn't last. Soon after they came back home, he began chiding her for "spendin' so much time with the kid."

Once he even pushed the little boy away when he tried to climb into his mother's lap. "You baby that boy too much."

Bobby Joe began to cry, and she picked him up. She was furious. "Well, he's not much more than a baby. He's only five."

"Five is old enough to know when to get quiet. Shut up, boy, before I give you something to cry about."

Seeing the anger dancing in his green eyes, she grew apprehensive. "Go to bed, Bobby. Mama will be in to tuck you in later."

This seemed to appease Clay, and he smiled and drew her into his lap. An hour or so later when she went into Bobby's tiny room, she sighed when she saw him clutching a tear-stained teddy bear close to his chest. It was to be the first of many nights that the poor tyke cried himself to sleep.

Life went on in a basic routine with Clay going off to work each morning to a Tulsa-based construction company. They soon had enough saved to buy a second-hand television set. The television brought a new aspect to their lives, home entertainment. Each night after supper, he would stretch his long frame on their worn, faded sofa, eyes glued to the magical box while Bonita washed the dishes and cleaned the kitchen.

Bobby had learned to play quietly in his room when it was too rainy or cold to play outside. It had only taken two swats from Clay's hard hand to teach him not to make noise close to the television.

She mused as she scrubbed the chicken grease out of her cast iron skillet. Even though it wasn't perfect, life was much better with Clay than it had ever been with Bob. Now she never had to worry about managing money. He took care of all financial matters and wouldn't hear of her looking for a job. It would be nice to make some money of her own, but he did give her a small portion of his weekly paycheck to buy groceries and other household necessities. Thrifty Bonita had even been able to save a paltry amount each week, unbeknownst to Clay. Still, she would dearly love to buy some new furniture for the house, but she was afraid he would get angry if she did. Almost all of their furnishings were worn out stuff that Granny had given them or they had bought cheap at the Goodwill Store, like their used television set.

For some reason, she could never make him understand her feeling about buying her own possessions, just like he couldn't understand her need to have friends. He scoffed at her when she said she would like to ask some neighbors over for supper some night. "Why do you want to ask anybody over? I been around people all day, and I'm tired of them. All I want to do is come home after work and relax."

"But I been here in the house all day, just me and Bobby, and I would like to talk to somebody else once in a while. When school starts in a few months, it's really going to be quiet around here."

"What's the matter? Ain't I enough for you, or are you hot to trot for somebody else?"

"Of course not, Clay. You know I only care for you. I'm sorry I brought it up."

"See that you don't bring it up again. Pop us some corn and come watch the fights with me."

"At least he doesn't drink," she mumbled as she continued to scrape at the hardened grease.

ONE MONDAY MORNING, after being cooped-up all weekend with Clay and Bobby, Bonita grabbed for a piece of freedom. That adventurous morning, after she put Bobby on the school bus, she called the number she had noticed in the phonebook right after they got their phone, R. Freedle.

The minute a lady answered the phone and drawled out a country, *"Hello,"* Bonita knew it was her old friend.

"Hello, Ramona. Guess who this is?"

"Bonita McKindle. Whatcha doin' in T Town?"

"Livin' here. I married Clay Stone almost two years ago, and we moved here."

"This is too good to be true. Today's my day off, and I hear from you. Can you come over and see me? My apartment is real easy to find."

"Well, we only have the one car, so I don't have a way."

"That's no problem. I'll just come pick you up. What's your address?"

She hesitated, worrying what would happen if Clay found out, but she decided to chance it. "Sure. It's 6413 North Trenton."

A few minutes later, Ramona greeted Bonita with an enthusiastic hug. "Bonita, it's been so long. You know you haven't changed a bit, still as pretty as ever."

"Well, I can't say the same for you. You look like a movie star."

Ramona patted her bleached hair, batted her mascara-covered lashes and agreed. "Yeah, I don't look much like that skinny, little, dirty girl that I useta be, huh?"

"You sure don't. And I love your black dress. Where did you get it?"

"At Renberg's. I do all my clothes shoppin' there."

"Renberg's? But I thought that was an expensive place."

"It is, but when you have a feller who likes to buy you pretty things, you can afford it. Come on and jump in the car. We'll be in my place in less than twenty minutes."

She stroked the soft leather seats. "Is this a Cadillac?"

"Sure is. I got it ordered special just for me."

Later, she looked around the tastefully-decorated apartment. The soft mauves and blues that dominated the living room were a sharp contrast to Bonita's battered, time-worn furniture. "I like the way you decorated this."

"Pretty classy, huh? It was all Hermy's doin'."

"Who's Hermy?"

"My boyfriend. There's his picture."

Ramona motioned to a large, gold-framed picture, sitting on her mantle. A gray-haired, bespectacled, pleasant-looking man grinned down at them.

"I know he's not much to look at, but he's been real good to me. If it wasn't for Hermy, I would still be livin' in that little cracker box I used to live in, slavin' on the line."

She sat down on the plush, floral sofa and patted a place beside her. "Sit down and let's talk."

She took the offered place. "So, where do you work now?"

"Oh, still at the fact'ry, but now I work part-time in the office as Hermy's secretary. He paid for me to have the secretary trainin' and everything."

"Are you plannin' on marryin' him?"

"Lord, no. *Marry* Hermy? He's already married, and that old bat he's married to won't give him no divorce. Not that I would marry him if I could. He's a nice enough feller, but can you imagine cookin' and waitin' on him and takin' care of him when he gets old and sick? Not this gal."

"So, you don't really love him?"

"Sure, I love him, and I'm good to him. I would never think of cheatin' on him, but I'll love my next man just as much. It's like that old sayin', 'I'd rather be an old man's darlin' than a young man's slave.' Well, that's spells out the way I feel.'"

She shook her head. "That's just hard for me to imagine. You know I been married twice. First to Bob Smith and then to Clay Stone."

"Well, I'm not surprised about Clay. He was always makin' eyes at you, even when we was kids. I always thought he would make a handsome man. I figured you would either marry him or his brother. I heard what happened to Ross. What a shame."

Bonita dropped her eyes. "I blamed myself for that for a long time."

Ramona wrinkled her brow and frowned at her. "What for? Didn't he just get drunk and drown?"

"Uh-huh, but he came to me before he went to Tenkiller, beggin' me to bring Bobby Joe and go with him. If I had, I might have been able to talk him out of jumpin' in the water." Bonita wiped a tear from her eye.

Ramona reached over and patted her hand. "You oughta know better than that, girl. Was you ever able to talk your dad out of leavin' the house when he was so drunk he couldn't see straight?"

"No, I never could."

"Same difference. Only Ross might have drug you and your baby both out in the middle of the lake, just playin' around. Then all three of you would be dead."

She gasped. "I never thought of that."

She grabbed her friend in a fierce hug. "Thank you, Ramona. You don't know how you helped me today."

Extracting herself, Ramona stood up. "Glad I could help. Do you want some coffee? I got some made in the kitchen."

Over coffee and store-bought cookies, Bonita shared her worries.

"I love Clay with all my heart, but he's powerful jealous of me. I guess that's because he loves me so much."

"Huh. From what I know of jealousy, it's closer to hate than love. My first boyfriend here in Tulsa was good-lookin' and young, but he about drove me crazy with his jealousy. Got to followin' me to work just to see who I would talk to. This was before Hermy. Then one night he slapped me just because I had to work late. He accused me of sleepin' around. Well, that tore it. That night I packed all of my things and cleared-out. Oh, he tried to say he was sorry, but I know how that type is. He would have done it again, and I ain't puttin' up with mistreatment no more. I got enough of it when I was young. Hey, how about us shoppin' and eatin' lunch later, my treat?"

"All right. Long as I get home before Bobby gets home from school."

Bonita had more fun with Ramona than she had experienced in years. Ramona knew all the best places to shop and eat. She even insisted on buying Bobby a football. "Think of it as my baby shower gift since I couldn't make it to your first one."

"I never had a baby shower."

"All the more reason I should give you something."

"I guess I could pass it off as somethin' I found in the park. Clay knows I walk to the park for exercise sometimes." Bonita studied Ramona's smiling face. "Do you ever wonder about your little boy?"

The smile slipped, and Ramona hesitated for a moment. "No, not really. To me that old life is dead and gone."

Ramona dropped her a block away from the Jordan house at Bonita's insistence. "If they should say anything to Clay about seein' you, I would have to answer a bunch of questions."

"Yeah, I can imagine. 'Who's that street walker you been runnin' around with?'"

"No, nothin' like that. Clay just don't like me bein' with anybody, except him."

"Sounds like my old boyfriend. Listen, Bonita, you helped me once, and I would be glad to do the same for you. If you ever need me to get away from Clay or anything, all you have to do is call."

"Oh, Clay's not so bad, really. But please don't be offended if I ask you something."

Ramona took off her sunglasses and looked at her. "I won't be. What is it?"

"Please don't call me at my house. I'll try to call you every Monday because I don't want to lose touch now that I found you. I really need a friend, but Clay wouldn't understand."

"I understand and I won't call, but don't you forget what I said either. Bye, Bonita. Call me next Monday, and we'll do something else."

Ramona and Bonita enjoyed several weeks of adventure until the morning Bonita sprang from her bed to keep from gagging on last night's dinner. She slumped weakly beside the toilet after retching her insides out and pondered on the possible cause of her sickness. Oh, no. She was overdue on her period and sick in the morning. That could only mean one thing.

Clay was not as happy as she thought he would be when she broke the news to him.

"A kid, huh? Guess that means another mouth to feed." Seeing her disappointed face, he added, "Oh, well, it had to happen sometime. Maybe it will be a boy."

Bonita mentally hugged herself. She was going to have another baby—Clay's baby. And it would be beautiful. She had always liked babies, and being a mother suited her.

Six months later, as she pulled her bloated body out of bed and waddled into the kitchen to make Clay's breakfast, she wondered at her earlier feelings. She was hideous. Clay didn't take her anywhere anymore. He acted like he was ashamed of her. He gobbled his eggs and bacon down, gulped the hot coffee, and headed out the door.

"Clay, when are you going to be home tonight?"

"When I feel like it. Why?"

"I don't know. I just wondered. You came home so late last night that I know you had to eat a cold supper."

"That's all right. I ate a burger with the guys after the union meeting. We got one again tonight, so don't wait up."

He hastily slammed the door behind him and took off, swinging his lunch bucket, down the street. She watched him from the living room window. That same blonde hussy was looking at him. This time he waved and grinned. She better wait up tonight.

Shortly after midnight he quietly slipped the door open and turned on a living room lamp. He didn't see Bonita right away, but she gasped when she saw him. His hair was all mussed, and his white shirt was unbuttoned half-way and sticking out of his pants. Red lipstick marks were still visible on his neck. That explained the telltale stain she had noticed on his collars.

When he saw her, he cursed and straightened himself. "What are you doin' still up?"

"Waitin' for you."

"What for?"

"I wanted to see if what I thought was true."

"Yeah, what was that?"

"I wanted to see if you was steppin' out on me like I thought."

He grabbed her by the hair and pulled her to the bathroom mirror. "Look at yourself, Bonita. You're fat and ugly. A man's gotta have somethin' he can stand to be with, and that ain't you no more."

"Leave me alone. You're hurtin' me."

Bobby Joe cried out, and she hurried to quieten him before Clay could turn on him. She pulled the child to her and kissed him. "Hush, baby. It's all right. You just had a bad dream."

She looked up to see Clay standing in the door, his face pale with rage or regret. She couldn't tell which. He spoke quietly but firmly, "Go ahead and stay with the kid. I'll leave for a few days and let things cool off. Don't worry about money. I'll be home Friday evening and give you some grocery money."

He hurriedly packed a suitcase and left without saying anything. He was true to his word. He came home every Friday, ate supper, and gave her part of his paycheck. She didn't ask any questions.

Bonita visited the neighborhood gossip one morning, and the woman confirmed what she had already suspected. "I hate to tell you this, honey, but that husband of yours has been stayin' with that Pomroy woman, who lives on the corner. He ain't the first married man she's tried to take away from his family. It's sure a shame, you expectin' and all."

She thanked her for letting her know and secretly vowed to get the blonde whore after the baby was born.

RAMONA WAS HER rock. Every Monday morning she came by in her fancy car and took her for a day of shopping and visiting. Bonita asked the Jordans to watch Bobby if she didn't get home before the school bus arrived.

Once when they went to a matinee of a particularly sad love story, Ramona looked over to see her wiping tears. "Bonita, Lord. It's only a movie, nothin' to cry about."

"I know. I know. But the hero reminds me so much of Clay. He's so handsome. You don't know how much I miss him."

"Must be hormones or something. Seems to me it would be a good miss not to have to put up with that hateful thing."

"You just don't understand."

"Guess not, but I'm glad I don't."

ONE FRIDAY CLAY came home to an empty house and a hastily-scrawled note lying in the middle of their chrome kitchen table.

Took Bonita to the hospital. Bobby's staying with me and Hank.
Come to the hospital when you get home.

Betty Jordan

He threw the note down, jumped in his car, and drove to the nearest hospital. Yes, they had admitted a woman named Bonita Stone early that morning. She was in the recovery room. He would have to go to the maternity ward to find out any more information.

He stalked from the desk and soon arrived at the maternity ward waiting room. He frowned when he saw Bobby Joe sitting with the Jordans. The little boy shrank back from his intended head pat.

Hank held out his hand in greeting. "Glad to meet you, Clay. Bonita's told us a lot about you."

Clay ignored his hand, and Hank finally dropped it. "Yeah, well, why didn't you call me at work and tell me she was here?"

"We just done what she asked us to," piped up Betty. "Come on, mister. Don't you want to see your daughter?"

THE PETITE, GRAYING lady took his arm and escorted him to the viewing window. She pointed out a blanket-swathed infant near the front. "Isn't she beautiful? Look at all that dark hair." She smiled coquettishly at Clay. "Tell you what, fella, if you don't want that sweet baby, me and Hank will take her in a minute. We can't have children, you know. Oh, look at those pretty, bright eyes. Why, she's lookin' straight at her daddy."

Clay felt himself being drawn into the darkest blue eyes he had ever seen. His eyes misted with the intensity of a feeling he had never experienced before—pure love—shining like a bright light through his soul.

When he finally got around to calling his former girlfriend three months later to tell her they were through, he could barely believe such a pretty woman used that kind of language.

She wound up her diatribe by screaming, *"And if that wife of yours ever touches me again, I'll have her arrested."*

He chuckled, hung up the phone, and hurried home so he could spend some time with his daughter, Miranda, while her mama fixed supper for the family.

IX

MIRANDA

AMELIA LISTENED TO her daughters and daughters-in-law talk about children and husbands and old times while she secretly observed the child sitting across from her. That Miranda. Such a funny little thing, sitting quietly in the corner, listening to the grown-ups talk while the other kids were outside playing games. She cast a quick furtive glance at the child, not wanting to embarrass her.

She stared openly when she noticed Miranda was too wrapped up in a story Mary was telling about life in the old days to notice someone was staring at her. She wasn't really a pretty child, too big for that, just like Clay when he was a boy. Yet she had an interesting face, a clear indication of her mixed racial heritage. Her fair skin showed her mother's blood, but that was all.

Amelia remembered how intently she'd looked at Miranda as a newborn. She had to make sure the child was Clay's since the mother had been so questionable. It had not taken her long to see the unmistakable dark blue eyes that would later change to hazel, and still later, to golden or dark brown. Most of her children had been born with those eyes, and the abundance of dark hair was a sure proof of Indian blood as were the heavy dark brows and lashes and high, sculpted cheek bones.

The long arms and legs were a bequest from her father through his Swedish blood from Martha and perhaps the Scot, Anderson. Amelia remembered Anderson with mixed feelings. Yes, she had always liked him, but he was a weakling when it came to drink. Something about the baby's mouth, that precise upper lip, reminded her of Michael and that old harridan, Martha, but the full lower lip was Clay's and Amelia's.

At eight, Miranda still looked much the same, an interesting blend of people, groups, and cultures. Cherokee, English, and Swedish, and hadn't she heard that there was Cherokee and German, as well as Scottish and French, from Bonita? And she almost forgot her Irish grandfather, Zach O'Dell. No wonder the child was odd. Still, she had the most interesting face of any of her grandchildren, and Amelia was glad Clay had moved his family back home five years ago. She enjoyed watching Miranda grow up. The girl would be a beauty when she got older if she overcame the tendency to be heavy, but she would never be what the television people called an All-American Beauty. There were no blue-eyed blondes in Amelia's family.

The child finally noticed her staring. "Grandma, will you tell us about the time you heard the baby crying, and you didn't have a baby?"

"Now, Miranda, why do you want to hear that old tale? You've heard it a hundred times."

Abigail joined in. "Come on, Ma. It's been a long time since you told it."

"No, it's not really my story, anyway. Emily or Mary can tell it. They were awake for the whole thing, and I was passed out most of the time."

As Mary started her narration, Amelia walked away to get a drink of water.

WHEN CLAY CAME into the kitchen to get a slice of pie for dessert, he noticed Miranda, sitting with the women of the family, listening to them talk. "Are you still here? Go on outside and play with the other kids."

"Do I have to, Daddy?"

"You heard me."

She gave a loud sigh and ran outside.

Mary stopped in the middle of another story and looked up at him. "We don't mind her sittin' with us."

"Yeah, but I do. She needs to act her age."

Emily rushed in to smooth things over. "You know, Clay, I've taught school for some time, and I think Miranda is mentally a lot older than she is physically."

Clay finished cutting himself a large slice of apple pie and turned to face her. "Yeah, no doubt she's book smart. Taught herself how to read before she started school, but she don't have no common sense. Can't even fry a decent skillet of potatoes. Fact is she can't do nothin' right. Can't make a bed, can't mop a floor, can't milk a cow. You name it, and she can't do it. Her mama has just about spoiled her rotten."

Bonita blushed and cleared her throat nervously. "Well, maybe I *do* go a little overboard with my kids, I guess. But they'll never doubt I love them."

Clay scoffed at her words. "Miranda needs a lot more trainin' and a lot less lovin'."

By this time, Amelia had rejoined the group. "Well, somebody must have taught her how to behave. She's so quiet you hardly know she's here."

Clay shrugged his shoulders. "Can one of you women get me a cup of coffee? Pie don't taste the same without it."

MIRANDA SAT ON a tree stump, watching her cousins play tag. She hated that game. No matter how hard she tried to get away, someone always tagged her, naming her as "it." Maybe she could change things.

She stood and called out. "Anybody want to hear a scary story?" She smiled as they stopped their game and gathered around her, all except for Bobby Joe.

He turned to the oldest cousin, Tommy Jack, and punched him in the shoulder. "Come on, Tom. Let's get away from these babies."

As the two boys strolled away, he called back, "Have fun, listenin' to your nursery rhymes. We're goin' to take a walk down by the tracks."

With big, dark, scared eyes, Katie, who was just a few months younger than Miranda, looked over at her older sister Lydia. "Do you think we ought to tell the grown-ups? They said we're not supposed to go near the tracks because of the bums that camp there."

Lydia shook her head. "Nah, they'll be all right. The bums all like Grandma. She gives them egg sandwiches when they come to the house and beg. Go ahead and tell the story."

"All right. I'm goin' to tell you a true story about the mysterious, crying baby."

One of the younger cousins, Ronnie, Mary's son, started sniffling. "I don't want to hear this story. I already heard it, and it's scary."

His slightly older sister Pauline shook him. "Oh, quit cryin', baby, or go in the house with the grownups."

He wiped his eyes and scooted closer to Miranda.

Miranda ended the story almost in a whisper. "This time when Aunt Mary told the story she told somethin' I never heard before."

Almost in unison, they asked, "What?"

"She said that Uncle Ross saw a little man under the house that night, but later he said he just imagined it."

Studious Micah, Emily's only child, looked up from the book he was reading. "I never heard that before either. I wonder if he saw one of the Little People."

Miranda nodded. "I think he did."

Katie shivered. "That's creepy."

ON THE WAY home, Miranda got her feelings hurt. It all started when Daddy looked over at Mama and said, "Why are you so quiet tonight?"

"Just tired."

"Yeah, well, you insisted that you wanted to work again when we moved back home. But you know, if you had a girl to help you the way Lydia helps Susan, you wouldn't be so tired. Susan said Lydia fried the chicken, made the tater salad, and baked the pie they brought today. Too bad we don't have a smart girl like that at our house."

Mama looked mad. "Did you ever take into account that Lydia is three years older than Miranda?"

"True, but Lydia's been cookin' since she was Miranda's age, and Katie is just a little younger than Miranda and she helps Lydia with the cookin'."

"Daddy, my grades are a lot better than Lydia's. She usually makes C's, and I make A's."

Daddy snorted. "You still don't get it, do you? Lydia's smart in the way that counts."

Miranda swallowed her tears and pretended to be asleep.

The following Monday went down in Miranda's diary in all caps as *ONE OF THE WORST DAYS EVER.* The day turned sour early when Mrs. Gates made her stay in during morning recess and clean out her desk after shaming Miranda before her classmates.

"Girls, if you ever want to get married, don't be like Miranda. Anyone who keeps such a filthy desk would make a terrible housewife." They all laughed and ran outside to freedom.

Miranda bit her lip to keep from crying and quickly filled a large metal trashcan with old papers, pencils, and candy wrappers. She smoothed out one wrinkled, smudged math paper and timidly showed it to her teacher. "I found an old math assignment. Would you still take it?"

Mrs. Gates scarcely deigned to stop reading *The Morning Chronicle* long enough to glance at the messy paper. "You know that paper is not acceptable, Miranda. Throw it away with the rest of the trash."

Lunch was particularly nasty that day. The cooks filled her tray with sauerkraut and wieners, brown beans, cornbread, carrot sticks, and a small chocolate brownie. She ate the carrot sticks, a little of the cornbread, and all of the chocolate brownie. Everything else got tossed in the large gray trash container.

On the way home "Jess the Mess," the mean, old bus driver told Miranda and her group to "Shut up that noise" when the girls were singing their favorite songs.

Miranda retaliated by softly crooning, *"Jess, Jess, you're a mess. We don't like you, JESS MESS."*

The other girls tittered and joined in. This was one of Miranda's own creations and a great bus favorite.

Unfortunately, today Jess knew he was the subject of their laughter since he heard his name being called. He summarily separated the girls and sentenced them to solitary confinement for the duration of the hour-long trip home.

Miranda was already in a bad mood when she walked into the living room and saw Bobby Joe patting his flat stomach, his silent way of calling her "fat." She didn't take the bait, but noticed he was holding her father's favorite fishing pole.

"Why didn't you ride the bus all the way home? You know Mama doesn't like you to take the shortcut."

"She's not home from work yet. Besides why should she care? I'm here in time to mind the baby."

"I'm *not* a baby. And what are you doing with Daddy's fishing pole?"

Bobby screamed in her face. "None of your beeswax. Now go away and leave me alone."

Miranda ran to her room. She threw her books and notebooks on her bed, except for her library book, and went outside to sit under her favorite tree to read until her mother got home.

She had only read one chapter of *The Lion, the Witch, and the Wardrobe* when she heard Daddy call her by her funny nickname. "Luce, do you know where my fishin' pole is?"

After briefly wondering why Daddy was home before Mama, she

jumped at the chance for revenge. "Bobby Joe was holding it a few minutes ago."

"He better not."

She followed him to the creek, which ran less than a quarter of a mile from their house. Bobby Joe was fishing with the forbidden pole and couldn't have been caught at a worse moment. The line of his stepfather's prized possession was heavily entangled in a cottonwood tree that grew near the creek. Bobby jerked the rod hard when he heard Clay's bellow, and the pole broke under the pressure.

He was instantly on Bobby, cuffing his ear and yelling. "You, worthless thief. I'll teach you to keep your hands to yourself."

Miranda gasped when he slammed his big fist into Bobby Joe's nose. She watched frozen in horror until blood began to run from Bobby's nose. She couldn't sit still and watch her brother be beaten. "Daddy, stop it. You're killing him."

She ran between her father's upraised fist and Bobby's face. He lowered his fist and drew a trembling hand across his sweaty brow. "Well, let that be a lesson to you. Leave my things alone."

After he left, Miranda found a hanky in her pocket, rinsed it out in the cool, clear creek water, and washed the blood from her brother's face. At first, he suffered her to help him.

Suddenly, he stopped crying in mid-sob and pushed her down. "Go away and leave me alone. It was your daddy that done this to me. I hate him and you."

Shocked that her brother would say something like that, Miranda ran away in tears to her tree, and Mama found her still there, sitting in the dark, sobbing.

Mama looked sad, but she smiled at Miranda. "Come on in and eat, sweet girl. Bobby told me what happened. He didn't mean what he said. He was just hurtin' and mad. And your daddy didn't mean to hurt him either. He shouldn't have done it, but he just gets real upset sometimes. He promised it won't happen again."

Miranda dried her eyes and allowed herself to be led into the neat, cozy house. She piled her plate full of one of her favorite meals—

good-tasting meat loaf, pinto beans, fried potatoes, extra crispy the way she liked them, golden cornbread, and best of all, chocolate pie in one of Mama's inimitable, flaky pie crusts. She always made the filling in a hurry and poured it into one of the homemade crusts she never seemed to run out of. It was missing meringue, but Miranda didn't care. The delicious food warmed her stomach and soul, and she ate two large helpings of everything.

She pushed the sad memory into the back room of her mind. It was just an accident. Daddy had promised it wouldn't happen again, and he always kept his promises. "That was yummy, Mama. Can I go outside and play with Thor now?" Thor was her new kitten, whose name was a result of her newest reading interest, Norse mythology.

"Go ahead, but don't go too far from the house. I don't want you to step on a snake."

In the corner of their big yard, beside her mother's fire bush, she spied Bobby, with a bruised face, and his old tomcat, Tom Tiger, a yellow-striped tabby. "What are you doing, Bobby?"

"Just goin' rattin' with Tom in the hay."

"Could Thor and me come?"

"I guess, if you don't get in the way."

The black and white Manx kitten's eyes shone bright with curiosity as he watched the master mouser sniff the hay with interest. He struggled to escape Miranda's grasp, and she barely kept from dropping him.

"Go ahead and let him down."

The kitten bounded toward Tom but stopped short when he laid back his ears, gave a low feline growl, and flicked his tail. Suddenly the tabby's paw slashed at a pile of nearby hay, and a large brown mouse ran for its life. The cat neatly cut off the rodent's escape with one blow to the animal's head, temporarily stunning it.

"Will he eat it now?"

"No, he'll play with it for a while first."

The kitten sprang into action as the mouse, recovered from the blow, made a dash across the barnyard floor. Tom Tiger was faster, and he attacked the mouse again before it had covered more than five feet. This time he bit the mouse in the neck, killing it instantly. He growled again as Thor approached his prey, took a big bite and severed the head from the mouse's trunk. He chewed on the head a bit, ate the rodent brain, and began grooming himself, leaving the body for a later snack.

The kitten sniffed at the corpse and lapped the blood from the floor.

Bobby patted Thor in approval. "He likes it, all right. Guess he'll be a mouser just like Old Tom."

The siblings spent the next hour in the company of their cats, shining the flashlight to watch the cats hunt. The kitten wasn't much help, but Tom tolerated its presence as long as it gave him the first serving of the kill.

Shining a flashlight, Bonita came out to call them in. "What are you kids doin' out here? Don't you know it's time for bed?"

"Oh, do we have to? Bobby Joe and me's havin' so much fun."

"Yeah, Mom, let us stay up a while longer,"

Smiling at their happy state, she agreed. "All right, but just a few more minutes."

Miranda watched her mother walk slowly back to the house and turned back to playing with Bobby. Everything was all right again.

THE NEXT MORNING, Miranda decided there was something nice about family fights, but only one thing. Whenever her daddy really blew up, he would always do something nice soon after. After he finished eating breakfast, Daddy tweaked her ponytail and said, "Let's go ridin' around."

"Oh, boy. Can we stop at a store somewhere and get baloney and pop? *Please,* Daddy?"

"Sure we can. Now go tell Bobby."

As she ran off, she heard him call out to Mama. "Bonita, are you about ready to go?"

Bobby wasn't as enthusiastic as Miranda, but he didn't complain. Daddy even let them buy a couple of funny books to read on the way.

"Now, if your belly starts hurtin', Luce, you stop readin'. We don't want any accidents like we had before."

"Oh, Daddy, that's when I was little. I haven't puked since I was five-years-old."

"Well, see that you don't."

It was so much fun driving around for miles and miles, eating the sliced, red-rind bologna on fresh, white bread, drinking orange Nehi pop, or sometimes lemon pop with salty peanuts mixed in, and listening to the country stars belt out their honky tonk hits on the radio. From time to time, Daddy would find a pretty spot to show them, and they would get out and stretch their legs. It was great. No fighting. Just a nice, warm feeling of family.

Sometimes, like today, Daddy took them back to the places where he and Mama grew up. "See that old, abandoned building there, kids? That's the old Jubilee School. That's the first place I saw your mama."

"Was it love at first sight, Daddy?"

"'Course not. She was a skinny, little, bushy-headed thing then, but she improved with age."

Mama laughed. "You weren't much to look at either in those days, but you improved, too."

Since the weather was warm, they stopped along the creek and went swimming. Mama just took off her shoes and wiggled her toes in the cool water, but she and Bobby jumped in, clothes and all. Daddy took off his shirt, rolled up his blue jeans, and jumped in with them. Daddy held Miranda by the waist and told her to practice swimming.

After that, he crossed the creek with strong, powerful strokes. When he came back, he got out, located his cigarettes and lighter, and sat smoking on the bank beside Mama.

She and Bobby got into water fights and swam around. After about an hour, Daddy said, "Time to go home."

They got home, right before dark, and Mama fixed them a bite to eat. Miranda crawled in bed, feeling tired, happy, and loved.

THEN A YEAR later, Bobby was sixteen, Miranda was nine, and things got bad again. This time it was Mama who lost her patience with Bobby. Mama had got her out of school one afternoon, saying the high school principal had called her in to talk about Bobby's behavior at school. Miranda sat in the corner of his office, supposedly reading a book, but she was really listening.

The principal said Bobby was always picking fights and wouldn't stop punching and kicking after his opponent was beaten. "I hate to do it, Miss Stone, but we may have to suspend him from school."

Mama looked grim, but she just said, "That won't be necessary. I believe Bobby Joe might need to live somewhere else for a while."

Miranda cried all day that dreary, rainy May morning when Daddy drove Bobby to Tahlequah where Grandma Smith lived. A lonely summer vacation loomed ahead because she liked having someone to talk to, even if that person griped at her for being a pest.

THE SUMMER WAS a summer of change. Daddy quit his construction job and took a job as the Assistant Police Chief of Aiden. That meant he got to stay home more. They also moved from their rent house on the creek to a larger, older farmhouse in the Strawberry Hill community. One day, her father sat her and her mother down and said he needed to talk to them about something important. Miranda wondered if she was in trouble, but then her father smiled.

"Luce, when I was a boy, my pa always had horses, and he was good at trainin' and racin' them. I miss that, so I'm thinkin' about takin' it up. He always gave me a horse of my own to take care of. If I give you a horse, will you feed and water it, groom it, and ride it?"

Miranda's eyes glowed. "I sure will. I'll do anything if I can have a pony of my own."

Mama didn't seem to like the idea. "Your daddy said a horse, not a pony. Are you sure you want a horse to take care of? And, Clay, are you sure we have the time and money to fool with horses?"

Daddy grinned big. "I can find the time and the money when it comes to horses. How about you, Luce? Do you want a horse?"

Miranda did a little happy dance. "Yes, I want a horse. My friend Bridget has one, and we can go ridin' together."

It was one of the best summers of Miranda's life. When she looked into Pride's warm, golden eyes and stroked her soft, velvet nose, she recognized a deep, loving communion. When she leaped on Pride's back and galloped across the pasture, she was as free and as graceful as any bird in flight.

Bobby came back in August, just in time for school to start. His grandma had decided she wasn't ready to take on a rebellious adolescent for more than a few months. Miranda welcomed him back, and everything was fine for a time. Bobby appeared respectful around their father, but Miranda saw him slip a five-dollar bill out of her father's billfold, which he always placed on the kitchen table before bedtime.

She never told because she couldn't stand to see Bobby get hurt again. She hated the stubborn cries Daddy squeezed from Bobby after he had lashed him again and again with his heavy leather belt. But more than that she hated Mama's begging voice when she pled for him to stop. She had learned at an early age that fights must be avoided at all costs. They made your stomach hurt, even if you were just an observer and seldom a participant.

The worst fight of all occurred on Christmas Eve when Daddy caught Bobby with his hand in his billfold. As Daddy twisted his arm, Bobby kept screaming, "It was just for Christmas presents."

He didn't stop twisting until Miranda grabbed her stomach and fell to the floor. As he knelt to check on her, she said, "You're ruining Christmas, Daddy."

He grunted and walked away.

Mama called Grandma Smith Christmas night. This time she offered money if she would just take Bobby Joe off of her hands for the rest of the school year. Money was exchanged, and peace prevailed again. But Miranda soon learned that her mother wasn't happy at all about the arrangement.

ONE SATURDAY WHEN Daddy was working, Mama said, "We're goin' to see Aunt Kate today. Get you some books together to take along."

After Aunt Kate hugged her and talked about how big she was getting, Miranda was dismissed to a corner of the living room to entertain herself. As always, the grownups forgot she could overhear their conversation.

Mama started right in. "You know when Granny O'Dell passed right after Miranda was born, I lost my best friend. I'm so glad you don't mind me comin' by and bendin' your ear with my troubles."

Kate patted her on the arm and said, "You're welcome here anytime. Now what's the problem?"

"I just can't live with Clay when Bobby Joe's around. Every time Bobby does the least little thing, he's on him—hard. And he punishes him like he was a man instead of a boy. "

Miranda watched as Aunt Kate took Mama's hand. "I was married to a hard man, and I know somethin' about them. I should be ashamed of myself, but when Jed died in a car wreck five years ago, he done me a favor. Well, anyway this is what I think. Maybe when Clay looks at Bobby Joe, he don't really see him. He sees Bob, instead. And when Bobby Joe ain't around, he can forget you ever belonged to Bob."

Mama's eyes were spilling tears. "What can I do? I can't turn my back on my son."

"You have to make up your mind. Stay married to Clay and leave Bobby with Pearl Smith to live or divorce him."

Mama started crying, and Aunt Kate hugged her. Miranda watched them hug and rock each other for a while before returning to her book.

BOBBY JOE BOUNCED between their house and Grandma Smith's until his senior year in high school. He was living with his grandma at the time when he was caught writing hot checks in Tahlequah. The judge gave him a choice, join the army or go to jail. Bobby chose the army.

Oddly enough, Bobby Joe's enlistment in the armed services and eventual moving out didn't solve Bonita's marital problems. Now most of Miranda's parents' fights grew out of her mother's fear that Clay was unfaithful to her. They all ended the same way. She would accuse him, and he would blow up. Sometimes he would push her, pinch her, or hurt her some other way.

After it was over, her mother would almost always say, "If it wasn't for you, I would have left him a long time ago."

When Miranda entered junior high, she noticed her father was coming home later and later. Her mother never smiled or laughed anymore, and Miranda grew anxious. "Mom, why does Dad always come home after we've gone to bed?"

"He says he's working, but I think he just doesn't want to see me."

"I don't understand. Why?"

"Because he thinks I'll find out what he's doin'."

Miranda frowned. "What's he doing?"

"Cheatin' on me again. If it wasn't for you, I would have left him long ago, but good mothers sacrifice themselves for their children. I need to get away from him for a while. Let's go visit Aunt Esther and Uncle Wade."

Miranda's stomach churned with the guilt she always experienced when her mother blamed her for her unhappy marriage.

THEIR VISIT LASTED two days. On the third day Bonita got

a call from home. She knew something was wrong when her mother held out her arms. "Come here, baby. I got some bad news for you."

All at once, Miranda couldn't breathe. "What is it?"

"Your grandpa passed away a few minutes ago."

The news was bad, but it could have been worse. She had thought the news was about Clay. Grandpa Michael had suffered a mild heart attack the year before and had been told to take it easy. His response had been, "We all got to go sometime, and when I go I wanta be livin', not just passin' time until I die."

At Grandma Amelia's insistence, he had cut down on the number of pipes he smoked, but that was the only change he made. He was working with a young horse, which he had just purchased, when he was overtaken by chest pains. He managed to close the corral gate and stagger a few feet away before collapsing.

Her mother handed her a handful of tissues, and she wiped her eyes. Bonita hugged her. "At least your grandpa died doin' what he loved. We'll go back home for the funeral."

When they got home, Bonita hugged Clay, and they both acted like nothing had ever happened. That night Miranda slept soundly in her own bed and heard her mother singing the next morning as she made them breakfast.

THE FUNERAL THAT afternoon was well-attended because Michael had lived in Jubilee his whole life and had made lots of friends. The family all sat together in the funeral home viewing room in almost complete silence. Mama had told her that the service was going to be much like the one held for Michael's father, Grandpa Josh, who had died before Miranda was born. Miranda looked around, surprised to see very little emotion expressed. She had been told that Grandpa Josh's death had been a relief for himself and those who loved him, but Grandpa Michael's death had been unexpected.

Her mother, crying silently, sat close to her father, patting him on the back from time to time. He sat with his head bowed, as still as a statue. The only emotion he betrayed was a slight trembling in his clasped hands.

She watched Aunt Susan hide her stricken face on her husband's shoulder. She had overheard Grandma calling Susan a "Daddy's girl." Later, Mom told her that Grandpa forced Grandma to accept Susan back in the family after she came up pregnant and unmarried.

Aunt Emily sobbed once, and her husband enfolded her in his big arms. Aunt Mary and Aunt Abigail dabbed at their eyes from time to time. Uncle Zack stared at his feet the entire time.

Grandma Amelia sat still, her face devoid of emotion, hands clasped in her lap, staring straight ahead. Only once when the Cherokee singers were singing, she raised a handkerchief to her eyes and wiped away a few tears.

AT THE FAMILY cemetery, when the grownups were talking, Miranda and her cousin Katie walked over to look at some of the older graves. Miranda picked up a small rock and began scraping off the lichen that clung to two of the gravestones. "These are the oldest, Grey Wolf and Bluebird. They came over on the Trail of Tears."

Katie took out a handkerchief, spit on it, and tried to rub the dirt away. "I know. Mom told me about them."

Miranda paused in her scraping. "Just imagine what they went through coming here."

Katie shivered. "I know. It must have been terrible. Mom said they tried to run away, and the soldiers caught them and tied them to the wagon wheels."

"Dad told me about that, too. Did Aunt Susan ever mention Bluebird bringing a rock with her over the Trail?"

"Uh-huh. Lots of times. Grandma Amelia still has it."

Katie's words aroused Miranda's curiosity. "She does? I've never seen it in her house. Where is it?"

Katie rolled her eyes. "I can't believe you've never seen it. She keeps it in her bedroom dresser. Mom showed it to all of us when we were visiting Grandma one time."

"I wish I could see it."

Katie frowned. "It's no big deal. Just ask Grandma."

Miranda fidgeted, tightened her grip on the rock, and scraped harder. She had seen Grandma scold other grandchildren for being too loud or for touching her keepsakes without permission. "I don't think so. If she said no, I might cry and embarrass myself."

Katie giggled. "I know what you mean. Grandma Amelia can be scary. I would ask Mom or one of the other aunts."

Mama came over and took the rock from her hand. "Time to go home. Bye, Katie. Come and see us."

"Bye, Aunt Bonita. I will."

DAD WAS QUIET when they went back home, and Miranda noticed his eyes were red like he had been crying. She remembered Mom saying he had always been close to his father. Miranda thought about how she would feel if her daddy or mama died. It almost made her cry to think about it, so she wrote a poem in her diary about her grandpa's funeral instead. Then she went to bed and dreamed about Grey Wolf and Bluebird on the Trail of Tears.

THEY SOON SETTLED back into their home and daily routine. Bobby Joe was stationed in France and sent Miranda post cards from all the places he visited when he was on leave. In one of them he told her about visiting the Louvre, something Miranda ached to do.

Me and my buddies spent all day at the Louvre yesterday. I looked at the Mona Lisa, and I was surprised how small it is. I liked the picture of St. Michael Vanquishing Satan a lot better. Say hello to Mom and Clay for me.

Love, Bob

She wrote long letters to him, which he responded to with post cards and short notes. When she told him how much she liked the new British band, the Beatles, he told her he had once seen them play in person in Liverpool, England.

When she read this, she threw down the letter and called one of her best friends. "Meredith, my brother saw the Beatles in person. Can you believe it?"

When she wrote back to Bobby, she told him, "I have never been so envious of anyone in my life. First, you got to tour the Louvre, and now you tell me you listened to the Beatles in person. These are two of my dreams that will probably never come true. You are so lucky."

HIS MOTHER WAS delighted when Bobby came home after serving six years in the military. When they met Bobby at the airport in Tulsa, she stood still and looked at him. "You're all grown up into a handsome man."

In a rush, she grabbed him and cried all over his crisp sergeant's uniform. Clay and Miranda stood quietly by, waiting their turn to greet him. Bobby smiled at them over Bonita's head and extended his right hand to Clay, which he shook briefly.

When Bonita released him, she turned to Miranda. "Come here, sweetheart, and see your handsome brother."

Miranda stared at the solidly built, clean-cut soldier, who looked nothing like the skinny, tousled brother she remembered. She suddenly turned shy until he gave her a saucy wink.

"Come here and let me get a look at you. Well, you sure have changed for the better. You've slimmed down and grown a foot." He put his hand on the top of her head. "Now, quit growin' before you get taller than me."

That night Mama cooked him all of his favorite dishes, and after supper, Miranda asked him questions about the places he had visited. Clay sat in his big Naugahyde recliner, smoking a cigarette, listening to them talk. He didn't say much unless someone asked him a question.

After Bonita finished the dishes and sat down between her children, Clay looked over at Bobby. "What do you plan on doin' next?"

Bobby grinned. "Got it all taken care of. I've already enrolled at Northeastern on the G.I. Bill. Startin' classes in two weeks."

"Yeah, that would probably be all right. You need to fix it where you can live over there and go to school. You should be able to do that on the G.I. Bill. Well, I'm goin' to drive back in to town to check on some things."

AFTER HE LEFT, Bobby shook his head and laughed sarcastically. "Well, I see Clay hasn't changed a bit. Just as friendly as ever."

Bonita patted him on the arm. "Don't you worry about what Clay thinks. I'm tickled pink to see you again, and I know Miranda is, too."

Bobby left the next week in a banged-up, used car that Bonita helped him buy. She paid his first month's rent in a small apartment near the college. As she kissed him goodbye, Miranda overheard her parting words. "Don't say anything to Clay about me helpin' you out. Let him think it was all done with money you saved up. It will save me a lot of problems."

"I get it. What Clay don't know won't hurt him, and he don't need to know about your secret savings account."

"Exactly."

Bobby found a part-time job at a Tahlequah hardware store and took classes in business administration. He made it through his freshman year all right with a 3.0 Grade Point Average.

When he was a sophomore, he got involved with a senior girl

who talked him into moving to Alaska with her when she graduated. She had landed a high-paying job, teaching school in a small remote village. After she met Bobby's fiancée, Carla, Bonita said, "I'm glad Carla has a job, but what are you goin' to do there?"

A beaming Bobby leaned over and gave his petite, perky girlfriend, who reminded Miranda of Sally Fields as *Gidget,* a kiss on the cheek. "Don't worry, Mom. I'll find somethin'."

IN THE 1960S, fashion had undergone a great change, and Miranda and her friends embraced it. They all read *Ingenue* and *Seventeen,* and they all wanted to look just like Twiggy with her boyish figure, big eyes, and short hair. Miranda realized she was going to have to lose at least 30 pounds to come close to looking like her idol. She starved herself the summer before her sophomore year, and she entered Aiden High School, pencil thin, with a new, stylish wardrobe, complete with fishnet hose, purchased by her mother.

Despite the change in her appearance, she couldn't break out of the mold she had been placed in, the quiet, different girl, who could never be popular. Miranda's friends were intelligent, talented, sensitive girls, who remained loyal friends during most of their school years, but none of them ever attained popularity. Even though her best friends, Meredith and Bridget, both became twirlers in the band where Miranda played clarinet, they still weren't part of the "in crowd."

Her stylish figure gave Miranda the confidence to pursue Adam, a handsome boy she had maintained a crush on since junior high. She made sure their paths crossed often, and she always wore her cutest outfits when she was around him. Flirting did not come naturally to her, but she always spoke to him and smiled a lot.

The way he looked at her she thought she was making progress until her cousin Katie, who had gained popularity by becoming a star basketball player, took her aside. "Miranda, Adam wants you to know he only dates popular girls."

SHE GAVE UP on dating in Aiden High School and joined her friends in driving to other towns to meet boys who didn't care whether they were popular or not. It was nice to have boys pay attention to her, and she dated a few times, mostly going out to eat and to one of the area movie theaters with this boy or that. When any of them acted like they wanted something more, she would tell him she wasn't interested in getting serious and would break it off.

She did, however, get involved in a long-distance relationship with a soldier who was stationed in Vietnam. He was the nephew of one of her mother's church friends, Rebecca, who had visited her Sunday School class to ask if any of the young people would write to her nephew Silas. "Silas is so homesick, and a letter from some of you young people would let him know someone from back home cares about him. I'll write his address here on the chalkboard."

MIRANDA, ALONG WITH a few others, wrote down the address, and Miranda mailed off a cheery letter to Silas the next day. Two weeks later she received a reply, in which Silas thanked her and asked her to send a picture. She sent the picture and another letter in which she asked Silas what Vietnam was like.

After chatting a bit, mostly telling her how pretty she was, Silas answered her question. "Vietnam is hell on earth. When it's not pouring rain, the sun is baking you. But that's nothing compared to being afraid all of the time. I don't mean to make you feel bad. Please keep writing to me. It really helps."

She cried when she read that and resolved to keep writing him as long as he wrote her back. They kept up regular correspondence several months until one Saturday she realized she hadn't heard from him in over three weeks.

WHEN SHE AND her mother arrived at church that Sunday, she moved to the front so she could sit by Rebecca and talk to her. "Have you heard anything from Silas?"

"Oh, Miranda, I had hoped you were goin' to tell me you had heard from him. No, his mama is real worried, and so am I." Rebecca's arthritic hands were shaking as she rose to her feet when the pastor asked if anyone had a special prayer request. "Please pray for my nephew Silas who is in Vietnam. No one has heard from him in nearly a month."

Brother Hallford assured her they would all pray for Silas, and she sat down. Miranda couldn't get her mind on the service for the rest of the morning, even though the singing and preaching were particularly good. She kept thinking about Silas and wondering if he were all right.

AS WAS HIS custom, Miranda's father had gone to the horse races at Sallisaw. He was in a good mood these days because he had a really fast filly that was winning all her races. She was sitting at her wooden desk in her little room, praying and thinking, when she heard him come in that afternoon.

She heard him ask Bonita, "Where's Luce?" She couldn't hear her response, but she heard his knock on her bedroom door a few minutes later.

"Can I come in?"

"Uh-huh."

He opened the door and looked around her room. "What are you doin' in here? It's a pretty day. I figured you would be out ridin' Pride."

"Didn't feel like it."

"Well, a horse needs to be ridden and handled, or they start actin' wild. You know you're not doin' that soldier any favor by stayin' in your room mopin'."

"I'm not mopin'."

He sat down on her bed. "All I want to say is I was a soldier once, and I know somethin' about what might be happenin' to that boy. He could be captured, missin' in action, or even dead, and you sittin' here ain't goin' to change that."

She burst into tears. "How can you say such mean things?"

He stood up and patted her shoulder. "Cryin' don't change anything, and I'm not bein' mean. Just think about what I said and go see to your horse."

THEY GOT THE bad news the next day when Brother Hallford called their house. Silas Fields's company had been found in a remote jungle area. They had all been shot when they were ambushed by the Viet Cong.

Even though she had never met him in person, Silas's death had a marked effect on Miranda. She couldn't understand why someone so young was taken before he had a chance to really live. All he had wanted was to survive until he could get back home, but instead he died, afraid, in a place he hated.

THE SUMMER BEFORE Miranda started her junior year, her mother began changing. She had put on weight, complained of hot flashes, and became irritable with Miranda, Clay, and everyone else. Worst of all, all she wanted to talk about was her suspicions that Clay was cheating on her.

One night she woke Miranda from a sound sleep. "Come on, Miranda. You're goin' to drive me around town while I look for your sorry father."

When they got to town, Miranda drove her to the police station first. "See, Dad's truck is right there. He's inside working just like he said he was."

"Maybe. Or maybe he's ridin' around in a police car. Drive me down Main."

They were soon spotted. Clay was parked in the alleyway behind the barber shop. He flagged them down. "What are you two doin' here at this time of the night?"

Miranda looked at her mother's ashen face and realized she needed to lie. "Mom's so miserably hot that she asked me to drive her around to cool down in the night air."

"Is that so? Well, I think you better take her home and let her sleep in the front room under the air conditioner. I'll be comin' home after my help gets here. We have been keepin' a close watch on the stores since we had that break-in last week."

"All right." She waited until he drove away and turned to Bonita. "Let's go home, Mom."

"You know he just told you that so he can slip off and meet his new girlfriend."

"Mom, I really don't think so this time. Besides, I need to go back to sleep. I am going job-hunting in the morning."

MIRANDA NOTICED WHEN she went to bed that Bonita was sitting at the kitchen table, drinking a cup of coffee. An hour later she heard her mother cry out and the front door slam.

She ran into the kitchen and found her mother, crying as she cradled her right arm with her left. "What happened?"

"He got mad when I asked him who he was seein', and he grabbed my arm and squeezed it. It'll be black and blue tomorrow. He drove off somewhere, probably to her house."

She leaned down and put her arm around her mother's shoulders. "You don't have to put up with this. You should leave him for good and make a new life for yourself. I know you've got some money saved up. We could move to Laurel Grove, and you could get a job at a bank or office over there."

"How about school?"

Miranda thought about leaving her friends and her pets, especially Pride. Mom was more important. She sighed and mentally gave them up. "I could finish there. I only have two years to go, anyway."

"How about your friends? Would you want to leave people you've known all your life?"

"I could probably make new friends, and if I didn't, I could manage on my own."

That night Miranda couldn't sleep, and two lines of poetry kept buzzing through her brain.

I am an unknown entity, floating in the Nameless Sea,
How can I give my hand to you
When it doesn't belong to me?

She spent another hour hammering out the rest of the poem that went before the ending lines. Deciding it was complete, she signed her name and fell asleep.

BUT BONITA WOULDN'T consider moving for real, and two nights later she told her Clay would be coming back home the next day.

"*Why*, Mom?"

"Good mothers sacrifice themselves for their children."

"I'm not a little girl anymore. I don't need a Daddy. Now be honest."

Bonita's smile vanished, and she saw a different side to her mother. "I took him back because I love him."

Miranda took a deep breath and let it out slowly. "Finally, you told me the truth. You lied to me all these years, making me feel guilty for wrecking your life. That's over. From now on I'm thinking about myself. Living for me, not you."

She stormed out of the kitchen, jumped in her old white Impala, and spun out of the driveway. She drove over to the house of a good friend and spilled out the story to her. Jessie listened sympathetically and said, "That's tough, Miranda, but that's the way parents are. Let's forget about them and go riding around."

"Where are your parents? Don't you need to leave them a message telling them where we're going?"

"They're doing inventory at the store. Nah, they trust me. Besides we'll be home in a few hours."

It was a magical night, her first night as a free spirit. Jessie and she drove around Tahlequah in Jessie's shiny, new red 1966 Mustang, as objects of admiration and envy. They attracted the attention of two strangers, driving an almost new blue Ford pickup. "Don't look now, but someone's following us, Jess."

"You think so? Only one way to find out."

Jessie put on her right turn signal, slowed down, and pulled into Tahlequah's crowded Dairy Freeze and parked. The pickup pulled up beside them.

"Oh, my gosh. They're coming over. Jess, what should I do?"

"Say hello, silly. And try to be cool about it."

A STOCKY, MUSCULAR young Indian appeared at her window and motioned for her to roll the window down. In her nervousness, red-faced Miranda opened the door instead as she got out a squeaky, "Hi."

"Hi. Nice-lookin' Mustang. I'm Darryn Steel. Mind if my buddy Steve and me sit with you girls and talk?"

He smiled, showing nice teeth and cute dimples. She surprised herself by saying, "Sure."

Jessie's whisper came out as a hiss. "Remember our rules?"

As the boys settled into the back seat, Miranda mouthed, "It will be all right."

Steve took over the conversation. "Sure glad you girls let us come over and meet you. We been lookin' at you for a while."

He realized his mistake and covered his mouth immediately. "Whoops. Just noticed how that sounded."

Darryn poked him in the ribs. "Man, Steve. They're goin' to think we're stalkers."

Jessie giggled. "Nah. You don't seem like the stalker type. I'm Jessie Drywater, and this is Miranda Stone. We're from Aiden."

"No kiddin'. Me and Darryn are both from Tahlequah, but I got kinfolk that live in Aiden and Stilwell. Ever heard of Everett Sanderson? He's my cousin. Has the same last name as me."

"I've heard of him, but I don't know him personally. How about you, Miranda?"

"Seems like I've heard the name somewhere. Maybe from my dad. He knows everybody."

Darryn raised his eyebrows. "Really? Who's your dad?"

"Clay Stone. He's the Chief of Police in Aiden."

Steve hooted. "Uh-oh, Darryn, you're gettin' friendly with the Police Chief's daughter."

Darryn elbowed him again. "Shut up, Steve. You'll scare her off. Sorry about my friend, Miranda. They keep him on the farm so much that he doesn't know how to behave around ladies."

Miranda laughed. "That's all right. I'm glad to meet you, Steve and Darryn." She extended her hand for a quick handshake with Steve.

When she gave her hand to Darryn, he hung on to it. "You have soft hands."

"Thanks. Can I have it back?"

"Oh, sure." He released her hand. "Say, you girls want something to eat or drink?"

"I'm not hungry, but a cherry limeade would be good."

"Miranda's never hungry, but I sure am. I'll take a burger basket and a Coke."

Steve leaned over and patted Jessie on the shoulder. "A woman after my own heart. You know what I want, Darryn."

"Same as me. Double meat burger basket with a Coke, right?"

"Right, only don't forget the cheese."

"Oh, yeah. I never eat cheese, so I forget anybody else wants it."

Somewhere during the night, the conversation turned to jobs. "Me and Darryn's been haulin' hay this summer when we ain't rodeoin'."

This piqued Miranda's interest. "Really? I love horses. I have a sorrel mare named Pride, and my dad trains and races horses."

"Sure enough? Well, I'm not that much, but Darryn here's a regular Jim Shoulders."

Another elbow jab followed. "Ow. Quit jabbin' me."

"Well, quit lyin'."

"I'm not. You know you're one of the best bronc riders around."

"Maybe around this area but not on a national or even state level. It's just a hobby and a way to earn a little spendin' money. What I'm really workin' on is my business degree at Northeastern. I just finished my sophomore year. What grade are you girls in?"

Jessie rolled her eyes. "I'm out of school. I graduated from high school last year, and I'm working for my dad at our grocery store, but I plan on starting at Northeastern in August. I'm going to be a teacher. Miranda here is a high school junior."

Steve slapped his forehead. "Wouldn't you know it? I'm the only high school dropout in a car full of smart people. You girls are goin' to kick me out for sure."

Jessie turned around and patted his hand. "Don't you know, brains aren't everything? Looks definitely count too, and I've always gone for blue-eyed blonds."

Steve stood up and kissed her lightly on the cheek. "Thank you, darlin'. Now as for me, I prefer little, dark-eyed beauties like you. Miranda, mind if I change places with you? I want to sit where I can look into Jessie's pretty brown eyes."

Miranda turned to Jessie with a question in her eyes.

"It'll be all right."

Miranda moved into the back seat with Darryn. For the next three hours the couples laughed, talked, and flirted. Around midnight the Dairy Freeze turned off its lights.

Steve, who had his arm around Jessie, asked, "You girls want to go ridin' around with us?"

Jessie sighed. "Guess we better not. That would be breaking a big rule."

Darryn chuckled. "We already broke one when you let us in the car, right?"

Miranda wrinkled her nose at him and grinned. "Yeah, and we broke another one by my getting in the back seat with you."

Steve turned to Jessie. "So, why not break a big one and go ridin' around with us?"

"Because I promised my mom we wouldn't go riding around with strange boys."

"Strange? I ain't strange. Are you strange, Darryn?"

"Nope. Last time I checked I was normal."

Jessie gave Steve's shoulder a playful punch. "You know what I mean."

"I think you and Darryn mean to beat me up. Why does everybody want to hurt me tonight?"

"Nobody wants to hurt you, Steve, but Miranda and me better get home before we get hurt by my mom."

"All right. Give me your phone number and a little goodnight kiss, and we'll go in peace."

Darryn turned to Miranda. "Can I ask the same from you?"

"Sure."

Darryn's kiss was not so little. Miranda went dizzy when their lips connected. She came to herself when Steve leaned over and slapped Darryn on the back of the head. "Hey, Romeo, let go of the girl."

She pushed Darryn away and blushed. Darryn squeezed her hand. "Sorry, Miranda. Just got a little carried away."

He reached into his pocket and brought out two wadded-up tickets. "Hey, I got an idea. Why don't you come to the Muskogee Fairgrounds tomorrow night and watch us ride? You can have these free passes."

Eyes shining, Miranda took the tickets. "What do you think, Jess?"

"Sure, why not?"

Steve leaned over and gave Jessie another light kiss and opened the car door. "Can't wait to see you tomorrow night, darlin.'"

Darryn hugged and kissed Miranda again and paused after exiting the car. "See you tomorrow night, Miranda, after my event."

"How will you find me?"

"I'll always find you. Don't worry about that."

A PASSIONATE, ALL-consuming summer courtship soon developed. Miranda told him she couldn't enjoy a date after working at the canning factory all day, so they limited their dates to Friday and Saturday nights. After each date, Miranda imagined herself blooming like a thirsty rose that had been neglected by its caretaker, gulping the refreshing, satisfying water Darryn provided.

After only a few dates, she made her confession to Jessie. "I'm like that princess in that story, you know the one that the witch puts to sleep, and only a handsome prince could wake her up. You know, Sleeping Beauty. That's me, I've been asleep or dead all my life, and now Darryn has brought me to life. Do you know what I mean?"

"Yeah, I know what you mean, but be careful."

"Why?"

"Sometimes loving somebody too much can hurt you."

"I don't see how."

Miranda, always a bit of a poet, found herself inspired by this new experience of love. She found herself writing old-fashioned, sentimental love poems, not at all like her angry, black poetry of previous years. On the back of her senior picture, she inscribed her latest poem.

STAR TRAVELERS
There are those who forever travel,
Straight as an arrow, ascending upward.

There are those who will never rest,
Until they see the smile of God.
They are the star-travelers, the true
Children of Heaven.
But what greater plane can man reach,
Than to be loved so greatly by one mortal being?
Therein lies all the stars of heaven
And all the smiles of God.

Darryn looked at the picture, read the poem, drew Miranda to him, and kissed her tenderly. "They're both beautiful, Miranda. Just like you. Have you thought about getting married?"

That April night Darryn and Miranda pledged themselves in engagement. Three months later, Darryn spent some of his savings on, what appeared to Miranda, as a dazzling diamond engagement ring.

JESSIE WAS THE first one she told. "It's so pretty. When's the date? Have you decided?"

"October 23."

"Why then?"

"I've always liked the fall of the year for some reason. All the pretty colors, the crispness in the air, the feeling of excitement, something about it makes me want to travel."

"Won't you both be in college?"

"We're getting married on a Friday evening, and neither one of us has classes on Monday. Both of us have part-time jobs, and that, plus our scholarships and student loans, should get us through until Darryn graduates in less than two years."

Her wedding would be simple but pretty. She chose yellow and white for her colors, and she ordered a basket of yellow roses to be placed in front of the altar. Two lit candelabras would frame the basket, and she would carry a bouquet of yellow roses. The wedding would be held in the small, white, community church Miranda had attended most of her life. Her only disappointment was that Clay refused to give her away.

"What a lot of foolishness. Why don't you go to the courthouse like your Mom and me done? It'll take just as good."

Bonita looked into the once-handsome face that now sported heavy jowls. "Now, Clay, Miranda wants a church weddin', and all young girls are entitled to a church weddin' if that's what they want."

Clay lit up a Pall Mall, took a big drag, and stared hard at Miranda. "All right, then. Go ahead and have your weddin', but leave me out of it. I don't have the time or the patience for such silliness."

Miranda gave him an even colder, harder look. "Fine. If you don't want to give me away, I'll call Bobby Joe tonight. He'll be glad to do it."

Bobby Joe, who had recently moved to Tulsa with his wife and young son, readily agreed to give Miranda away. "Sure, sis. Can't talk the old man into it, huh?"

"You know how he is. He never came to anything I ever did in my life, so why should he start now?"

"That's tough, kid. Not even your graduation?"

"No, the only family I had there was Mom, even though I gave the salutatorian address."

"Sorry I couldn't come, Miranda. But we couldn't afford to fly back here from Alaska."

"That's okay. I understand, but please, don't let me down this time."

"I won't."

Dressed in a silky, yellow and white floral dress, wearing black and white heels to make her look taller, Bonita scurried around making sure everyone was in their places. She frowned when she saw Miranda. "Miranda, go get ready. The girls are waitin' on you in the church nursery."

"Do you think Dad is coming?"

"He'll show up. Now, go get ready. The guests will be here in a few minutes."

Her bridesmaids, Jessie, Meredith, and Bridget helped dress her in a long, white satin gown trimmed with a flower-patterned lace. Bridget's eyes filled with tears as she pinned Miranda's white veil, trimmed with yellow roses, in her hair. "Miranda, you look so beautiful, but all I can see is that shy little girl I met in the first grade."

Meredith sobbed. "I know. I can't believe one of us is actually getting married."

Miranda put an arm around each of them. "And this is exactly why I have always loved you girls. Friends forever, right?"

Jessie put her hands on her hips and scowled. "So what am I, chopped liver?"

Miranda reached out and brought her into the embrace. "No, you're my funny, older friend, who always made me laugh, no matter how much I wanted to cry."

Jessie pushed herself back so she could look up into Miranda's face. "Well, you know we all love you too. If we didn't, we wouldn't dress in these frilly, yellow dresses your mom had made for us. I don't know about you girls, but yellow's definitely not my color."

They were still laughing when a knock sounded on the door. "Sis, are you ready to go?"

"I'm ready."

She opened the door, and he gave a soft whistle. "Wow. You look like a movie star."

"Thanks, big brother, and thanks for walking me down the aisle since my own father refuses to do it."

"It won't do any good to get mad at Clay. He's sittin' on the front row by Mom with his hand all bandaged up. Heard he got in a fight with a drunk earlier today. Anyway, like I learned a long time ago, he's set in his ways, and there's no changin' him."

"Well, it just makes me realize how little he cares for me."

Bobby shook his head. "I'm the one he don't care for. If he didn't care for you, he wouldn't be here at all. His hand probably hurts like thunder, but he's here anyway." He frowned, and his upper lip curled up in a derisive sneer for a fraction of a second before he resumed speaking. "Or maybe givin' you away just don't suit his tough guy

John Wayne image. Who knows? Well, even if that is the case, he still thinks the sun rises and sets with you and only you. Don't you ever doubt that fact. Now, come on, the music is startin'."

As Miranda walked down the aisle on her brother's arm, her eyes were focused on the handsome man who awaited her, beside the glowing candelabra, at the altar. Meisha, Mary's daughter, her little flower girl, dressed in a puffy, yellow floral dress, scattered yellow rose petals in her pathway. The little church was filled with family and friends, and everyone had their eyes on her, but she only had eyes for her bridegroom.

As her brother gave her into his arms, she looked into his adoring, love-filled eyes. Darryn whispered, "I love you forever," and Miranda took her place at his side.

X
THE TEACHER

FIFTEEN YEARS LATER, Miranda looked out her bedroom window to a snowy January morning. Good. Maybe school would be canceled today.

After wrapping her body in the comfort of her heavy chenille robe, Miranda slipped on her furlined house shoes, turned off the alarm clock, and opened and closed the bedroom door quietly. Darryn didn't have to get up yet, and she didn't want to awaken him.

As she looked out the bay window of the front room, she caught a glimpse of a speeding mass of fur cavorting through the snow. It was the family's white Himalayan cat, Thai, racing across the front yard. At first, he seemed oblivious to her watching him, so carried away was he with the pleasure of his snow play. She admired his long, lean, whitefurred body, almost camouflaged in the snow. His bright blue eyes danced with excitement as he hurled himself at an unsuspecting wren, only to miss as the bird flew away barely in time to escape his huge paws.

Her mind played back the memory of Bobby Joe and his cat Tom, instructing her kitten, Thor, in the art of rat hunting. Sometimes she yearned to go back to that time when life was simple and mostly fun.

When Thai began to look around for more possible prey, he noticed her at the window and bounded toward her. When she opened the front door, he stretched himself to his full, considerable length. This was one of their greeting games. "What a long cat, you are, Thai baby." She scratched behind his cream-colored ears and let him into the warming room.

After she filled the cat bowl, she opened the front door again and whistled for their black Labrador Retriever, Yona. In a matter of minutes, he crossed the snowy ground between the barn where he slept and the front door. When he reached the porch, he started shaking the snow off of his fur. She stepped back to avoid getting wet. "Hey, boy, what happened? Did you get some snow on you? Are you ready to eat?"

At the word "eat," Yona wiggled all over and wagged his tail. She reached over and scratched behind his ears. "All right. Just a minute. I'll open up the garage and let you eat in there."

After the pets were fed, she poured herself a cup of coffee, sank into the comfort of her favorite velvety recliner, and waited to scan the television screen for Aiden's name on the list of school closings. She would just let Byron and Lorna sleep, and, hopefully, they would get a good surprise when they finally woke up.

Thai soon joined her on the chair, kneaded her robe for a couple of minutes, found a comfortable spot on her lap, and was soon sucking contentedly on his paw as he slept. Poor baby. He must have been taken from his mother too soon and missed on some important suckling. Maybe that explained his neurotic behavior.

She patted his head and waited anxiously for the list to be shown. Ah, yes, there it was, near the top, since the list was alphabetized. She smiled as she thought of the happy day that stretched before her, a day away from the responsibilities and stress of work.

The phone rang from the kitchen, and she dumped a protesting Thai on the floor and rushed to answer it. A cheerful voice told her that there would be no school today and asked if she knew whose name was after hers on the inclement weather list.

Miranda said that she did, made the quick call, put Thai in the family room, closed the family room door to keep him from roaming the house, and started back toward her bedroom. Right before she opened the door, she remembered to place a heavy wooden chair before the family room's sliding door so that he couldn't slide it open with his clever paws.

She heard his tentative scratching just as she settled back under the covers. Darryn reached out and pulled her close to him in their king size bed. "No school today? You're cold. Come here, and I'll warm you up."

Miranda nestled close to Darryn's warmth much like Thai had rested on her a few moments earlier. This was one of the nicer things about marriage, someone to cuddle with on a cold winter morning.

About a half hour later, she awoke from her doze to see Darryn rummaging through his chest drawer for clean underwear. She hugged herself with glee at the thought of the leisure day, pulled the heavy quilts about her, and dozed off again.

She slept until she heard Darryn drive away, changed into some sweats, ran a comb through her short dark hair, washed her face, and made the bed. Wanting to get a head start on the kids, she went into the kitchen and began finishing the cleaning job that hadn't been completed the night before. As she cleaned the counter tops, she sang "Yesterday" and "The Sound of Silence."

Suddenly she switched into Patsy Cline's "Crazy." For some reason in recent years, she had rediscovered the earliest music she had been exposed to as a child, country. In her teens she would never have admitted listening to, much less singing, her parents' music, but deep down she knew that Cline, Cash, Williams, and others were all there, just waiting to be voiced.

After cleaning the kitchen, she decided to treat the kids to something sweet by making cinnamon rolls. There was something deeply satisfying about making and shaping bread with her own hands. She looked out the patio door and watched the wooden deck, rapidly being buried in snow. Why they might be out of school for a week, and that would suit her just fine.

Then she thought of the kids. Byron was like Miranda and could occupy himself with a good book or a writing project. Lorna was a restless spirit who demanded to be entertained. Two days max stuck in the house, and she would be driving them all crazy.

DARRYN CAME HOME a little after noon with some videos. "They let us off early so that people living in the country could make it home."

"Do you think people will work tomorrow?"

"Them that can make it in."

The only flaw in the perfect day was Lorna's disagreeableness. She didn't like the stew Miranda had fixed for an early supper. "Yuck, stew. You know I hate stew."

"Then have a cinnamon roll and fix yourself a sandwich."

"I'm tired of sandwiches. Why didn't you make something chocolate?"

Miranda's patience abruptly came to an end. "Lorna, you aren't the only one in this family, you know. If you're going to be so picky, you can find yourself something to eat."

Darryn came into the room and heard the conversation. "Yeah or do without."

Lorna grabbed a cinnamon roll and retreated upstairs to her room just as the phone rang.

Miranda heard the anxiety in Bonita's voice. "I need to talk to you about something."

"What is it, Mom?"

"Carla just called, and Bobby's in the hospital."

"What's wrong with him?"

"They're not sure, but he's hurtin' really bad in his stomach. Clay's gonna take me up there to see him. Do you want to go?"

"Sure. I guess so. What about all the snow?"

"You know your daddy never has trouble drivin' anytime. We'll be there in about twenty minutes, so be ready."

"Okay. I'll be ready."

As she was hanging up the phone, Darryn came in. "What's going on?"

"Bobby Joe is in the hospital, and Mom and Dad are going to take me with them to see him."

Lorna, coming downstairs in time to catch their conversation, started campaigning. "Mom, I want to go. It's boring around here."

"Ha. You think it's boring here. Wait until you sit in a waiting room for two or three hours."

"I don't care. I'm starving, and Poppa will stop and get me something good to eat."

"Sorry not this time, babe. You would get so tired of waiting on us that you would get aggravated. Besides, I don't know what condition Bobby Joe is in or when we'll get back home."

"I don't care. I want to go."

"Hush up, Lorna, and leave your mother alone. You aren't going."

Lorna's small, round face contorted with anger. "You never take me anywhere."

"Now, Lorna, that's not true. You know we went to Fayetteville a couple of weeks ago. Just calm down, and I'll get Poppa to stop somewhere on the way back, and I'll bring you something to eat. What would you like?"

"I want to go. I hate staying here in this borin' old house."

"Just quit talking to her and get ready, Miranda. Your folks will be here anytime."

Lorna stomped off upstairs. A few minutes later the lights of her father's Silverado truck shone through the trees of Miranda's wooded yard. She grabbed a heavy down coat and ran out the front door.

NOT BOTHERING TO say hello, Clay asked, "How are the kids doing?"

"Byron's fine, but Lorna's mad, as usual."

"What's she mad about?"

"She wanted to go with us."

"Well, why didn't you let her go?"

"Dad, you know how much trouble she is when she's bored. She would have driven us crazy wanting to go home."

Bonita nodded her head. "Miranda's right. A hospital's no place for a child."

Miranda looked at her father's sullen face. She knew he didn't want to drive them to Tulsa but was probably secretly hoping that Lorna would come to brighten the trip. Too bad. She had made the call to leave her bright but demanding child at home.

He maintained a stony silence for the rest of the hundred-mile trip to Tulsa, one huge arm emerging from time to time outside the car window, the hand flipping cigarette ashes onto the snowy highway.

Miranda was appalled at her first sight of her brother. Always a robust, stout man, he seemed pale and thin. Thin, except for his swollen stomach.

He held out his hand to his mother. She held it between her own and kissed the palm. "Hello, son. How are you feelin'?"

"Been better, but I'm makin' it." He turned toward Clay and Miranda. "There's a couple of chairs in the corner if you want to sit."

Clay moved them beside Bob's bed. "Y'all go ahead and sit. I can't stand to sit no more." He moved closer to the doorway.

Sweat poured from Bob's brow and dripped off his reddish beard, and he clutched his belly and roared with pain. Bonita gasped. "What's wrong, son?"

He smiled apologetically, "Don't mind me, Mom. It just hurts sometimes. Would you get a nurse? I think it's time for my pain shot."

Clay spoke up. "I'll go tell them."

Miranda tried to lighten the situation with humor. "Man, you're getting skinny. I bet you'll have to buy a whole new wardrobe after you leave the hospital."

"Yeah, I'm pretty bony except for this gut. How are the kids?"

"Fine, except Lorna's mad because she didn't get to come up with us."

"She's always mad, isn't she? Must take after Clay."

"Hey, you know you're probably right. Maybe that's why they get along so well. How's little Bob?"

Bobby dropped his head and looked sad. "Growin' like a weed. I don't get to see him as much as I'd like. Carla did bring him to wave at me through the window yesterday. They were on their way to a Little League game. Seems like his mother's always got plans for him. The divorce will be final soon and hopefully the judge will make her let me see him every other weekend."

"I hope so." She changed the subject. Bob didn't need to be thinking about divorce right now. "What do you think of the food here?"

"You know, hospital food, pretty tasteless. You know what I've been wantin'?"

"What?"

"A tall, cold, orange Nehi."

"Well, looks like your nurse is here. I'll go see if I can rustle you one up."

Miranda walked over to the waiting room where the vending machines were located. Clay spied her. "What are you huntin' for?"

"Oh, Bobby wants a Nehi, but all they got is Coke here."

"I seen a convenience store not too far from here. I'm outta smokes, so I'll go."

"All right."

While Bonita visited with Bobby, Miranda cornered Bobby's doctor and asked him to explain Bobby's condition. The short, balding man nervously shuffled the papers in his hands. "Your brother has cirrhosis of the liver, likely brought on by excessive drinking. The liver's inflammation causes pain, vomiting, and bloating."

"I knew he liked to drink, but I didn't think he drank excessively."

"Evidently, he has been drinking heavily for some time to cause this much damage."

"What is his prognosis?"

He finally looked her in the eyes. "Not very good I'm afraid. He's in the last stage."

"How long?"

"Can't be exact, but I would say less than a year."

Miranda realized she had just heard some catastrophic news. She went to the bathroom, locked herself in a stall, and cried until her tears were spent. After washing her face, she shared the doctor's words with Clay in the waiting room.

He took it stoically as she knew he would. "So this is it for poor Bob. Don't tell your mother. It'll just upset her."

"Well, I'm not giving up. Miracles can happen, you know."

"Very seldom."

CLAY INSISTED THAT they stop and eat Kentucky Fried Chicken on the way home, and he bought an extra bucket for her to take home for Darryn and the kids. By the time she got home that night, only Darryn was up. She offered him some chicken and asked him to refrigerate whatever he didn't eat.

Moving quietly down the hall, she cracked the door open to Byron's room. He didn't stir, and she stood in the doorway, admiring her firstborn. Byron was a tall, big-boned boy with long arms and legs. His eyes, which had been bright blue when he was born, had changed to an interesting hazel, and his complexion showed his Scottish-Irish heritage. In appearance and in personality, he was almost her twin. He had always been a quiet, intelligent, and sensitive child, and they got along very well.

As soon as she opened Lorna's door, she saw a pair of dark brown eyes, glaring at her. "You said you would bring me somethin' to eat."

"I did. There's Kentucky Fried Chicken in the kitchen, but I thought you were asleep."

"Nope. I just been layin' here, waitin' on you to get home." She sprang from her bed, turned on the light, and ran into the kitchen.

She heard Darryn say, "What are you doin' up?"

By the time she got there, father and daughter were tucking into some fried chicken. She almost laughed when she saw them, sitting at the table, side by side, with the exact same contented expression on their faces. Lorna looked as much like Darryn as Byron resembled her. Not only did she have Darryn's dark eyes, she had his thick, black hair and coffee-colored skin. Of course, Grandma Amelia said she favored her side of the family.

Byron and Lorna were almost polar opposites in looks except for the long arms and legs that they both inherited from her side. She was every bit as intelligent as her brother, but she was generally more vocal and not always considerate of the feelings of others. Lorna and Miranda naturally clashed, and she got along best with her Poppa. As soon as Lorna finished eating, she ran into the front room and started watching television with him.

"Lorna, your hands are greasy. Go and wash them and brush your teeth."

"Do I have to?"

"You heard your mother."

"All right, but I'm going to watch television when I get back."

As she ran away, Miranda called after her, "And wash your face too. And we'll talk about television when you get back."

She went to the bay window and looked out at the glistening snow. "Wonder if we'll have school tomorrow."

"How were the roads?"

"Not too bad, but it really depends on how the bus routes are in the morning."

"Well, I guess you won't know until the morning then."

They stayed home for another two days, and the kids made snow angels and built snowmen. Miranda cooked three meals each day and even made chocolate fudge. Her pants appeared to be tighter by the time she returned to school on Friday.

Miranda only told Darryn about Bobby Joe's prognosis. Somehow she believed saying the frightening words would only give them strength. She still prayed for a miracle every day.

THAT MORNING BONITA called Miranda up and relayed her latest plans. "I'm packin' a bag and gettin' ready to have your dad take me to the hospital. I think Bobby Joe will do better if he has me to look after him. I'll call you this evenin' and give you a report."

Two weeks later, Bobby had improved enough so that he was dismissed from the hospital into Bonita's care. She told Miranda, "He'll get to feelin' like his own self in no time when he gets back home."

MIRANDA DROVE UP to her parents' old farmhouse on Strawberry Hill one cool March morning to see Bobby Joe sitting on the front porch, drinking coffee and listening to the songs of the myriads of birds that dwelled in the woods nearby. "Good morning, Bob. Boy, you look good. Do you feel as good as you look?"

"Well, since I'm so handsome, that would be kinda hard, but I'm feelin' pretty good, sis. What are you doin' up so early? I figured you schoolteachers crashed on the weekends."

"I do sometimes but not this morning. Gotta go wild onion hunting today."

"Wild onions, huh? Haven't had any in years. When are we goin' to eat them?"

"We got to find, clean, and cook them first. That takes a while, especially the cleaning part, but maybe around supper time we'll have them with a big pot of brown beans, a skillet of fried potatoes, and a pan of cornbread."

"And some of Mom's peach cobbler. I know she's makin' the crust for it now."

"Lord, you and me both will weigh two hundred pounds if we stay around Mom much more."

"Oh, well, there's nothing wrong with bein' fat, dumb, and happy, is there?"

"Speak for yourself, boy. See you later. I got things to do."

She walked into the kitchen to see Bonita putting the finishing touches on a large peach cobbler. "I thought you said you were out of your home-canned peaches."

"I am. This is the last two quarts. Guess I'll buy me some more this spring to can if I can afford them. Doesn't Bobby look good?"

Clay spoke up. "He looks good, but I don't think he feels as good as he looks. He coughed most of the night last night."

"That don't mean nothin', Clay. You cough most of the night yourself from smokin' all them cigarettes. Come on, Miranda, we'll go get our onions and then put the rest of dinner on. This is sure a good year for onions. Clay went down to the branch yesterday to check fences, and he said he had never seen so many onions."

Clay looked up from his coffee and biscuits. "Just remember to pick enough for everybody. Darryn and the kids are comin' to eat, too, ain't they?"

"Yeah, sometime this afternoon. The kids are still in bed."

Miranda spent a good day helping her mother prepare an early supper and talking and reminiscing with Bob. "You remember the time you dared me to smoke a cigarette so that I would be as tough as the other boys' little sisters?"

"Oh, yeah, how could I forget that? You got so sick you puked all over the place, and Mom lit into me like a mad hen."

Clay frowned as if trying to recall something. "I don't remember that at all."

"Of course not, Dad. There's a lot of things you never heard of to save us all some trouble."

Bobby mumbled, "Not to mention pain."

Clay's countenance turned stony. "Sometimes that's the only way some people can learn."

Bonita butted in. "Oh, well, that's all in the past, and we don't need to bring it up. Miranda, you better call Darryn and tell him supper's almost ready."

"WE HAD A good day today, didn't we?"

Fluffing up his pillows, Darryn reached out a hand to caress Miranda's face. "Yeah, I guess, but Bob sure looked wore out by the time we left."

"Well, what can we expect? He just got out of the hospital two weeks ago, you know. I'm just thankful he can enjoy being with his family again."

"Speaking of family, where were Little Bob and Carla? Did anybody try to invite them?"

"No, now that you mention it, we never did even think of inviting her. It's just so far to Tulsa, and they're away most weekends anyway since Bobby and she separated."

"Did anyone tell her Bob is out of the hospital?"

"Mom called her before they brought him home. Carla's called and talked to him a couple of times."

Darryn looked her over. "Nice gown. Is it new? Come here, you. It's Saturday night."

Miranda feigned ignorance. "Just haven't worn it in a while. And what's the significance of it being Saturday night?"

Darryn grabbed her and pulled her to himself. "Guess I'll have to jog your memory."

THE NEXT MORNING, Clay called to say that Bobby was having trouble breathing, so they were taking him back to the hospital. "Could be pneumonia. We'll call you when we find out somethin'."

Miranda showered, threw on some jeans and a sweater, and was vacuuming the living room when she got another call about two hours later.

"Get Darryn to bring you up here. It don't look good. Better leave the kids with Darryn's folks."

When Miranda arrived at the hospital three hours later, she'd convinced herself that Bobby would be recovered by the time she got there. "You just wait, Darryn. I've been praying. I know he's going to be fine."

"Hope you're right, honey."

Carla met Miranda at the nursing station and ushered her into the conference room where Clay was sitting with Bonita.

He stood up when they came into the room. "Doc's going to be here any minute. Just sit down here with your mother and me. Shouldn't be long now."

"What happened?"

"We don't rightly know. Something must have gone wrong when they was examining him, and they moved him to Intensive Care. Said we can go visit once they stabilized him. Here's his doctor."

Miranda tried to force away her worry so she could concentrate on the doctor's report.

"It was the stupidest thing. Mister Smith passed out during the examination, and we quickly flopped him over on his side, but, unfortunately, aspiration had already occurred, and we were forced to hook him up to life support."

Miranda could feel hot anger rising from the pit of her stomach up to her mouth. "In other words, my brother is dying because you allowed him to choke on his own vomit?"

Clay rose to his feet to stand towering over the doctor. "Is that right, mister?"

Darryn and Bonita both reached out to calm the big man. "Now, Clay, nothing is to be gained from losin' your temper, even though you have reason to."

"Darryn's right, Clay. Please don't get mad."

Carla's voice was trembling. "Anger won't change the situation."

Miranda didn't speak but watched with satisfaction the fear, showing in the small man's eyes, that was replaced with relief when Clay sat back down.

"Mister Smith had already developed pneumonia, and in his weakened condition, aspiration could have occurred at any time."

Miranda's gaze could turn a man to stone. "How're you treating him?"

"We're pumping the vomit out of his lungs and have placed him on life support until he has improved sufficiently to breathe on his own again. At the present time he is considered in serious, but stable, condition."

Bonita sighed in relief. "So, can we see him?"

"Of course, if you abide by ICU visiting regulations. But remember he's in a somewhat comatose state and cannot speak nor perhaps even hear."

Carla reached out and shook the doctor's hand. "Thank you, doctor. I know you're doing all you can."

MIRANDA WAS APPALLED when it came her turn to visit. Bobby didn't seem to be aware that she was in the room. His head twitched continually as his unfocused eyes gazed at the ceiling.

She stroked his forehead and tried to soothe him. "It's going to be all right, Bobby Joe. The Lord's going to get you out of this."

She prayed aloud and experienced the comforting presence of God, but Bob's head never quit twitching, and his eyes never seemed to look at her. Now she understood why her mother was crying when she came to the waiting room.

Carla had tears in her eyes after her visit. She grabbed her purse and said, "I need to get home to put Little Bobby to bed and let Mom go home." She gave Bonita a quick hug. "Be careful driving home. I'll probably see you tomorrow."

Clay, who was next, spent less than five minutes with Bob. He came back with red, watery eyes. "Couldn't stand to see him like that. I'm afraid this is the end for poor Bob."

"It's not over until it's over, Dad, and where there's life there's hope. Didn't the doctor say Bob's condition had stabilized?"

"That and some other things I didn't like. Help me talk your mother into us goin' home after Darryn comes back. We ain't doin' the boy any good here, and she's about sick herself. We can call in the morning and see how he is, and then we'll come back and see him. Maybe by tomorrow he'll be hisself."

Bonita resisted at first. "Now I don't know, Clay. Think how I'd feel if anything happened to my boy and me not there."

"Daddy's right, Mom. You don't look so good, and I need to get home. I have to call my principal so that he can find me a substitute for tomorrow. We'll plan on spending the day with Bob tomorrow."

Reluctantly, Bonita finally agreed to going home to rest and returning the next day.

MIRANDA WAS SORTING laundry the next morning when the phone rang. When she turned, Darryn placed his hands on her shoulders. "Babe, that was your dad. Bob passed away a few minutes ago."

"No, it can't be. He's supposed to get well." She brushed his hands away and ran off.

She found herself opening the bedroom closet door. It was a walk-in closet, deep, quiet, and dark. She locked the door after her and turned out the light. She heard herself keening and screaming out the question, "Why? Why? Why?"

WHEN SHE EMERGED from the closet more than an hour later, Darryn shook his head in sorrow at her appearance. Her eyes were so red from weeping that every blood vessel seemed visible. Her voice was hoarse from wailing. He gently wiped the tears from her eyes and held her close.

She finally pulled away and got her car keys out. When he asked where she was going, she calmly said, "I need to be with Mom."

People remarked to her later about how well she took her brother's death, but no one knew how she had lost all control in the closet.

They tried to talk her out of it, but Carla had Bob's body cremated. Bonita cried for days and said, "She wouldn't even let me have a real funeral for him, just a short memorial service."

IT WAS EARLY May and two weeks until Aiden Junior High School was dismissed for the summer. Although she loved the thought of almost being out of school, Miranda dreaded the extra stress the last days of school always brought. That Tuesday, on the last class of the day, the students' level of mischief had reached its peak, and her level of coping had fallen to its nadir.

After repeatedly scolding a boy for throwing spitballs, poking another student with his pencil, and interrupting her lesson, Miranda found her hands on the sixth-grader's shoulders. Her voice was grinding out, "Why can't you ever be quiet?" as she shook him in rhythm to her words.

The other students looked at her in shock. Miranda was rather shocked herself. Even though her classroom was finally quiet, she knew it wasn't acceptable teacher behavior and prepared herself for the parental and administrative attacks that could come. This time she might be lucky, and no one would care enough to complain. But it was just a matter of time before she cracked again and maybe did something worse.

She walked into the teachers' lounge at the end of that day, fighting back tears. Seeing her stricken face, veteran teacher, Mr. French approached her. "What's the matter, Miranda, have a bad day?"

"Bad's not the word for it. I might have got myself on suing grounds today."

After she related the incident, Beryl French replied, "Don't worry about it. I've done worse and haven't been called on it. You said it was the Spencer kid? You're all right then. The Spencers never come to the school about anything. They're too happy to have that brood off of their hands for a while. Now if you had grabbed a Kincaid or a

Burgeste, you would have been in deep. Those people are just looking for a chance to sue the school. And our superintendent's so chicken that the word "sue" gets him to running scared."

"Yeah, but maybe tomorrow I'll grab a Kincaid or a Burgeste or some other special case. I've been this close to jumping right in the middle of Gary Gene Kincaid all week."

"Well, I'd hold off of that if I were you. Just think, less than two weeks, and we'll be out of this den of despair. And if you can't make it to Friday, there's always sick leave."

"I suppose I could take off tomorrow, but I have to give a make-up spelling test tomorrow. No, I better not."

"Suit yourself, Miranda, but you're far too responsible for your own good. You would be happier if you were like me. I wake up in the morning, my stomach's a little queasy, and I call up Jim Sweeney and say, 'Boss, I don't feel so good this morning. Get me a substitute. My lesson plans and grade book are on my desk. Thanks.'"

"But I'm giving that spelling test tomorrow, and the last time I left a test for the substitute to give, the kids cheated like crazy."

"So what? You're being gone might give some poor kid a passing grade for the last nine weeks. It's not like most of them want to learn anything anyway."

"There are a few."

"Mighty few."

At this point, Stephanie Shandell, intern teacher, spoke up. "I can't believe you teachers talk this way."

"Be quiet, rookie. One year in the classroom, and you'll talk just like us."

Francine Spyres, the counselor, patted Stephanie on the back. "Now, now, don't disillusion the poor child so. Stephanie, not all teachers talk this way."

Mr. French smirked. "Oh, yeah, name some."

"Well, when I taught in the grade school, some of the teachers seemed to enjoy their students, especially in the lower grades."

"Grade school doesn't count."

Chad Peterson, the eighth-grade science teacher, put away the newspaper he'd been reading and walked over to join them. "I enjoyed teaching chemistry in the high school before they moved me here."

"High school doesn't count, either. We're talking about junior high, home of the hyper, the destructive, and the weird. This place is a zoo."

Angela Bearpaw, choir teacher, giggled and raised her right hand. "Amen to that, Mr. French. Don't you think we ought to get extra pay for hazardous duty?"

"Absolutely. Lord, look at the time. I still got to get my desk cleared off, so I can be in my car when the bell rings. See you tomorrow." Mr. French made a fast break down the hall to his classroom.

Mrs. Spyres scowled. "Lord forbid he stay at school one minute past the bell."

"Do you blame him? Excuse me. I need to straighten up my classroom before the bell rings." Miranda grabbed a stack of papers from her mailbox and walked to her classroom.

When she got there, both of her children were waiting for her. Byron was reading a copy of Watership Down that he had found on one of her shelves.

Lorna was drawing kittens and puppies on her chalkboard. She stopped drawing when she saw Miranda. "Mom, would you take us to the Burger Bar before we go home? We're starvin'."

"I might if you and Byron will help me get this room straightened up in a hurry. You can start by erasing everything off of the board and picking all the paper up off of the floor."

Lorna hesitated. "Do we have to?"

"You do if you want to eat at the Burger Bar."

Since she didn't have to cook dinner, Miranda took a nap. She woke up when she heard Darryn coming in and considered telling him about the incident. She remembered the last time when she had confided in him about making a mistake. By the time he told her everything she did wrong, she was almost in tears. No, she would keep it to herself. She walked into the kitchen and warmed up some dinner leftovers for Darryn.

When she got discouraged like this, her thoughts sometimes wandered back to her good classroom experiences. She thought about Ben Spotted Horse when he came into her eighth grade English class as a shy, overweight underachiever. Some of his first words to her were, "I'll probably fail your class. I failed English last year."

She gave him an encouraging smile. "No, you won't."

And Ben didn't.

From the beginning she treated him like a top student, bragging on him when he turned in a good paper, chiding him gently when he began falling behind, never letting him get so behind that he would fall into the black hole of academic failure. Ben was really quite bright she discovered, but no one had taken the trouble to find out before. One of his creative writing papers was so good that she took it to one of her college night classes for the class to critique to Ben's utter amazement.

"You took one of my papers to your class? Why?"

"Because it was the best one turned in."

Ben finished the year with a strong A in eighth grade English and went on to graduate in the top ten percent of his senior class

But there hadn't been another Ben in three years. Now people occasionally threw her a crumb, parents thanking her for teaching their child how to write, get in front of an audience, use the library and the like, or more rarely, even an administrator commenting on the talent of a child she had worked hard with or giving her high marks on a teacher evaluation. But crumbs thrown to a starving person would not sustain life, and Miranda was caught in the death throes of a life-draining affliction. Something had to change.

Miranda was eating lunch on the last day of school in the teachers' lounge when a sudden movement from the playground caught her eye. She stood up to get a better view.

Mr. French, who was sitting beside her, seemed oblivious to what she was doing. "Did you know that the kids are out there spraying shaving cream all over each other?"

"Yes, I'm aware of it."

"Aren't you going to do anything about it?"

"Why should I? I'm not on duty. Let Spyres and McKinsey take care of it."

"They don't even know what's going on. They're over on the far side of the playground, gabbing. Well, I guess I'll just go break up the fun. Are you coming?"

"I suppose, if I must, but no one's going to appreciate our diligence."

A few minutes later they came back into the lounge with their hands laden with shaving cream cans. Miranda threw the cans into the trash, wiped off her hands on a paper towel, handed the roll of towels to Mr. French, and said, "Well, that takes care of that. Did you get the names of all of the perpetrators?"

"The usual. Devlin, Mason, O'Reilly, Pathfinder, Spencer, Burgeste, and Kincaid. I think there were a couple of girls who were smart enough to put their cans up when they saw us coming, but we don't have the proof on them."

"I'll go turn their names in to the office."

"He won't thank you for the information."

"That's all right. I will still have done my duty."

The bell rang, and Miranda found herself caught up in the crowd of pushing, noisy children. She finally made her way to the office only to be stopped by the secretary. "Mister Sweeney's busy."

"Do you know when I may see him?"

"It might be a while. He's in conference with parents."

"Well, I don't really have time to wait. Would you tell him that here is a list of kids that Mister French and I took shaving cream off of at noon. He can let me know when he wants to talk to me."

"That will be fine."

Miranda waited all afternoon for word from Sweeney. Gary Gene Kincaid gloated that "he hadn't got in trouble over the shave cream."

"Don't be so sure, Gary Gene. Mister Sweeney has been extremely busy today. He'll call you in when he has time."

But as the three o'clock bell rang, and the last student left the building, Miranda decided to check for herself.

"May I speak to Mister Sweeney now?"

"Go ahead. He doesn't have anyone with him now."

As usual, something about the principal made Miranda tongue-tied. "Mister Sweeney, did you get my note today?"

"Yes, I did."

"Did you want to talk to me about what happened?"

His voice sounded low and weary. "Go ahead and tell me."

After Miranda related what had happened, she asked, "Did you call the kids in to talk to them?"

"No."

"Are you going to call their parents?"

"I don't want to deal with it right now."

"But if the kids get by with this, they might try something worse next year."

"Maybe so, but as I said before, I'm not going to deal with this, not now."

"All right then." Miranda slunk from the room.

She met Mr. French in the hall. "You were right. He refuses to deal with it."

"I won't say I told you so, but I do hope you learned something from this."

"What, to stay in the lounge and ignore what goes on out on the playground?"

"Exactly."

"I'll try my best."

"Good. Then you'll make everybody a lot happier, including Mister Sweeney and yourself."

XI
FAMILY
MATTERS

MIRANDA AND HER family had a memorable summer, beginning with a long road trip to Florida. As they were coming home, she asked the question she always asked after all of their big experiences. "What was your favorite part?"

Without hesitating, Lorna replied, "Disney World."

Byron nodded his head. "Yeah, I can't wait to go back."

Darryn said, "It hasn't happened yet."

She frowned at him. "What does that mean?"

"It won't happen until I get back home and can relax in my recliner."

Miranda laughed. "Why am I not surprised?"

He grinned at her and showed his dimples. "How about you?"

"Hmmm... if I had to pick one thing, it would have to be the ocean. It is unbelievably beautiful, and I can't wait to see it again."

They went camping at Lake Tenkiller, floated the Illinois River near Tahlequah, watched some good movies at the Stilwell Eagle Theatre and the Tahlequah Drive-in, hosted sleepovers, and attended a big family reunion at Grandma Amelia's house.

Miranda never asked "what was your least favorite part?" about any experience. If anyone had asked her that question about this particular summer, she would have to answer, "Lorna." One minute her daughter thrilled her with her exceptional ability and intelligence, and the next minute she fought back tears of frustration and despair.

Lorna's greatest fan was her grandpa Clay, whom she and Byron called Poppa. He liked Byron, but he doted on Lorna. As soon as she was potty trained, he had taken her on the backroads of the rural areas of Jubilee, Adair, Cherokee, Sequoyah, and the adjoining counties. She learned the location of every pretty view and every good place to fish and hunt.

He would sometimes even drive her around Aiden in his police car, and he bragged about her toughness. "That girl's as mean as a snake."

Lorna was a frequent visitor in her grandparents' home, where she was treated like a princess. All she had to say was "I'm hungry for shrimp, Poppa," and Clay, Bonita, whom Lorna and Byron called Mema, and Lorna were off to one of her favorite seafood restaurants in Fort Smith or Fayetteville.

He often took Lorna fishing and bragged, "She baits her own hook and can catch more fish than most men I know."

Why he so clearly favored Lorna over Byron was a mystery to Miranda. Once he told Miranda "You baby that boy too much. If you ain't careful, you'll turn him into a sissy."

He had turned Lorna into a tough little tomboy, who hated to be touched. Her daughter pushed her away every time she attempted to hug or kiss her.

Darryn assured her it was nothing to worry about. "The people in my family aren't the touchy-feely kind either, and Lorna just takes after Clay and us."

She suspected Lorna and she would never experience the close bond she had always shared with her mother. Bonita was not only her mother but also her best friend. Lorna treated Miranda more like an enemy than a friend. She never seemed to accept anything she said without arguing about it.

When Miranda told her she needed to clean up her room, she said, "Why? I like it this way."

When she told her there would be no more sleepovers until she did, she shrugged her shoulders and said, "Who cares?"

Once she asked Darryn, "Why does everything always have to be a battle with that girl?"

His answer disappointed her. "Because you've always let her get by with it, Miranda."

Her problems with Lorna took a backseat to what happened to her father that year. It started when Clay began limping. She noticed it one day when she saw him walking to his truck after bringing back Lorna from one of their excursions.

After he had driven away, she called Bonita. "What's wrong with Dad?"

"He says his right leg just gives out on him sometimes, and it pains him somethin' awful."

"Well, he needs to go to the doctor."

"I know. I think I finally got him talked into goin' to the Veterans' Hospital in Muskogee. He told me I could make an appointment, and we are supposed to be there on Friday."

"Do you want me to go?"

"No, that's okay. You just started back to school, and they won't let you off very easy."

"That's true, but I am going to call you as soon as I get home from school, all right?"

"All right."

They talked about other matters until Bonita said, "Here he comes. Guess I better see what he wants for supper."

THE NEWS WASN'T good on Friday. Bonita called Miranda. *"The doctors say his right femur bone looks like a honeycomb on the x-ray."*

A chill came over Miranda's soul. "What caused it?"

Bonita sighed. *"Cancer. And they say it is in one of kidneys, too. They're sendin' him to what they call an oncologist."*

When they spoke to the oncologist after Clay's examination, he didn't give them much hope. "Removal of the diseased kidney is necessary to keep the cancer from spreading further. As you know, it has already metastasized to the right thigh area, which is why you have been experiencing pain when you walk."

Clay scowled. "What are you goin' to do about the leg?"

"We'll try to remove the tumor if we can and will then insert a metal bar in the leg in an effort to compensate for the destroyed bone."

Miranda fought to keep her voice steady. "How about chemotherapy treatment?"

"I'm afraid chemotherapy is ineffective against this type of cancer. Perhaps we'll try radiation when it's needed."

Clay patted Bonita's hands as she sobbed. "Just tell me my chances, Doc."

"Not very good, I'm afraid. The five-year survival rate for your type of cancer is less than twenty percent."

"If I got a chance, I'll make it."

Miranda hoped he was right.

AFTER RECOVERING FROM surgery and radiation, Clay worked at his job as Aiden's Chief of Police for another three years until the doctors had to amputate his cancerous leg. Even after the amputation, Clay learned to manipulate the heavy crutches as he put his weight on his good leg, swinging the small stump that remained with each step.

When his cronies came around, he put on a brave show. "Boys, do you really think a missin' leg is goin' to get me down? How many men do you know that can say their"—he hesitated in the presence of Miranda and Bonita—"part is longer than their legs? I'll be back at City Hall as soon as Doc makes me a new leg."

After they left, he turned cranky. "Get over here, Luce, and fix my pillows, will you?"

She did her best, but he threw one at her. "Still can't do nothin' right. Bonita, can you fix these pillows so they will be more comfortable?"

At least Miranda didn't cry until she got to the car.

He didn't say anything at his next appointment when his doctor told him an artificial leg would be cumbersome and practically useless for a man in his condition.

When Bonita teared up, he joked. "Aw, come on now. I ain't the first one-legged man you ever took care of, am I?"

She smiled through her tears. "No, of course not, Clay. And it will be nice to have you home more. I will tell the bank that I will be takin' an early retirement."

"Do what you want. It'll be all right as long as I can drive my truck and go when I want to."

Miranda hugged Bonita and patted Clay's shoulder. "Tell you what, Dad. If you don't feel like driving, just let me know. I'll get Darryn to take you where you want to go."

After he healed, Clay had his truck modified with hand controls. He drove like he had always done, going to work and taking Bonita and Lorna as far as Fayetteville to try out a new place to eat from time to time. But as the months went by, he had less and less strength to get out of the house, even when Darryn drove. His appetite lessened and finally vanished.

One day Miranda walked in the kitchen to find Grandma Amelia comforting a crying Bonita. "Now, Bonita, you're just going to have to take hold of yourself. You got to be strong for Clay. Women have to be strong for their menfolk at times like this. I don't care if Clay's cussing you, you have to take him to the hospital."

She turned to look at Miranda. "Miranda, tell your mother that Clay's got to go in the hospital. They can feed him through his veins and get him built-up again. Why, he's nothing but a bag of bones."

Miranda looked at the long, thin skeleton that her once robust father had become. She watched in pity as the fragile fingers worked to bring the sheet over the stub that had once been his leg. He had been cut to pieces.

"All right, Grandma. Maybe they can do something at the hospital that we can't do here."

Grandma Amelia was right. After being hooked up to an I.V. for a few days and getting shots to stimulate his appetite, Clay was raring to go back home. It wasn't long before he asked them to visit.

Over a fried chicken supper, he outlined his idea. "I want to take the kids to the Kiamichi Mountains. They haven't been there, have they?"

"No, but you need someone to drive you, and we can't all go in our car."

"Already thought of that. Darryn. If I rented a van, would you mind drivin' it?"

"No, I'd be fine as long as I didn't have to miss a lot of work."

"Don't worry. I'll rent it for a weekend. How about next Friday afternoon? We would come home Sunday night."

"Sounds good, Dad."

Miranda sat in the back seat of the plush van, taking in the splendor of the colorful trees and the glorious views up ahead. She watched Clay's eyes sparkle as he told them stories she had never heard. "We're on Windin' Stair Mountain right now. The first time I saw this spot was from my horse Champion, and I was headed to the Palo Duro Canyon in Texas. Talk about pretty. Darryn, you gotta take the kids there someday."

"I'll do that. Why were you in Texas?"

"My cousin Manuel has a ranch close to the canyon. His grandpa, Junebug Clay, was a brother to my grandpa."

"Hey, I heard of him. He was supposed to be some kind of cowboy. Worked for Charles Goodnight, didn't he?"

"That's the one. "

"Man. I bet you heard some tales."

"I know a few."

Lorna's dark eyes glittered. "I want to hear a war story. How many men did you kill, Poppa?"

Miranda winced as the enthusiastic tone was replaced with something else. "More than I can count, but I only regretted one."

"Tell us about it, Poppa."

"It was a German soldier, who begged me to spare his life. He begged me while he showed me pictures of his wife and child."

Miranda detected a new note in Lorna's tone, and she was glad to hear it. It was pity. "You didn't really do it, did you?"

Byron answered for Clay. "Poppa had to. He was a soldier, and soldiers have to obey orders."

Darryn signaled a right turn and pulled the van to a pullout. "I think it's time we had a stretch break. How are you doin' back there, Bonita?"

"I really need a break and some fresh air. My stomach feels a little queasy. Guess I ate too much spaghetti at that Italian place in Krebs."

THEY GOT HOME Sunday evening, and they were all tired but happy, especially Clay. A sleepy Lorna allowed Miranda to kiss her good night as she leaned over to tuck her in. "Mommy?"

She smiled at Lorna's use of her old nickname. "What is it, honey?"

"Poppa's getting better, isn't he?"

Miranda started to tell her the truth, but she couldn't squash the flickering candle of hope. "We hope so, baby."

A FEW WEEKS later, Miranda visited Clay in the hospital. He had been admitted the night before, complaining of dizziness. When he saw her, he moaned and croaked out, "Where's Bonita?"

"Down in the waiting room, resting."

"Go get her. I need to tell her something."

When Miranda and Bonita walked into the room, Clay spoke hoarsely, "Come closer. I want to tell you both something."

"What is it, Clay?" asked Bonita.

"I won't die in no blamed hospital. Take me home."

"But they can take better care of you here, Daddy."

"Don't matter. Gonna die, anyway. Take me home."

"Whatever you say, Clay. As soon as they finish giving you blood, we'll take you home."

THE LAST YEAR of Clay Stone's life was spent in his own bed, which he ordered moved into the living room in one of his moments of clarity. Toward the end there were fewer and fewer of those.

ONE MORNING MIRANDA was summoned to the school office. The secretary said her mother needed her right away. Fearing the end, Miranda pulled up to a yard overflowing with all types of vehicles. All the family was here. It must be bad.

But when she walked in the front door, she heard her father's raspy voice. "Is that Luce? I gotta talk to Luce."

"I'm here, Daddy. What do you need?"

"It's Lorna. She's run away to a bad place. You gotta go get her."

She tried to humor him. "What kind of place?"

"It's like a slaughterhouse, way out in the country. Kids run off, and they catch them. And when they do, they cut their heads off and put them on the wall. You gotta get Lorna out of there before it's too late."

Reaching out a soothing hand, she said, "It's all right, Daddy. You just had a bad dream. I talked to Lorna during her noon hour, and she's just fine."

"Oh, yeah, she's fine, and you're fine, but you won't be for long if you keep wavin' your hand around like that. Don't you see them snakes that just come out of the wall? There. See 'em? That one almost got you."

Miranda's Aunt Emily comforted her sobbing Aunt Mary. Her father continued to scream in his delusion. "Miranda, tell Ross to take my truck and catch Bonita. She run off with a salesman last night."

"Daddy, don't you remember Uncle Ross is dead? He drowned in Tenkiller years ago."

"That's what you think. He's really just hidin' in the woods. He always was a sneaky feller."

Aunt Susan's daughter, Lydia—a nurse—gave Clay an injection.

"Luce, bring me my gun. I'm tired of this crazy woman shootin' drugs in my body."

Miranda took Clay's bony hand and watched the frightened eyes fighting the drug-induced sleep. "Don't you remember, Daddy? Grandma Amelia borrowed your gun for a while. Said she might need it for protection against prowlers."

"Oh, yeah, guess she needs it more than me right now."

Miranda held her father's hand while he slept. "That was a good idea, Grandma. Taking Daddy's gun home with you. He scared us to death with it a few days ago."

"I never heard the like, letting a sick, crazy man have a gun. What if he had shot you with it?"

"Then I would have been out of my misery," said Bonita. "Oh, I know it was a mistake, but he wouldn't hush until I let him hold it a while. The home nurse said today that it can't be much longer. His feet are as cold as ice."

"As stubborn as Clay is, there's no telling," said Amelia. "Well, the crisis is past. You all can go home now. We'll call you if we need you."

Everyone left but Amelia, Aunt Abigail, and Aunt Emily. Miranda continued to hold Clay's hand, peering closely into his face and waiting. As dark grew near, and the three other women left to prepare supper in the kitchen, Miranda sensed another presence in the room. She whispered, "Come, Death Angel, and take him away."

He opened his eyes and spoke clearly. "I love you, Luce."

Miranda sobbed, "I love you, too, Daddy."

"Remember, Luce, always think for yourself. Don't let other people force you into doin' anything you don't want to do. Don't make no hasty decisions neither. You'll regret them later. Don't forget, you hear?"

"I won't forget."

"Oh, Luce, two more things before I go to sleep."

"What's that?"

"Put a picture of a horse on my tombstone and bury me in town, not way out in the country in the Jubilee or the Stone Family Cemetery."

"I understand the horse, but why do you want to be buried away from all your kin?"

"Someday nobody will be around to take care of my grave, and it will become just another old cemetery, out in the woods that nobody remembers."

"I'll do it, but it'll probably be a fight."

He grinned up at her. "You can handle it."

Those were the last lucid words Miranda ever heard her father speak. She sat by his bed, holding his hand until he was snoring again. As she watched him sleep, her mind played back a familiar memory.

IT WAS NIGHTTIME in Miranda's childhood in the house on Strawberry Hill. Then, as now, she was sensitive to nocturnal sounds. She couldn't sleep until that strange noise went away. What was it? Could it be a murderer who would slaughter them in their beds? Or something even worse, some supernatural being that couldn't be detected or stopped? She got up and cracked the door.

Across the hallway, she glimpsed, through the partially open door, the red flare of her father's cigarette lighter as he lit another Pall Mall and lay smoking and thinking in bed. Now she could go to sleep because if Daddy were awake, everything was fine. She could relax, knowing that nothing could harm her as long as he was on guard. She had never felt as safe since.

SHE MUST HAVE nodded off because she became aware that

her mother had been repeating her name for some time. "Miranda, wake up."

She opened her tired, blurry eyes and focused on Bonita's face. "What is it?"

"You need to go home and get some sleep."

"I'm all right."

"No, you're not. It's two in the mornin', and Abigail took your grandma home about half an hour ago. You go on home now and come back early in the mornin'. Emily will need to be relieved by then."

"How about you?"

"I'm all right for now. I got some sleep last night before your daddy had this last spell."

WHEN MIRANDA GOT home that night, she fell into bed, clothes and all. She had barely gotten into a deep sleep when she had one of her strange waking dreams. A very small Indian man, dressed in old-fashioned clothes and moccasins, came skittering across the room. When he got to her bed, he stopped, leaned over, and looked intently in her face. She sat up in bed and screamed, with eyes wide open.

She looked all around the room. Nothing was there.

Alarmed, Darryn sat up, "What's wrong?"

"Nothing. Just one of my crazy dreams. Go back to sleep."

Miranda contemplated her dream before falling back to sleep. Aunt Mary would say it was a warning dream. Something bad was going to happen, and she was afraid she knew what it was.

The next morning she started when the phone rang in the kitchen. Darryn, who was already up, must have answered it. She looked at the alarm clock on the nightstand by her bed. Oh, no. She had overslept. She had meant to be at her mom's house by six, and it was almost seven.

She noticed Darryn's wet eyes as he came into the room. He sat on the bed and took her in his arms. "He's gone, honey."

She pushed him away. "No, he can't be. I was supposed to be there to hold his hand and say goodbye. I was supposed to close his eyes. I'm his only child, and that was my job. He can't be dead."

"He is, but your mom, Grandma Amelia, Aunt Emily, and Aunt Abigail were with him. They did those things."

She bit the inside of her mouth to keep from screaming. "I can't do anything right, not even when it comes to death."

"Quit beatin' yourself up, Miranda. You did your best. You want me to wake the kids up and tell them?"

"No, let them sleep a while longer. I need to take a walk."

When she got back some thirty minutes later, she was more in control of her emotions. "Darryn, will you wake them up and tell them to come in the front room?"

When Miranda told the kids the news, Lorna flew at her, hitting and scratching. "I dreamed Poppa died last night, but I didn't believe it because you told me he was gettin' well."

Byron pulled her off of his mother. "Mom never said that. She always said she hoped he would get well."

Lorna screamed, ran to her room, and locked the door.

Darryn embraced Miranda, patting her back like she was a baby. "Byron, go get a bandage from the medicine cabinet. Your mom's got a little scratch on her cheek."

Miranda mumbled into his neck. "I just lost my daddy, and my daughter hates me."

He rocked her in his arms. "Lorna doesn't hate you. She's just hurt and confused. Give her time. She'll come around."

By the time Miranda showered, changed clothes, and arrived at her mother's house, the funeral home had picked up her father's body. Her aunts had taken down the bed and moved it back into Clay's bedroom, had vacuumed the whole house, and cleaned the living room. Abigail was lighting a lemon-scented candle.

"That smells nice, but what's it for?"

"It helps get rid of the smell of death."

"I guess I got so used to it that I didn't notice it anymore."

"Visitors would notice it, and I'm sure your mom will have several."

Miranda sat at the kitchen table with her mother and grandmother eating homemade pie and drinking coffee, feeling guilty, while her aunts scurried around, cleaning the entire house. She stood up to help, and Grandma Amelia put her hand on her arm. "Sit down. They want to do it."

"All right." She paused, peering into her grandmother's face before proceeding, to see if she was up to questions. Seeing no sign of emotional distress, she asked the question.

"Grandma, I always wanted to ask Daddy something, but I never did. Could I ask you instead?"

The thick black eyebrows rose, and the dark glittering eyes shone with curiosity. "You can ask me anything, and I'll try my best to answer."

"Why did my dad always call me Luce?"

Bonita, who had barely touched her pie, put it aside. "That's easy. You know how your dad always loved television? He called you Luce after Lucy Ricardo in the *I Love Lucy* show."

Amelia shook her head. "No, I think it was more than that. I think it goes back to Clay's army days. You know he was stationed in Texas before they sent him to Europe?"

Miranda and Bonita both nodded their heads.

"Well, Ross told me once that Clay had a Mexican girlfriend when he was there. She was teaching him Spanish so he could impress her father when they finally got to meet. Trouble was, he got sent off before that could happen."

Bonita giggled. "Good thing for me that he did."

Amelia frowned. "Yes, I suppose. Anyway, Miranda, do you know what *Luce* means in Spanish?"

"No, but if I had to guess, I would say, maybe clear, because of the word *lucid*."

She smiled. "Close but not exactly. It means light."

"Why would he call me light?"

Bonita chuckled. "Don't you get it? You were always the light of his life. Each day started and ended with you."

"You know Bobby Joe said almost the same thing to me the day I got married."

She stood up, tears spilling from her eyes, reached down, and hugged her grandmother. "Thank you, Grandma. I should have asked you that question a long time ago."

Amelia brushed tears from her eyes and smiled up at her. "I might not have known the answer then, but I'm glad I could help you today."

When she turned to her mother, Bonita stood up, and they fell into each other's arms, laughing and crying at the same time. Miranda experienced a warm feeling of healing sweep through her body and soul.

When Bonita released her, she stepped back. "I feel better."

Her mother asked Uncle Zack and Aunt Emily to go with them to make funeral arrangements. Zack just agreed with everything they discussed. All Emily said was, "I hope you get something in blue for the coffin. Blue was always Clay's favorite color."

Miranda had brought a small picture of a running horse that she had cut from a magazine. "Do you think you can find someone who can chisel an image like this in the tombstone?"

The funeral director, a soft-spoken, kind, balding man, took the picture and put it in a folder with all the arrangements. "I know just the man for the job. Have you written the obituary?"

He took it over and quickly read it. "Hmm, he was the same age as me, sixty-six. Well, this is excellent, well-written and not one mistake. You'd be surprised how many people can't write a decent obituary." He placed it in the folder. Let's see what else? Oh, yes. Here's a plot map. Where in Jubilee Cemetery do you want your father buried, or have you decided on the Stone Cemetery?"

"He told me he wanted to be buried in the town cemetery."

Uncle Zack finally had something to say. "Are you sure about that? Why would he want to be buried there?"

"It was one of his last requests. He said, 'I want to be buried in town because someday nobody'll be around to take care of country cemeteries.'"

Bonita nodded her head. "She's right. I've heard him say that same thing more than once."

Miranda could tell Grandma, Uncle Zack, and the aunts weren't too happy with her during the funeral, but they didn't say anything. Earlier that morning, she had found one of her favorite pictures of her father and Lorna, with its frame broken, lying in Lorna's floor, along with a hand mirror. She cleaned it all up and didn't say anything to Lorna since she still wasn't speaking to her. It seemed like she had somehow offended almost everybody.

Finally, it was all over. Her father was buried, the funeral meal was finished, everything was put away, and everyone had left. "Mom, do you need me to spend the night?"

"That would be nice."

"All right. Let's have some coffee and pie. I got a story I want to tell you about a strange dream I had a few hours before Daddy died."

XII

LORNA

THREE YEARS LATER, they had two high schoolers in the house. Byron was eighteen, a high school senior, who talked a lot about where he might go to college. Lorna was fifteen, a freshman, who didn't talk much about anything. After Clay's death, Miranda had noticed Lorna's increasing withdrawal from the family. As she poured over test papers, she pondered the subject of Lorna. What was wrong with the girl? She had been such a strong, confident baby and toddler, almost too strong-willed for the gentle Miranda. But adolescence had brought on a host of illnesses, most of which Miranda suspected were psychological, rather than physical, in nature.

It was nearly eleven o'clock, time for bed, if she was to have enough energy to cope tomorrow. She had to deal with a flash of anger directed toward herself when she realized she had forgotten to call her mother tonight, and now it was too late. Maybe she could pay her a short surprise visit tomorrow after school.

THE FOLLOWING DAY, after her workday ended, Miranda

enjoyed the six-mile trip to her mother's country home. The dogwoods and redbuds were in full bloom, and somebody had been baling hay. The air was full of its sweet, clean smell.

She got stuck behind a slowmoving tractor at the bottom of Strawberry Hill, just two miles from her former home, and fretted about the delay until the friendly farmer motioned her around him as soon as they reached the top. He grinned and waved, and Miranda recognized him as Bill Dooley, one of her mother's neighbors. He and his wife, Lillian, had been so good to see about Mom since Daddy's death, and Miranda was glad she hadn't shown her impatience to him.

When she drove up, she caught a glimpse of a bright red cloth and, with a closer look, identified it as a bright scarf Bonita had tied around her head. She was occupied with one of her favorite activities, working in her flower beds.

She looked up when she heard the motor of Miranda's car and walked over to where Miranda had parked. "Hi, babe. Come on in the house, so we can talk."

Miranda looked around the small, neat house as her mother slipped out of her gardening shoes on the front porch. The house was immaculate as always. Her mother had told her many times, "Always put things back in their places, and you'll have a neat house."

As Bonita's words echoed through her mind, Miranda guiltily considered the state of her own house. She hadn't mopped in a month, the bathtub had a semipermanent brownish ring in it, and as always, the carpet needed vacuuming. Neither Darryn, Lorna, nor Byron behaved as though he or she had heard of objects having places, much less actually putting things back where they got them. Someday she hoped to follow her mother's mantra.

Her mother sang, "If I knew you was comin', I would bake a cake...." She kissed Miranda on both cheeks. "But you would rather have pie, anyway, right?"

"You know me well. I like cake, but nobody can make pie like you."

"Well, if you have time, I could probably come up with a pie that you could take home with you."

"I wish I could stay, Mom, but this has got to be a short visit. I need to get home so I can do the laundry and work on the house a little before we head out to Tulsa tomorrow."

Bonita's eyes lit up. "What are you goin' to do in Tulsa? "

"Watch a movie, eat out, and shop."

Bonita's sigh was long and sad. "Well, if you wasn't watchin' a movie, I would like to go with you. It gets lonesome out here on Saturdays."

Miranda tasted the guilt that rose up to choke her and tried to ignore it. "We've been waiting a long time to see this one, but you're welcome to come with us. Of course, we won't be back until late."

"Then, I better not go. I like to be home before dark."

"Tell you what, Mom. Why don't just you and I go somewhere next Saturday, maybe Fort Smith or Fayetteville. That way we can leave as early as we want and stay until we're ready to come home."

"That sounds good. By the way, did you see the county paper this week?"

"No, is there something I should see?" She picked up the newspaper that was lying on the coffee table."

"Look at the Classifieds."

She located the ad she thought her mother was talking about. "So, old Miss Brinkley has finally retired as the elementary librarian. What has that got to do with me?"

"Didn't you take some library classes at Northeastern once?"

"Yes, I actually earned my library certification." She put the newspaper back on the coffee table. "It would be nice to manage a quiet library instead of putting up with unruly kids all day. But who am I kidding? They would never give it to me."

"And why not? Your dad used to work with Ted McQueen, and he's on the school board. I could remind him of that if you want me to."

"You could if you don't mind doing it. I will apply for the job, but I don't have a lot of hope since I'm not one of the favored. The school board always goes along with whatever Mr. Spyres recommends, and I've already heard Mrs. Spyres has a niece who is graduating this spring. I bet she gets it somehow. But I'll try anyway. Maybe, by some miracle, I can win them with my eloquence and my looks."

"Well, you certainly have more than Miss Spryes's niece of both of those."

"Mom." Miranda laughed out loud. "You don't even know her niece."

"It doesn't matter. You'll always be the prettiest and smartest in any crowd."

"Oh, that all the world could see me through my mother's eyes." Miranda laughed again and was suddenly much lighter. "Mom, you're good medicine for me, but I better be getting home. Byron and Lorna will be back from school and looking for food. I'll call you tomorrow when we get back."

"Before you go, let me tell you the latest on Junior Horton."

"What has Junior done now?"

Bonita began launching into a description of her latest run-in with the Hortons, her neighbors to the east. "Junior said he would keep my pasture brush-hogged and my fence fixed for allowin' him to run his cows on it. Well, did you see it when you came up? It's all growed up, and the fence is almost down to the ground in some places. I had to run one of his cows out of my yard this morning. Old heifer was eatin' my peonies. If your daddy was alive, Horton wouldn't have dared to act this way. Why, Clay would have slapped his jaws."

"That's for sure. Have you tried talking to Horton?"

"Won't do no good. I tried talkin' to him, and he got red in the face and talked real mean to me. People take advantage of widows, Miranda. Hope you never have to go through what I've had to go through."

"I hope not either, Mom. Let me think about it. Maybe I can write him a legalistic letter or something."

Bonita hugged and kissed her. "Thank you, sweet girl. I knew you would help me."

"All right. Just give me a little time to work on it. Well, I been here an hour, so I better go."

Having completed another successful negotiation of time and energy, Miranda drove home.

SHE ARRIVED HOME to find Lorna and Byron raiding the refrigerator in a vain attempt to scavenge snacks.

Lorna started complaining as soon as she walked through the door. "Mom, when is the last time you bought groceries? There is never anything good around here to eat."

"Well, it's true I've been too busy to shop much, but you could fix yourself a healthy snack. We still have rice cakes, peanut butter, honey, and fruit, and you can always pop some popcorn."

"No thanks. I probably have an old candy bar or something layin' around in my room." She started up the stairs.

"Lorna, wait a minute. I need to tell you something."

She stopped in the middle of the stairs and turned around with a scowl on her face. "What?"

"Bring your dirty clothes down to the laundry room in a few minutes. I'm going to do laundry since we will be gone tomorrow."

"I don't have anything for you to wash."

"Now, Lorna, that's what you said last week. I know you have to have dirty clothes that need washing."

"I'll do them myself when I feel like it."

Darryn had come in when they were having their conversation. "Well, when are you going to feel like it? That shirt you got on looks pretty grungy."

"When I do. Besides this is an old shirt, anyway."

"She can do her laundry herself. It'll mean less work for me."

"I just hope she doesn't go around stinkin'."

"Well, so do I, but I would rather not have a big fight about it. You want something to eat? I was just going to warm up some of the soup I made yesterday."

"I'll take some."

Byron came in with a basketful of dirty laundry. "Can I have some, too?"

"Sure." She pushed his hair out of his eyes. "I forget sometimes how teenage boys are eating machines. By the way, when's the last time you got a haircut?"

"I been thinkin' about growing it out? Do you mind?"

"No, as long as long as we can see your pretty green eyes."

Later on, after she had started the laundry and cleaned the kitchen, she listened to Darryn and Byron laugh at the comedians' antics. As usual, Lorna was up in her room.

"Mom, come and watch this. Kelso is trying to break into Miriam's apartment."

"All right. Just let me put my broom away."

Miranda spent the next few minutes unwinding with her family. It was so good to laugh and forget everything for a while. Soon, just a few more weeks, and her life would be her own again. Summer vacation would be here, and she could awaken from her zombie-like existence that she lived in for nine months of the year and fully come alive again—alive for two and a half months out of twelve, not counting weekends. Maybe she should update her resume tomorrow night.

THEY HAD A fun day in Tulsa. Lorna was happy because she got to choose where they ate lunch. Since she chose Red Lobster, and it was more expensive than their usual restaurants, Miranda offered to help Darryn pay for it. It was worth it to see Lorna smile.

After that they watched the new movie, *Edward Scissorhands.* Fifteen minutes into the movie, Darryn whispered, "Wake me up when it's over."

She whispered back, "Come on and give it a chance."

"I did, and it lost."

Lorna, who was locked into the movie, scowled. *"Shhh."*

FOUR MONTHS LATER, on a Sunday morning, Lorna claimed she was cramping and stayed home from church. When they got home, Miranda went up to check on her. She knocked on the door but got no response. She quietly opened the door and looked inside.

She gasped at what she saw. Lorna was lying sprawled out on top of her bed, her long dark hair, spread out against her pillow. At the top of her head was a noticeable bald spot and a large pile of black tresses lay beside her.

"Lorna, baby, what have you done to yourself?"

For a moment Lorna stared at her like she didn't know her. She covered her head with a pillow and murmured, "Nothing."

"Don't tell me nothing. You've got a bald spot, and there's hair all over the bed."

"Nothing's wrong. I just like pulling it out, and when I start, I can't stop, but it takes a long time to fix it where nobody can tell. Please don't make me go to school tomorrow."

"You don't have to go, but I am going to take you to my hairdresser after I get out of school and have your hair cut so the bald spot doesn't show. "

"All right. Thanks, Mom. Just don't tell Dad, okay?"

"I won't tell him now, but you have to promise me that you will quit pulling your hair out."

"I don't know if I can."

"Sure you can, and I can get you some help if you need it."

"I'll try."

Miranda met Darryn at the bottom of the stairs. "How's Lorna?"

"Still cramping. I'm going to let her stay home from school tomorrow, let her get better."

"Is that a good idea? She's already missed quite a bit, and she could just be fakin' it."

"I don't think so. I'll write her a note on Tuesday, and she should be fine."

Lorna seemed to like her new hairstyle. Darryn wasn't so pleased. "Why did you get her hair cut? Her long hair was beautiful."

Lorna went on the defensive. "You mean it's ugly now?"

"Of course not. I just liked your long hair. It looks fine now, too."

ABOUT TWO WEEKS later Darryn discovered Lorna's secret. He came home from work early one Friday because the power was out in his office, and the boss sent everyone home. When he got home, he decided he would help Miranda out by doing laundry. When he went upstairs to check Lorna's hamper, he found numerous wads of black hair hidden away.

Before she could walk in the house that day, Miranda was met by Byron, who had come home early from OU. "Mom, I just wanted to warn you that Dad and Lorna had a big fight, and she's locked herself in the upstairs bathroom."

"A fight? What about?"

"Dad says she's been pulling her hair out, and she's going to have to go to the doctor. Lorna said she's not going anywhere, and she's going to stay in the bathroom until he tells her she doesn't have to go."

"Oh, no. I better see if I can help."

Darryn came downstairs when he heard her come in. "Did you know about this, Miranda?"

Miranda closed her eyes for a minute. When she opened them, Darryn was right in her face. "Did you?"

"I did."

"Why didn't you tell me?"

"Because Lorna said she would quit doing it if I didn't tell you."

"Miranda, won't you ever learn? Don't you know that Lorna will say anything to get her way?"

"I'm sorry."

"Well, you should be, but maybe you can talk her into comin' out. Will you try?"

Miranda pled with and cajoled Lorna for half an hour. Finally, Lorna agreed to come out if Darryn wouldn't bother her anymore. As soon as she came out, she disappeared into her room and stayed there for the rest of the night.

The three of them ate dinner and discussed what to do about Lorna. Byron paused from shoveling food in his mouth long enough to say, "Let her stay upstairs. It's a lot more peaceful when she's not around."

Miranda scolded him. "Don't talk about your sister that way."

Darryn looked up from sipping his iced tea. "Well, I think we better get her some help. I'll look at some of those old phone books we saved. I'll make a list of psychiatrists for you to call and arrange for her to visit as soon as you can get an appointment. My work insurance should cover most of the cost."

"I'll do it, but Lorna won't like it."

"This time she doesn't have a choice."

MIRANDA AND DARRYN took turns driving Lorna to see a psychiatrist in Fort Smith once a week for the next three months. At the end of the three months, Dr. Wortman had a conference with the three of them. "I believe the antidepressants and the therapy have helped Lorna. As long as she stays on her medication and doesn't have a relapse, I believe I can cut her visits down to once a month."

They were all relieved, and Lorna promised she would let them know if she lost control again.

Miranda had only told two people Lorna's secret, her hairdresser and her mother. Bonita cried when Miranda told her. "I knew something was wrong, but I didn't know what it was. If there's anything I can do to help, just let me know."

"I think we're getting it under control, but if we need you, I will be sure to let you know."

Bonita threw her arms around her. "I mean it. I would do anything for you and your children in this life or, if I can, in the next."

Miranda stayed in her mother's embrace for a minute, inhaling the sweet rose perfume her mother always wore. She finally stepped back and kissed her on the cheek. "I know you mean it, Mom, and I thank you for the offer."

THAT NIGHT SHE had trouble falling asleep. At last she drifted off only to, seemingly, awaken with a start, to see a large, black bird flying above her bed. Miranda gave a low scream, and her eyes flew open. To nothing. Another weird dream.

Her scream had awakened Darryn. "What is it?"

"Oh, nothing. I just had another dream. Go back to sleep."

Mercifully, he did, and Miranda could soon hear him snoring again. For a long time she stayed awake, afraid she had been sent a warning dream and fearing what bad thing was going to happen.

XIII
DANGEROUS
GAMES

AS HER MOTHER lay awake below, upstairs, Lorna struggled with her own night phantoms. The old woman had come to her again, grabbing her clothes, pulling at her, working to draw her away out into the night, where she would float above the earth, unfettered and unanchored.

"I don't want to go. Leave me alone."

Her screams fell on deaf—or more likely, *dead*—ears. The old crone persisted until she loosened the grip Lorna had on the bedstead. Out she went through the window, skimming above the family home and the woods that surrounded it, over the pastureland that lay close by, and up into the clouds that covered the night sky.

She flew like a bird, eating up the miles minute by minute. Looking below, she saw Aiden High School where she had spent so many hated hours, hiding in the shadows from those who tormented her and from those who claimed to be her friends.

As she approached the center of the small town, there wasn't much traffic, which didn't surprise her since it was well before dawn. Once she dipped down close enough that the policeman who sat in his car, nodding off and jerking awake every few minutes, could have easily spotted her, but she sailed on by a few feet above him. He never looked up as she continued her nocturnal flight.

Not for the first time she wondered where she was going and when she would return. Her inward compass turned her eastward, and she soon recognized the place that lay ahead. It was Grandma Amelia's big, ramshackle house, where she had once lived with her husband and a houseful of children, including Lorna's Poppa, and now lived with her youngest daughter, Abigail.

In a heartbeat, she had entered and was moving inside the house. What was she doing here?

Now she was in Amelia's bedroom, on the ceiling, looking down on the sleeping body of her ninety-something great-grandmother. She looked so frail when her eyes were closed, nothing like the strong, commanding matriarch who influenced her children, grand-children, and even great-grandchildren's lives. She moaned in her sleep, and Lorna held her breath, praying she wouldn't awake. The shock of seeing her there, hovering just above her bed, would likely stop her heart.

Lorna let out a sigh of relief when whatever was in charge of her transport took her out Amelia's bedroom window and spun her to-ward the south. This journey was shorter, and Lorna thought she knew where she was going. As she approached Mema's neat little house, she noticed a black cloud was hanging directly above it. Some-thing about the cloud filled her with a dark feeling of dread, and she knew this place was her final destination.

For the first time since her journey had begun, someone saw her, and for the first time her feet touched the earth. Mema was sitting in the swing on her front porch, waiting for her.

She smiled and held out her arms for a hug. "It's good to see you, sweet girl. I wondered who was coming to tell me goodbye."

It was so much like what had happened with Poppa. She could see Mema, talk to her, feel her body as she hugged her, and even smell the rose perfume she always wore. "I didn't want to come, Mema."

For the first time, she looked sad. "I know, but sometimes we all have to do things we don't want to do. I don't want to leave my daughter and her children either, but it's my time to go."

"She will be lost without you."

"No, she won't. She will have you. You will take my place as her best friend."

Lorna's eyes filled with tears. "I'm sorry, but I just can't."

Mema kissed her cheek. "Not now but someday. And who knows, I might just come back for a visit someday if I can. Goodbye now, sweet girl."

SHE AWOKE IN her own bed, shaking and crying. Was Mema really dead, or was it just one of her weird dreams? She had strange dreams often, but only once before had she experienced one like this, and that was the morning Poppa died. Please, don't let it be real.

Her head was pounding so she went downstairs to get some aspirins and almost collided with her mom who was on her way upstairs.

"Good morning, Lorna. I'm so glad you got up on your own this morning. Do you want some breakfast? I think it's early enough for me to fix you eggs or oatmeal or pretty much whatever you want."

Lorna's stomach churned at the thought of food. "No, I don't feel like eating. I actually have a headache and am lookin' for some aspirins."

"Oh. Well, there's some in the medicine cabinet. Just be sure you drink some water and maybe eat a little something when you take them. They're hard on your stomach."

"All right. I suppose I could manage a banana or a couple of crackers or something."

As Miranda started to leave, Lorna called her name. "Hey, Mom."

Miranda whirled around to face her. "What is it, sweetie?"

"Could I stay home today? My head and stomach both hurt."

Miranda sighed and shook her head. "I don't think so. You have missed so much lately that it's going to affect your grades."

"But I've only missed four days this nine weeks, and we're allowed to miss five. Please let me stay home. If I go to school, I will just throw up or stay in the nurse's office all day because of my aching head."

Lorna noticed her mother's hesitation and was certain she was going to let her miss until her dad came along. "What's this about missin' school again?"

Lorna gritted her teeth. She was going to have to explain it all over again. "My head aches, and my stomach hurts. I need to stay home today."

"Nope. Not goin' to happen."

A burning anger grew in Lorna's soul. She wanted to scream, but she held back. "Why not?"

"Because you have already missed too many days."

Lorna rolled her eyes. "Well, like I have already explained to Mom. I have only missed four days this nine weeks, and we are allowed to miss five."

"Have you thought about what would happen if you really got sick and needed to miss that fifth day but didn't have it anymore?"

"Have you thought about what's going to happen when I go to school sick, embarrass myself by throwing up in class, the nurse calls you or mom, and you have to leave work to come and get me?"

He started wagging his finger at her. "Don't take that tone with me, young lady."

Her anger exploded. "I hate you." She ran upstairs.

When she got to the first stair landing, she hid behind the drapes like she had always done whenever she wanted to hear what her parents were saying.

"Darryn, was that really necessary?"

"Yes, I think so. You're too soft on the girl, Miranda. She needs some discipline."

"Oh, and what about some understanding?"

"She gets more than enough of that from you."

Miranda mumbled under her breath. "Well, she sure doesn't get it from *you.*"

"What was that?"

"Nothing."

Her mom was still on her side, even if her dad wasn't. Too bad her mom would probably have to suffer for his cruelty. This time she really was feeling sick, but that wasn't the main reason she needed to miss school. The nurse would be calling her mother to come and get her before lunch time, and Miranda's jerk of a principal wouldn't be happy about it.

LORNA COULD TELL her mom felt bad about making her go to school. Once Miranda reached her hand out like she was going to check for a fever, but Lorna turned her head away so the hand slid off.

When they pulled up to the drop-off place, Miranda handed her a five-dollar bill "in case she needed some extra drinks or something special that would be easy on her stomach." She put it with the stash she kept in her backpack.

Lorna had hoped her sophomore year would be better, but it had actually turned out to be even more stressful. She liked her first class, English, so she didn't want to miss it. Mrs. Batteau could make any piece of literature interesting, and she never allowed bullying of any kind in her class.

Second hour was band, and since music had always been second nature to Lorna, she excelled at it. Even though she was only a sophomore, she was already third chair in the clarinet section. Mr. Muskrat, the band director, told her at the rate she was going she would probably make first chair next year.

Third hour could be trouble, World History. She chose it because the subject appealed to her. If she had known some senior jocks took it mainly to get away with murder, she would have taken another class. The teacher was old, and the class was too big, which was always a bad combination. Everyone knew Mr. Trask should have retired years ago, but he showed up every day with a new history video for them to watch and, supposedly, take notes on.

About half-way through the video, he would always nod off, and that's when everything went south. Depending on their mood, the jocks would bring out their chewing tobacco, pelt the younger boys with spit wads or give them wedgies. If anyone protested or tried to fight back, that person was bullied unmercifully for the rest of the year. And when they weren't tormenting the nerds, they were making out at the back of the room with the cheerleaders or trying to cop a feel on some poor girl.

That's what happened to Lorna on Friday, and that's why she had to miss the class today. She thought she was safe by making herself unattractive to them. She kept her head down, never wore makeup, and changed into the dirtiest clothes she had every day right before third hour.

On Friday, her band class had played for a special school assembly. Mr. Muskrat had told them to dress in their Sunday best, so there she was in a nice dress with pantyhose and heels. Her mom had made her fix her hair that morning because "no one can see your pretty face." The jocks must have got an eyeful. There was no time to change clothes because Mr. Muskrat told them to "put up their instruments and go straight to class."

She tried to sneak into class, but the leader of the jocks, Keith Kincaid, spotted her, stood up, and whistled. Mr. Trask ignored his behavior. When the film started, and it was dark, she moved from her usual place to the back of the room.

It didn't work. The jocks were watching her, and as soon as Mr. Trask nodded off, they moved in for the kill. Keith first tried to kiss her, and she pushed him off. He laughed and tried to grab her breast. She slapped him as hard as she could, which stunned and enraged him. When he raised his hand to slap her back, she ducked, and he fell on the floor.

Everybody laughed, which made him even madder. He yelled, "You'll be sorry."

Mr. Trask woke up, stopped the movie, turned on the lights, and gave the whole class a worksheet to do because someone had disrupted the movie. Before the class was over, Lorna was passed a note, which read—

You better watch your back because we <u>WILL</u> make you pay for what you did.

SHE THOUGHT ABOUT showing it to the principal or counselor or somebody, but her new friend Roz told her not to. "If you tell on them, they will figure out it was you, and they will hurt you even worse. That's why Stewart Chambers left school last year. He told the counselor that the jocks were threatening to beat him up when he took up for his girlfriend. They waited until they caught him at the skate park, and they beat him so bad that he had to stay in the hospital for a month. His family moved to Arkansas when he was dismissed."

"Why didn't they get in trouble?"

"Oh, they got a few days of detention for the threat, and the principal made them apologize to Stewart and promise to never do anything like that again. They just waited a few days and carried out their threat off of school grounds."

"So what should I do?"

"You can either apologize and let them do what they want, or you can skip the class until they forget all about you."

"How about if I just change classes?"

"Yeah, you could do that, but they're only makin' class changes at the end of the first semester, and that's five weeks away. Sorry, girl, looks like there's no easy way out. Buy some weed from me and smoke it all weekend, and before school on Monday morning you'll be so stoned by third hour you won't care what they do to you."

She bought a small amount of weed, but after the dream , she didn't dare to smoke it.

She had a plan to avoid the class, but she didn't have to put it into play because before first hour was over, an announcement came over the intercom. Lorna Steel was needed in the office.

WHEN SHE SAW her father sitting in the front office, looking shaken up, she knew her dream had come true. "Your mother is waiting in the car. We have some bad news for you."

As they walked to the car, she asked, "It's Mema, isn't it?"

He stopped and stared at her. "How did you know that?"

"I dreamed about her last night."

Her mother was totally messed up. She was hiding her face in her hands and rocking back and forth. It was like she didn't even know they were there.

He spoke to her mother like she was a little child. "We'll all go home now. I called Byron in his dorm, and he'll come in tonight."

She never looked up.

WHEN THEY GOT home, Dad took charge. "Miranda, why don't you go lie down? I'll take care of the cooking and cleaning today."

After her mother had left the room, he turned to Lorna. "Lillian Dooley went over to check on Bonita when she didn't answer her phone this morning. When she wouldn't answer the door, she called the sheriff. They kicked the door open and found her sitting in her recliner like she was asleep. The doctor thinks a heart attack took her."

"I didn't know she had a weak heart."

"No one did, but her doctor said she had complained about her heart fluttering a little the last time she came in. He ordered an EKG, but it didn't show anything."

He stopped talking and wiped his eyes. "Are you hungry? I can fix you something to eat."

"No, I'm good. Maybe later. My stomach is still a little messed up."

"Oh, all right. Maybe you should rest, too."

Lorna waited for the anger and the pain to sweep over her like it did when Poppa died, but it didn't happen. The weed she smoked had numbed the pain. She cried some because she loved Mema and knew she would miss her, but the overwhelming sorrow didn't take her under like it did when she lost her grandfather. She was mostly relieved because she wouldn't have to deal with school for the rest of the week.

Miranda stayed in her bedroom most of the day. Darryn talked her and Lorna into coming to the kitchen table to eat the light lunch he prepared. She still wasn't talking and ate even less than Lorna, who only ate a small bowl of soup and half a ham sandwich. By that afternoon, relatives, neighbors, and friends were bringing in all kinds of food. Her father ordered her to help him by writing down who brought what on a list he made. At least he didn't seem to mind if she stayed home from school now, and some of the pressure faded away.

BYRON CAME IN by supper time. When he came in, Darryn gave him a quick hug and said, "I'll tell your mother you're here."

Miranda came out, all disheveled from where she had been sleeping most of the day. She walked over to Byron and fell into his arms, crying.

Byron patted her back and said, "It's going to be all right, Mom."

When she finally released him, she stepped back, reached up, and patted him on the cheek. She said the first sentence she had spoken in hours. "I'm glad you're here, son."

Her father must have noticed the hurt on Lorna's face because he put his arms around all of them in a kind of group hug. "We'll get through this together." He held them close together for a few minutes before releasing them.

"You should see all the food people have been bringing in. Lorna has been keeping a list of who brought what."

Miranda smiled. "Good work, Lorna."

Lorna shrugged her shoulders.

Byron said, "I'm starved."

Darryn clapped him on the shoulder. "Well, come on in the kitchen then. There's something for everybody. I even saw a big batch of fry bread."

Miranda joined them when they ate, exclaiming over each dish she sampled. She pushed her plate away and looked down as if to gather her thoughts. "You know Mom planned and paid for her own funeral and a double gravestone right after Dad passed, so there won't be much to do when we meet with the funeral director. What do you think about having the funeral on Friday if they have an available time?"

Darryn stopped eating long enough to answer. "Sounds good to me. I made an appointment with the funeral director at 2:00 on Tuesday afternoon. Hope that suits everyone."

Lorna cast a sidelong glance at her father. "Do I have to go?"

"Not if you don't want to. How about you, Byron?"

"I'll go if you want me to."

Miranda smiled. "You've always had an artistic eye. You can help me select the things your grandma didn't choose, like the flowers and the service handouts. That reminds me I need to get started on her obituary. I think I'll go get on the computer and work on it."

THE FUNERAL WAS just like Mema would have wanted. She had chosen a nice pink casket with pink roses on the silky interior. Everything coordinated nicely, with a large casket piece made of fresh pink roses, roses on the funeral handouts, and roses were to be chiseled into her side of the gravestone. A large crowd of Bonita's relatives and friends filled the funeral home sanctuary.

All grieving was quiet and subdued until only the family, the pall bearers, the flower girls, and a few others remained. Lorna walked a few steps behind Byron as they approached the open casket. Byron stopped, reached over, patted Mema's folded hands, and wiped his eyes before exiting through the side door.

It was Lorna's turn. She couldn't bring herself to touch the cold body. She looked into the face that appeared to be sleeping and whispered, "Goodbye, Mema."

When it was time for Miranda to view the body, she stood at the coffin for a few minutes with Darryn supporting her. She leaned over and said aloud, "Goodbye, Mama. I will miss you." She kissed her mother on the forehead and walked way, sobbing.

TOO SOON IT was Monday, and her parents wouldn't let her stay home anymore. Time to put her plan in action. As soon as band was over, she ran into the bathroom, stuck her finger down her throat, and gagged herself. What little she had in her stomach came up. She took out a washcloth and a grungy shirt from her backpack, smeared the vomit on her shirt, and put it on.

When she went to the nurse's office, she had proof she was really sick. The nurse called her mother, and she showed-up all flustered and worried. "I'm so sorry, baby. I should have let you stay home like you asked me to."

She could afford to be generous. "That's okay, Mom. Just believe me next time when I say I am sick, okay?"

"I will, and I will have a talk with your father too."

They let her stay home another day because she was so convincing. But on the third day, her father messed up her plans again. "If you're still sick, Lorna, you need to see a doctor. Your mother will take you to the emergency room at Hastings and have you checked out when she gets home from school."

When her mom got home, she told her she was feeling much better and could go back to school on Thursday. She had come up with a plan, which she hoped would get her out of the mess she was in, but first she had to talk to Roz.

SHE CALLED HER up that night from the phone in her room. "Roz, how much pot can I buy off of you?"

"That depends on how much money you have."

"How much will a hundred dollars buy?"

"That'll buy a lot of weed."

"How about if I trade something that's worth $200 for a hundred dollars' worth of weed?"

"Maybe, what are you talkin' about?

"My diamond bracelet you like so much. My mom paid two hundred dollars for it, but I'll let you have it for a hundred dollars in weed."

"I'm interested, but my partner will kill me if I don't get some money on the deal. Give me fifty dollars cash and the bracelet."

Lorna sighed. "I guess I can scrounge up fifty dollars. Can I get it before school tomorrow?"

"Yeah, I think so if you can meet me early, say 7:45, behind the cafeteria?"

"All right. I'll figure out some story to get Mom to bring me early."

Lorna counted every bit of money she had stashed in her backpacks, purses, and dresser drawers and came up with $21.53. Since Byron was back at OU, she went through his room and found some hidden dirty magazines but little cash, just a little over six dollars, still way short. Where could she find another $23? She was afraid to sneak into her parents' room and get into her dad's wallet. If he caught her, he would never forgive her. Her mom usually left her purse on the fireplace, but sometimes she had money, and sometimes she didn't. Since this was the end of the week, there probably wasn't much in it.

If that was the case, she would have to get into the change jar. Her mom kept a glass gallon jar in the top shelf of the linen closet. From time to time, she and Dad tossed all their change in the jar. After the jar was full, they used the money to treat themselves to something like a short trip. If Roz refused to take a bag of change, she would just give her the cash she had and the bracelet and take part of the pot. She would get a ride to the bank, where she had a savings account, and ask them if she could exchange her penny bank money into cash.

Then she would meet Roz and exchange the cash for the rest of the weed. She had thought of everything. Her plan should work. Now all she had to do was get the jocks to go for it.

Step one, getting Mom to take her to school early. Miranda was busy grading papers on the kitchen table when Lorna approached her. "Mommy, I need to ask you something." Miranda looked up and smiled the way Lorna knew she would when she called her that name.

"What is it, baby?"

"One of the kids from my algebra class called and said Mister Scofield is giving extra points for kids who will meet him in the cafeteria at 7:45 on Thursday mornings. He is taking them to his class for extra tutoring, and if you just show up, you get twenty extra points that you can use on your lowest grade. I could use the points and the tutoring since I have missed so much school. Could you please get me to school around 7:40 so I can do it?"

"Why, of course, I can. All you have to do is set your alarm and get up at 6:00 instead of 6:15. That way we can get out of here by around 7:15 instead of 7:30, and I don't mind getting to my school a little earlier than usual either. I'm so glad to see you're taking more of an interest in your grades."

Lorna put on her best fake happy face. "Okay. Thanks, Mommy."

AFTER SHE THOUGHT her parents had gone to bed, she waited thirty more minutes, checked to see if the bedroom lights were out, and stole over to the fireplace where her mom's purse sat. She carried the purse to the bathroom where she could search it. There were several loose one-dollar bills scattered throughout her purse. Lorna took eight of these and a five-dollar bill she didn't think her mother would miss. As usual, her mom's change was thrown in the bottom of her purse, so she took $3.00 of that. Good. Now she only needed to take about $7 from the change jar.

After almost dropping the heavy jar, she brought it into the bathroom and counted out $10 in quarters in case she needed to buy something for herself tomorrow. There was so much money that her parents would never miss it. She got a gallon bag and put all the change in it and placed all of the money in her backpack.

All set.

THE NEXT MORNING Roz wasn't alone. She had a muscled-up Indian guy with her. This wasn't in the plan. "Who's this?"

"This is my half-brother Ned Raven. He's a junior and my partner. He wanted to meet you before we make the deal."

Ned looked her over. "Nice to meet you, Lorna. Let's move over to the trees where we can talk in private."

Lorna was getting nervous. She didn't know Roz that well and didn't know if she could trust her, but she followed her into the trees.

"All right. Let's see what you got."

She showed him the bracelet first. "Nice, but I guess you know it's only worth fifty bucks in trade."

"I know. Here's the cash." She handed him all the cash she had.

He took it and quickly counted it. "What the hell's this? You're short ten dollars."

She brought out the gallon bag of change. "It's all there, ten dollars in change."

"What do you think this is, kindergarten? We don't take change for weed."

"In that case, let me explain plan B." Lorna went on to tell him how he could get the rest of the money on Friday if he would wait until she could get to the bank.

He laughed. "No, we don't do layaway. But there is another way."

"What's that? "

"You can keep the change and work it out."

Lorna's quick mind raced through his proposition. "I don't think so. I can't take the chance of selling weed at school. I would probably get caught, and my parents would kill me. Just give me seventy-five dollars of weed, and we'll call it even."

Ned put his big, dark hand on her head. "Not so fast, little girl. That deal ain't on the table. Listen, I can give you somethin' a lot better than weed. I can give you protection from those jocks who are makin' problems for you."

"How can you do that?"

"Well, first of all, I don't know if you noticed, but most guys back off when they see me with a girl. I'll be your official bodyguard."

"That's great, but you can't be with me all the time."

"True, but I have a lot of eyes in this school who will watch over you. Besides, after I call Keith out and give him a beatin', they'll all leave you alone. Tell you what. I like you, and because I do, you can keep all your money. Just give me the bracelet, and as long as you work for me, you can have all the weed you want."

Lorna gritted her teeth. This wasn't going the way she planned, but maybe she could do it for just a little while. "What if I don't want weed?"

His laugh started out as a chuckle and turned into a full belly laugh. "Kid, you are so funny. Then we'll just find you somethin' you do like. Here's your cash back. Just go to class like nothin' has happened. I'll get word to Keith to meet me after school. By tomorrow he'll be treatin' you like the princess you are."

Lorna was nervous, but she did what Ned said. Keith gave her dirty looks before the movie started, but he didn't come near her. The next day he showed up with a nasty black eye. He never bothered her again or any of the girls who sat close to her. Lorna acquired several new friends this way.

Because she had become more popular and provided a product that was in demand, Lorna no longer hated to come to school. She learned how to relax and have a good time with her friends. The only drawback was her grades dropped, but only her parents cared about that.

Ned kept his promise and introduced her to a lot of new experiences, including booze, uppers, and sexual foreplay. She didn't overdo it, though, because she learned too much could lead to more terrifying dreams, and those were hard to handle. Even harder to handle would be a pregnancy, so she put a limit on that, too. Sometimes she told Ned she might want to quit the business, but he would always talk her into staying with him a little bit longer.

THE NEXT YEAR Ned wanted to expand their business. He aimed to bring crack into the high school and told her he was looking for some new salesmen. Two prospects were a girl who had always been mean to her since grade school, Mariah Panther, and Kyle Kincaid, the younger brother of her former tormenter.

"Why them? Why choose two people who hate me?"

"What am I supposed to do? I need somebody who'll help me move crack, and you refuse to do it. Besides, you're just bein' paranoid. They don't even know you."

"It's bad stuff, and they're bad people. If you let them in, they'll bring you down."

"Not goin' to argue with you about it. You don't have to like them, but you have to work with them."

Lorna's eyes turned black as she hissed at him. "I don't have to do anything I don't want to do." She ignored him as he called her name, and she stomped through the leaves of their meeting place toward the school.

THAT NIGHT NED called her at home. Her mother picked up the phone downstairs on the first ring. She called up, "Lorna, it's for you."

Usually Ned called her at a later time when her parents were watching television in the living room, so she knew to watch her upstairs phone. He must really want to talk to her to call her before seven. "What is it, Ned?"

He rushed into his spiel. *"I'm sorry for the misunderstandin' today. I don't want to lose you as my girl or as my partner. If I promise you don't have to work with Panther or Kincaid, will you stay with me at least until school is out this year?"*

"All right, one more year, but I'm not sellin' crack."

"That's all right. As long as you keep peddlin' weed and pills, I'll be happy."

Things went on exactly as before. She still met each Monday behind the cafeteria with Ned and Roz to discuss sales for the week. All that was different was Mariah and Kyle met with them.

Everything was fine until October when her mom and dad went on an overnight anniversary trip to Eureka Springs. Even though Byron was home because her parents didn't want her to be alone, Lorna knew it would be easy to slip away with Ned. He had bought a new motorcycle and had been itching to take Lorna on a long ride. Her parents weren't getting home until sometime Sunday evening, so they would have plenty of time.

That afternoon Byron knocked on her door. "Are you ever coming down today?"

"Go away. I got a headache, and I need to sleep as much as I can."

"Whatever. I'm going to town to rent some movies."

She looked out the window and watched him drive away. Good. This was their chance.

She called Ned. "Come on out. I'll meet you at the end of the lane."

TWENTY MINUTES LATER the crisp autumn air was blowing through her hair, and she was holding tight to Ned as they made their way down the narrow country roads. He rode the back roads that took them through the communities of Wauhillau and Caney. All around them were splashes of autumn color, and Lorna made Ned stop twice just so she could stop and take it all in.

When they came out on Welling Road, she said, "I didn't know you could get to Welling this way."

"My dad showed me this way when I was little."

"You never talk much about your dad."

"Not much to talk about. Let's go to the river."

As they sailed over the curves of Highway 10, they were so close to the water that Miranda almost believed she could lean over and touch it. She yelled so Ned could hear her. "We used to take float trips on this river when I was little."

"Yeah maybe we can do that someday. Looks like there's lots of places you can float from. Are you hungry? I know a good place we can stop and eat."

"Yeah, I haven't eaten anything today."

After some hamburgers and malts, they were back on the bike. "I got a friend who lives on the river. He said I can stay at his place whenever I want. I thought we might spend some time there. It's still a ways, though, and I know a place we can stop and buy food and beer on the way."

THE SUN WAS slipping behind the horizon by the time they found their destination. It was a small, neat cabin, hidden behind some tall oak and sycamore trees. Ned parked the bike by the front porch and got the key from its hiding place under a statue of a topless girl riding a fish. He opened the door and helped Lorna carry the grocery sacks inside.

"This is really nice, and it's spotless."

"Yeah, Ian is a neat freak."

"Well, it's nice of him to let you stay here. Why doesn't he live here?"

"He has a job and house in Siloam Springs. He just comes here mostly in the summer to fish and have parties with his friends. "

Lorna frowned. "He must be a lot older than you if he has a job and another house."

"Yeah, he's probably close to forty."

"So why does he want to hang out with teenagers? He must be weird."

Ned's voice had a note of annoyance. "Why do you have to analyze everyone, Lorna? Who cares how old Ian is? As long as he lets me stay in his place and invites me to his parties, he's my friend. Now come on, put the beer in the fridge, and I'll see if I can find us some music. He's got a great stereo system and a big screen TV, too, with lots of movies to watch."

Lorna was flipping through the movies, looking for something to watch. "Did you know that most of these are porno films?"

"So? That ain't goin' to hurt anything, and it might just loosen you up a little." He grabbed her around the waist and pulled her down into his lap.

They kissed and petted for a while, but when he tried to lay her on the couch, she resisted. "No, not that."

"Why not?"

"You know why not."

"Even if I brought protection?"

"I'm not ready."

"When are you goin' to get ready?"

"I don't know. Quit pressurin' me. Let's smoke weed and drink some beer."

"All right. I guess that will do for now. We'll have to smoke on the back deck, though. Ian don't like smokin' in his house."

"That's fine with me. Nothing I like better than sittin' outside, listenin' to the night sounds."

Lorna found some warm blankets, and Ned cleaned off some lawn chairs for them to sit in and smoke. "Oh, this is nice."

"Yeah, it's pretty cool. Let me know when you're ready for bed."

Lorna didn't answer. She listened to the calls of the whippoorwills and the croaking of the frogs. She waited until she heard another sound, snoring. After checking to make sure he was really asleep, she wrapped her blanket around her and went into the cabin to lie on the bed for a little rest.

IN NO TIME, the sun was streaming through the window, bringing her out of her dreams.

Uh-oh. She hadn't meant to sleep until morning.

When she went into the kitchen, she found Ned making himself a bologna sandwich. "It's about time you woke up. We need to get back to your house before your brother knows you're gone."

"Relax. He's used to me stayin' in my room all the time. He'll think I'm just sleepin'. My parents won't be home until dark."

"Where did you put the bean dip?"

"In the cabinet where it belongs."

"I'd say it belongs where it's easy to find."

After they finished eating, Lorna put everything away and walked out on the back deck. "Did you see this view? The river is practically in his backyard."

"Yeah, it's really nice in the summertime. He has this big tire swing he's tied to a tree in the back. I like to swing out as far as I can go before I splash down in the river."

"Let's walk down there."

"All right."

After they reached the tire swing, Lorna grabbed it and released it over the water. "I can't wait until this summer. You'll bring me back, won't you?"

"Sure, Ian always has a big party the first weekend in May? You want to go?"

"Yeah, I do. Let's walk around a bit."

"Okay. What time do you want to leave?"

"We should be okay as long as we leave around noon. We'll go back on the backroads, and I'll slip in the backdoor. Byron will never know I've left."

LORNA KNEW SHE was in trouble when she saw her parents' Oldsmobile in the driveway. She couldn't slip in the backdoor because they were standing in the kitchen. The windows were up, and she could hear her dad yelling at Byron. "What do you mean you don't know where she is?" Her dad was almost screaming.

"You know how she sleeps until noon on the weekends? Well, I didn't figure out that she wasn't still sleepin' until about an hour ago."

"Why didn't you call the sheriff?"

"I thought you would be home anytime, and you would know what to do. I was afraid you might get mad if I let anybody know how she is."

"Typical. Nineteen-years-old and still can't make decisions."

"Darryn, quit picking on Byron and call the sheriff."

"Yeah, that's right. Do what you always do and take up for him. Isn't that her standin' in the backyard?" His anger shifted to Lorna. "Get in here."

LORNA TRIED TO act nonchalant. "What's all the yellin' about? I was just taking a walk. What's wrong with that?"

"Haven't we always told you to let someone know when you leave the house? It's dangerous to go off by yourself. Something could have happened to you."

"Byron was in the bathroom, and I didn't think he could hear me. Besides you're just being paranoid. Nothin' is going to happen to me."

"That's what they all say. No one ever thinks anything is going to happen to them until they're dead."

"That's so stupid."

"We'll see how stupid it is when you're grounded for a month."

"Come on, Dad. All I did was take a walk."

"No, you broke a rule, and you got your mother all upset."

"Well, she shouldn't get upset so easy."

"Go to your room."

"Gladly."

MIRANDA SIGHED. "DO we really want her sitting up in her room even more?"

Darryn closed his eyes and gritted his teeth before turning toward her. "It's either send her to her room or whip her butt. Which do you want me to do?"

Miranda remained silent.

"All right. You can handle her next time she misbehaves." He went into the living room, slumped into his recliner, and lost himself in channel surfing.

AS SHE CLEANED the kitchen, Miranda thought about her marriage and her family. Some days, like today, she wanted to get in her car and drive as far away from Darryn and Lorna as she could go. She would make a new, peaceful life for herself, far away from their harsh words and selfish behavior. But she wouldn't because of who she was, a good wife and a loving mother.

She walked upstairs and knocked on Lorna's door. "May I come in?"

"I don't care."

Miranda sighed and considered how to get through to her daughter. "Your dad told me you had a bad dream about your mema before she died."

"Yeah, I did."

"I had a very strange experience when we stayed at the Crescent Hotel last night. Do you want to hear about it?"

Lorna's eyes lit-up. "Yeah. That place is supposed to be haunted."

"Well, after what happened to me last night I might agree." She sat down on the bed beside Lorna. "I don't know if I was asleep or awake, but I kept hearing a voice in my head, saying, 'Christina.' Somehow I knew Christina was a little girl."

"The lights kept going on and off, and at one point, I felt something tugging on my foot. Finally it all went away, and I fell into normal sleep, but it wasn't over yet."

Lorna's eyes shone bright and curious. "What else happened?"

"The next morning I told your father my dream. He looked at me funny and said, 'I had a dream about a little girl named Christina too.'"

Miranda reached out and smoothed Lorna's hair. "Isn't that the strangest thing you ever heard?'"

"Yeah, it's pretty weird."

Smiling at Lorna's obvious interest, she said, "Now I'm going to tell you a strange story about you when you were a very little girl if you want to hear it."

"Go ahead."

"We were walking down the lane, and you were so small that you still held my hand when you walked. Suddenly, you stopped, threw your right hand into the air and said, 'Hi, man.' Just like you saw someone that you wanted to speak to. Of course, no one was there."

"I don't remember."

"I'm not surprised. You weren't even two yet. You know I think you and I both are more sensitive to the supernatural than most people. I just wanted to let you know that. And if you really need to go somewhere this month, just let me know. We'll find a way to get you there."

"Thanks, Mom."

Miranda said a silent prayer of thanks. "You're welcome, sweet girl."

THE MONTHS WENT by, and the school year drew to an end. Ned asked her to go to the prom with him in April, and he actually met her parents for the first time when he picked her up. It was fun to dress up and go on her first real date. The experience made Lorna yearn for a more normal social life. But, of course, after it was over, they went to a party at Ned's house, complete with beer, weed, and other drugs.

Once she noticed Kyle and Mariah over in the corner, smoking crack, and talking to people she didn't know, but she ignored them. After an hour, she told Ned to get her home before midnight, or she would get grounded again. He told Roz to take her home.

Lorna grabbed her purse and blew up. "You ditch me on our first real date? I'm leavin', but I'm not goin' to forget about this."

The people sitting closest to Ned all laughed, and he looked embarrassed. He grabbed her arm and walked her to the door. "I'm sorry, baby, but I got business to take care of. I promise I'll make it up to you."

He leaned over to give her a kiss, but she turned her face so it landed on her cheek. She would be cold for a while to pay him back for disrespecting her.

IT WAS MAY and time for the big party at Ian's house. She had been looking forward to it ever since she had been there in October. She looked around and recognized some of the same people she had seen at Ned's prom party, but she didn't know any of them, except for Mariah and Kyle.

When Ned introduced her to Ian, he gave her the creeps. He looked old with his balding head and thick glasses. It bothered her how he wanted to hang around her and the other girls that were there. He kept asking if they wanted a beer and when they were going swimming.

It didn't bother Mariah, though. She jerked off her top, kicked off her cutoff shorts, and paraded around in her bikini for several minutes. All male eyes were glued to her body, especially Ian's, who looked like his eyes were about to pop out.

Finally, she walked down to the river and climbed up on the tire swing. She yelled, "Whee." before launching herself into the middle of the lake.

Lorna waited until she came back up to the deck before walking down to the swing. She kept her clothes on until the last possible minute. She wasn't ashamed of her figure in her modest one-piece swimsuit, but she didn't want to show off either. Since she was a good swimmer, she kept increasing her jumping distance with each swing she made. It felt good to test herself, and she did it over and over.

She was starting to wonder where Ned was when he showed up at the swing. "People are startin' to say you're not very friendly. Come on back to the deck and be sociable."

"I don't know any of them, and I really don't care to."

He ran his fingers around the sides of her face. "Please, Lorna, for me."

"All right. I guess I could use somethin' to drink."

"That's my girl." He leaned over and kissed her.

AS THEY WALKED up on the deck, Ian spoke to her. "I've been watching you, Lorna. You're a really good swimmer. Why don't you come in and cool off with a drink?"

Lorna sat in the corner, slowly sipped a beer, and watched some of the others get loud and obnoxious. Kyle got everyone's attention when he brought out a bag of white powder. "Ladies and gentlemen, would you care to sample our newest sales item, high quality cocaine?"

Ned came over and got in Kyle's face. "I told you before we ain't sellin' cocaine. It costs too much to buy, and we can't make enough profit sellin' it."

"We ain't sellin' it. *I* am, and I'm takin' all of your weed, pills, and crack, and sellin' them too."

"No, you ain't. You work for *me.*"

"Not no more."

Lorna gasped when she saw a flash of steel as Kyle plunged a knife into Ned's chest.

Ian, who was sitting near her, whispered, "Run."

She slipped away while everyone was focused on Ned and ran out the back door, down the deck, and into the woods. She had to get to the main road and find some help. She was just a few yards away when she heard Mariah's voice say, "Not so fast."

Something struck her on the back of her head, and everything went dark.

XIV
BLOOD
WILL TELL

MIRANDA SAT UP in the bed, looked at the clock, got out of bed, and went to Lorna's room. She wasn't there. Maybe she was downstairs. After searching the entire house, she came back to her bedroom and shook her husband. "Wake up, Darryn. It's three in the morning, and Lorna's not home."

Darryn groaned and blearily looked up at her, "Why did you wake me up? What did you say?"

"It's three in the morning, and Lorna's not home."

"What? All right, keep calm. Where did she say she was goin'? It was a party at somebody's house."

"Roz Devlin's, but her brother's name is Ned Eagle. He's the one who took her to the prom. I think she might have gone off with him somewhere."

"Well, get the phone book and look under Devlin and Eagle. Call every single one of them until we get an idea where she could be."

There were six Devlins in the phone book. The first two numbers were disconnected. The third number answered, but Miranda got a cussing from the owner. She got lucky on the fourth listing. A husky female voice answered the phone. *"Yeah, I'm Roz Devlin's mother, and*

Ned Eagle is my son. Roz is in bed, but I don't know where Ned is. He stays out all hours."

"Our daughter went to a party at your house and didn't come home."

"I don't know nothin' about no party."

"Could I talk to Roz? It's important."

"I guess you can—if I can wake her up."

Miranda held her hand over the phone and spoke to Darryn. "She's getting Roz."

"Ask her if her brother took Lorna someplace."

A sleepy voice mumbled, *"Hello."*

"Roz, this is Lorna's mother. Do you know where Lorna might be?"

"Not really."

"Did Ned take her someplace? Please tell me where you think they might be."

"He said something about goin' to a party at his friend's house on the river. I think he said it was outside Tahlequah on Highway 10."

Darryn, who had been listening, grabbed the phone. "Roz, what was the friend's name?"

"I don't remember."

"Think. You can remember if you try hard."

"Something weird, Igor, Ivan? No, I think it was Ian. He has a cabin in the woods close to the river. I never been there, so that's all I know."

"If you think of anything else, call us back, all right?" Darryn hung up the phone and looked over the notes he had scribbled on a scrap of paper.

"Call the sheriff, Darryn."

"I am, but I don't know if he can help."

"Why?"

"The cabin's in Cherokee County."

"Let me call Sheriff Adair. He was a friend of my dad's. He'll help us."

The sheriff wasn't in, but when Miranda explained who she was, the deputy took down their information and told them to expect a call back. Miranda looked over at the clock in the kitchen. It was nearly four o'clock.

Darryn came in, dressed in sweats. "You better get some clothes on. I'll watch the phone."

Miranda prayed aloud as she got dressed. "Please bring Lorna home to us."

A few minutes later the phone rang. Sheriff Adair wanted them to come in and give their statements. He had sent someone over to question Roz and her mother.

E.C. ADAIR'S WHITE mustache quivered in sympathy. "Don't you worry, Miss Miranda. Your father had a lot of friends among the lawmen in this county and Cherokee County. We'll find his granddaughter and bring her home. I made a call, and they're already out checking on a cabin belonging to a man named Ian Craig on the Illinois River. Maybe they'll have news for us soon."

"Thanks, sheriff. I appreciate all your help."

"It's the least I can do for Clay Stone's family."

Darryn patted Miranda's shaking hands and directed a question to the sheriff. "Did the Devlins give you any more information?"

"A little more. The girl remembered her brother had mentioned playin' around on a big tire swing behind Craig's house that went out over the water. It might help them identify the place."

The phone rang. "This is Sheriff Adair."

Miranda watched his face as he was listening. His face turned white. Something was wrong.

"I see. Thanks for your help."

Darryn had picked up on her fear. "What is it, sheriff?"

"They... they found two male bodies on the back deck. They both been stabbed."

Miranda fainted.

Lorna came to in the trunk of an oil-burning, dirty, yellow Malibu with an aching head. She touched her forehead and discovered her hair was sticky with dried blood. The fabric between the trunk and the back seat was worn so bare that she could pick up some of the words the driver and passenger were saying. "This is crazy. Why do we have to drive all the way to Tenkiller to dump the girl when there's a river right here we could dump her in?"

"Oh, something about it being harder for them to find a body in a lake than in a river."

"Well, screw it. There's an easy place to get to right over there. I'm goin' to stop there, and you can help me throw her in."

The car slowed and Lorna debated what she should do. If she had a little more time, she could probably kick the old trunk until it came open. But she'd run out of time. Maybe she should jump out and try to run away as soon as they popped the trunk open. No, they were stronger and probably faster and would recapture her in no time.

As a child, she had always been the best at hide and seek because no one could "play possum" like she could. She did it by imagining she was dead and couldn't move a muscle, not even to breathe. No one could ever find where she was because they could detect no movement or sound. By the time the creeps got the trunk open, she would look like a corpse.

"We gotta get her far enough that she don't wash right back up. Best I remember there's a good drop off pretty close. Let's wade out a ways until we find it."

The trunk popped open, and Lorna played dead. She took small, shallow breaths as they carried her out into the water. The men were so concentrated on finding the drop-off that they never noticed she was alive. They suddenly stopped walking. "There it is. Let her drop."

Lorna sank into the deep, dark water. She had to hold her breath and not surface until they could no longer see her. She sensed herself slipping away, letting go of consciousness. A whiff of a familiar, rose-scented perfume filled her nostrils, and she heard a well-known voice. *"Hang on, Lorna. Just a few more seconds, and they'll be gone. Now, sweet girl. Kick hard now."*

Lorna kicked, using her strong arms and legs to propel her to the surface. As her head cleared the water, she took a big lungful of fresh air. She murmured, "Thank you, Mema."

She was shaking from the cold and loss of blood where Mariah had hit her, but she was alive.

Now to find some help.

First, she needed to figure out where she was so she wouldn't go the wrong way and run into Kyle or his friends. Maybe she should walk along the shoreline instead of walking up to the highway.

She hadn't gone too far until she made out the figures of two men fishing from an aluminum jon boat. She emerged from the bushes and waved her arms. "Help."

Two Indian men paddled close to where she stood. The big man spoke. "What's wrong, girl?"

"Someone tried to kill me. My name is Lorna Steel. My parents are Darryn and Miranda Steel from Aiden. Could you take me to Hastings Hospital? Someone hit me in the head, and it's bleedin' pretty bad."

The small man said, "Oh, my. Who would do such a thing to a young lady? Let me help you in, and we'll take you to the truck. I'm Henry Wolf, and this is my brother Gene."

They half carried her to their truck and placed her in the middle, wrapping her up in a faded old quilt. In a few minutes, the warmth of the heater and the quilt lulled her to sleep.

WHEN MIRANDA CAME to, she was lying on a vinyl couch in the sheriff's office. Darryn was sitting beside her, looking worried. She dreaded what he was going to tell her.

"Miranda, are you all right?"

"I suppose. How long was I out?"

"Oh, not that long. Maybe ten minutes. Probably just stress. The sheriff wanted to send you to Hastings on an ambulance, but I talked him into waiting a few minutes. He's checking with the dispatcher to see if any new reports have come in. Here, I'll help you sit up. How about a little water? The sheriff gave me a couple of bottles."

Miranda took a few sips of water. Darryn put his arm around her. "Are you cold?"

"A little."

"Here. Maybe this will help." He took off his jacket and draped it across her shoulders

The sheriff walked in, all smiles. "Folks, I got some good news for you. Your girl's in Hastings Hospital, alive, and mostly well."

"Oh, thank God!" Relief poured through Miranda's soul.

Darryn grasped the sheriff's hand. "Thank you, Sheriff Adair. You saved our daughter."

He chuckled. "Well, she kinda saved herself. She attracted the attention of two fishermen, name of Wolf, and told them to take her to Hastings. They're still there with her if you want to thank them."

TWO INDIAN MEN were sitting outside Lorna's room, talking in Cherokee and drinking coffee. Darryn grabbed their hands. "Wado. We're so thankful you brought our daughter back to us."

The smaller man spoke first. "I'm Henry Wolf, and this is my little brother, Gene." He chuckled. "Only he ain't so little. Anyway, we're just glad we could help."

Gene nodded his head. "Yeah, she's a tough girl, but she's been through a lot."

Miranda smiled at them. "You said your name is Wolf. My grandmother was Amelia Wolf before she married. Do you know her?"

"We sure do," said Henry. "She's our cousin, and that makes you our cousin, too. Good to meet you."

Miranda gave them both a quick hug. "I am so very thankful that Lorna met you tonight, cousins."

Darryn reached into his billfold and pulled out two twenty-dollar bills. "Here have breakfast on us."

Gene chuckled. "That's a mighty big breakfast."

"Save some of it for lunch if you want to. Just take it, please."

Gene reached out his hand. "Well, if you put it that way. *Wa-do.*"

Henry said, "I know you can't wait to see your girl. We'll go now but come and visit us when she gets well." He handed Miranda a slip of paper. "Here's our phone number."

"Thanks. We will."

MIRANDA KNOCKED SOFTLY on the closed door. "May we come in?"

"Come in, Mom."

She rushed to Lorna's bed, crying and laughing at the same time, and leaned down and kissed her on the cheek. "Oh, Lorna. I was afraid I would never see you again."

"Me too. Hello, Dad."

"Hello, sweetheart. How are you feelin'?" Darryn pulled two chairs up for Miranda and him to sit in.

"Not too bad. I had to have some stitches in my head."

Miranda gently examined her head. "Where are they?"

"You can't see them. They're in the back where she hit me."

Darryn's voice vibrated with anger. "Who hit you?"

"Mariah Panther."

"That girl that used to bully you in the seventh grade?"

"I'm surprised you still remember."

"Well, of course I do. I never forget anything important that happens to you, good or bad."

Darryn interrupted. "Do you want to tell us what happened?"

"Yes, if you promise not to get mad at me."

"I promise."

Lorna told them about the party, including the drugs. When she got to the part about Ned, she started to sob. "I saw Kyle stab him, Dad. Is he all right?"

Darryn hugged her. "I'm afraid not, honey. When they found him and Ian, they were both dead from knife wounds."

Lorna started shaking and crying hysterically. Despite their best efforts, they couldn't get her to calm down.

A nurse came in and pointed to the door. "I'm afraid you'll have to go. Your daughter's been through so much, and she needs some medicine to help her rest for a while. Come back this afternoon or tonight, and you can visit her again."

"We would like to stay, but I suppose you know best. Please call us if there's a change in her condition." He turned to see Miranda still standing by Lorna's bed.

"Do I have to leave her? I just got her back."

He put his arm around her and led her away. "I know, honey. Let's see if we can talk to her doctor."

DR. MASTERS, WHO was at the nurses' station, motioned for them to follow him into a small conference room. "Take a seat, and I will tell you what I know. Except for getting stitches for a head wound and some minor scrapes and bruises, Lorna is recovering nicely, but she needs to stay calm and get some rest. Since she had a hard bump to the head and was unconscious for a period of time, I want to keep her in the hospital overnight for observation. Barring any unforeseen circumstances, I plan on discharging her tomorrow morning."

Darryn shook his hand. "Thanks, doctor. We appreciate all you have done for our daughter."

Miranda smiled and nodded. "Yes, thank you."

"That's quite all right. You should be proud of her. Not many sixteen-year-olds would have the presence of mind to save their own lives under those circumstances."

Darryn smiled. "We are very proud of her."

THAT AFTERNOON, MIRANDA sighed with relief when she saw Lorna, dressed in a clean hospital gown, watching television. "How are you feeling now, baby?"

"Much better."

Darryn pulled the chairs back to Lorna's bedside. "Do you feel like finishin' your story?"

When Lorna got to the part about almost drowning, she stopped. "What I'm going to tell you next really happened, but it's pretty unbelievable. When I knew I was fadin' away under the water, I smelled Mema's perfume and heard her voice. She told me not to give up. When she said that, I had the strength to wait until it was safe to swim to the surface. Do you believe me?"

Miranda smoothed her hair and thought of her own warning dreams. "Of course, baby."

"How about you, Dad?"

Darryn frowned, thinking it over. "I believe you think that happened, but it might have just been something you imagined because your brain was starved for oxygen. I wouldn't tell that to the police when they question you."

"I won't."

She finished the story with, "Did you meet Henry and Gene? They were so nice to me. They were still here to make sure I was all right after I had the stitches."

"Yes, we met them, and it turns out they're kin to you and me. We're cousins."

"Somehow that doesn't surprise me."

About that time Grandma Amelia came in with Aunt Abigail. She came over to Lorna's bed. "Your mother told me what happened to you. How are you feeling?"

"I'm okay. I get to go home tomorrow."

"That's good. Have you talked to Sheriff Adair?"

"Not yet, but Henry and Gene said they would tell him what I told them when they put me in their boat."

Darryn smiled. "Those two are good men. Lorna's going to give a formal statement to Sheriff Adair tomorrow."

"Have they arrested that Kincaid boy yet?"

"I think they're waiting to hear from Lorna. How do you know his name?"

"This is Aiden. There are no secrets in this town."

BYRON CAME TO see Lorna the next morning before she was discharged and hugged her, much to her surprise and embarrassment. The next few days passed in a blur of activity. Almost everyone they knew came by their house to offer them support. Darryn's father, Jack Steel, offered some interesting insights. "You have to consider what kind of people make up Aiden. You need to remember where most of these people came from originally."

"Where was that?"

"From the criminal white trash who were run out of the southern states. Did you know that the patriarch of the high and mighty Kincaid family was a dirt farmer who fled Georgia for his life when he was caught stealing hogs from his neighbors? He came to Oklahoma in the territory days when no one cared or dared to ask a man about his past. Ever heard of the bushwhackers?"

Lorna nodded. "Oh, yes. I remember Grandma Amelia talking about her grandfather, the first Sam Clay, having a run-in with some bushwhackers on his way home from the Civil War. They tried to jump him and steal what he had. He shot one dead, but the other one got away with his favorite horse."

"Well, that's the way the Kincaids got their start. This Kyle is a descendant of lawless people. Blood will tell."

Lorna gave her testimony, and Kyle and Mariah were arrested. They both said they were at the party, but when Ned and Ian started fighting, they left. They didn't know what had happened to Lorna. She had just disappeared before the fight started. At the hearing, all of the other attendees supported their story.

At the recess, their lawyer told them things were not going their way. "The rumor is the Kincaid family bribed all the witnesses to tell the same story. They're trying to paint Lorna as Ned's unstable, underage girlfriend. They said when Ian came on to her, Ned got mad and started attacking him. Lorna ran away because she was scared. Unfortunately, the pornographic videos the police took from Ian's cabinet support the theory that he may have been a pervert."

Lorna's mouth dropped. "What? That's *not* how it happened."

Miranda shook her head in disbelief. "Lorna had to get stitches for a head wound. Do they think she gave that to herself?"

Darryn spoke up. "Let me guess. She fell on the rocks and hit the back of her head."

"You guessed it."

Lorna gripped her hands into fists and watched her mother hold back tears as the Kincaids and Panthers cheered in the courtroom when the charges were dismissed. Grandma Amelia stood up with the help of her cane. Her strong, clear voice rang out over the courtroom. "I found a dead owl in my mailbox this morning, probably put there by the Panthers. I also saw some new trucks in the courthouse parking lot this morning, probably bought by the Kincaids. Bad medicine always rebounds on the ones that use it. There is still good medicine in the world, and blood will tell."

Lorna ignored the angry buzz from the Kincaid and Panther families. Amelia sat down next to her and her mother and turned to them. "Come to my house tonight for supper. All your aunts and your uncle will be there. Abigail is fixing brown beans and fry bread."

MIRANDA LOOKED AT Lorna as they sat at the large wooden dining table. She had put on a brave face, but Miranda could see the pain behind her smiles. After their food was cleared away, Amelia said, "Stay where you are. It's family meeting time."

Mary frowned. "What's goin' on? We haven't had a meeting since Pa died."

"I just want to let everybody know what I am going to do, so there won't be any confusion. Abigail, bring me my strong box and keys."

Abigail appeared with a medium-sized metal box. "This has some of my important papers and keepsakes in it. I'm going to give some things to Miranda today."

Miranda's mouth dropped open. "Why me, Grandma? I'm just a granddaughter, one of many."

"You're Clay's daughter, his only child, and I owe Clay more than most. Besides, I have a strong feeling I am supposed to do this here and now. First, I am giving you this lease to a place I bought several years ago in Georgia. It's a small modern house that I had built on the same land Bluebird was forced to leave in 1839. I've been talking to some of our kin who are kin to us through Bluebird and Grey Wolf. They helped me find the land."

Zack spoke up. "Where did you get the money to buy land and have a house built in Georgia?"

Amelia winked at him. "Don't underestimate me. Before Grandpa Josh passed away, he put the store in your father's name. We sold it and got a good price for it. I persuaded your father to let me invest most of the money in stocks and bonds. I hung on to them until I could make a very big profit. I applied part of those profits toward the cost of the property and house. Someday the house will belong to Abigail because she gave up her opportunity to have a home and family to care for me all these years, and she has always wanted to live in Georgia.

"But first I'm leasing it for free to Miranda for the next two years. She needs a place of refuge from the Kincaids and the Panthers. Our people in Georgia and North Carolina have promised me they'll watch over you while you live there. They have sent me pictures of the place, and it is beautiful."

Darryn shook his head. "Grandma Amelia, don't think I don't appreciate this, but how can we just leave our home and move somewhere without any jobs?"

"I have confidence that you both'll find new jobs soon, but if it takes a while, that's all right. Miranda may draw on the money I have reserved for her to inherit as Clay's daughter. It should be sufficient for your needs for two years."

"Grandma, what about our house? I'm afraid what might happen to it if it sits empty."

"It won't sit empty. Zack's boy, Jeremy, called him last week from Little Rock with some news. He's been laid off, and he and his bride are moving back to Aiden. Zack, do you think they would like to live there?"

"They sure would. They been lookin' everywhere for a place to live."

"Miranda, would you agree to let them live there free if they will take good care of the place."

"It seems you have thought of everything. Yes, I would agree." She turned to Darryn, "How about you?"

"Anything you want."

Amelia looked at each of her children. "And are the rest of you all right with this?"

They all nodded. Abigail offered her siblings a flustered apology. "Honestly, I knew about the house, but I didn't know she was going to give it to me."

Susan laughed, leaned over, and gave her a hug. "Don't worry about it, sis. You earned it."

Emily stood and patted Amelia on the back. "I like the way you think, Ma."

"Good. One more thing. I want you to take this back to where it came from." She unwrapped the red stone.

Susan gasped. "You're givin' her Bluebird's stone. That's not right. It should go to one of us."

Amelia's thick eyebrows lowered until they almost covered her coal-black eyes, and Miranda saw fear in Susan's eyes. "It will go to who I say it will go to. Don't you remember Bluebird didn't give it to her daughter, Starr? She gave it to her grandson, Sam Clay. Besides, I'm not giving it to Miranda. I saw Granny Bluebird in a dream the other night. She told me I needed to send her rock home. Maybe in two years, I will know who it's supposed to go to.

"Now I have something to say to you, Lorna."

Miranda looked over at Lorna and saw her instantly change into a scared, little girl. "What is it, Grandma Amelia?"

"You must make me a promise."

Lorna's voice quavered. "About what?"

"Promise me you will never do anything else that will harm your body or spirit."

Almost unconsciously, Lorna raised her hand in her old Girl Scout pledge. "I promise."

DARRYN, MIRANDA, AND Lorna loved their mountain home. Other than enrolling Lorna in school and setting up their new household, Miranda and Darryn spent all of the first month in unwinding and healing. The log house, nestled in the tall pines, was a wonderful place to just sit and take in the sights and sounds of nature. Miranda and Darryn got in the habit of getting up early, sitting on the back deck, sipping tea or coffee, and watching as the sun rose over the mountain tops. On one such morning Darryn looked over and smiled at Miranda. "You know we really should start looking for jobs before too long."

"I know, but I hate to leave this place and join the rat race again."

"Maybe we can join a slower race this time."

Miranda found a job as a teacher/librarian at a small rural school. She had never applied for the full-time librarian job in Aiden. Miranda's problems and her mother's sudden death had sidetracked her from that action. Her salary wasn't as large as what she made in Aiden, but the children were better behaved, and she got to spend half her day with some of her best friends, books.

Lorna soon settled in the small junior class and started dating David, a quiet, studious fellow musician. David, who had lost a brother to drugs, was passionate about helping others who had fallen victim to them. Lorna joined him in modeling a drug-free lifestyle.

Darryn found work as the business manager of a small local hospital. After he had worked there for a month, Miranda woke up to find his spot in the bed empty. She walked out on the back deck.

Far below, she saw Darryn, speeding down a mountain path. It was the first time she had seen him on a morning run in years. He had always claimed his job took so much out of him he had no energy left for any kind of exercise. Miranda resolved to join him on his next run.

ON MOTHER'S DAY, when they had been in the mountains for almost a year, Byron called her from OU to wish her a happy Mother's Day and to tell her he was coming there for a visit and bringing a special girl with him.

After she hung up, Miranda walked into to the kitchen to find an envelope, lying on the table, marked, "To Mommy."

Miranda cried when she read what Lorna had written inside of it.

Grandma Bonita said someday we would be best friends just like the two of you were. She was right about that like she was everything else. I love you, Mommy.

LATER THAT NIGHT as Miranda and Darryn were sitting on the deck, listening to the night sounds, Lorna came outside. "Grandma Amelia is on the phone for you."

Miranda frowned. "That's odd. She never calls at night."

The line fairly crackled with Amelia's excitement. *"I want to read you this headline from* The Tulsa World. *It says, 'Panther Changes Testimony.'"*

"Oh, my gosh. What happened?"

"It basically says the Panther girl got mad when Kincaid dumped her, and she confessed that everything they said was lies. She says Kyle stabbed Ned and that other man and set it up to look like they attacked each other. He made her hurt Lorna and gave orders for Lorna to be dumped in the lake. His father was worried when Lorna survived, so he bribed all the witnesses to support Kyle's story. Judge Richards has ordered a new trial."

"Well, that's encouraging news. Of course, she's probably lying about being forced to hurt Lorna. But the rest of it sounds true. You keep us up on all of the developments. We'll likely find our way back to Aiden for the trial."

"I sure will. That good medicine is working."

"You know I never thought you believed in supernatural things like medicine."

"Well, guess I can have a few secrets at age ninety-nine."

"I guess you can."

"Do you still like living in the mountains?"

"I love it, but I miss my kinfolks and friends in Oklahoma and my house in the woods."

"Well, you can stay there as long as you want. I'm in no hurry to die and leave the house to Abigail."

"Glad to hear you're in no hurry. The world still needs Amelia Stone, and so do I. Goodbye. Grandma. I love you."

"Love you, too. Goodbye."

Miranda went out to tell Darryn and Lorna the good news.

XV
THE GRAND FAREWELL

ONE YEAR LATER, Lorna hugged David one more time before her dad said, "Time to go. We got a long drive ahead of us."

Lorna sighed, put in her earbuds, and settled into the comfortable back seat of their almost-new 1994 Lumina. It had been a year since they had gone back home for the trial, and she had mixed feelings about this journey. It would be great to see all of her family again at Grandma Amelia's 100th birthday party and to stay in the house where her poppa grew up. But she knew it would be sheer misery to not see David or her friends for nearly three weeks.

As usual, her mother and father were making light conversation about first one thing and then another, and she half-way listened to them while she tried to concentrate on her music. Mom kept obsessing about the party.

"Do you think we should stop and buy her a gift?"

Dad frowned at her. "No, the invitation plainly said, 'No gifts.'"

"I know, but do you really think anybody's going to pay attention to that? What if everybody else buys her something, and we are the only ones who don't?"

"Then we'll be the only ones who know how to follow directions.

Your grandma is always complaining about having too much stuff, so I think she said what she meant."

"I suppose so. I did buy her a special, hand-painted 100th birthday card. I don't think she will mind that. Can you believe she is actually going to be 100?"

Dad put on his turn signal and passed the slow-moving SUV in front of him. "Sure as heck don't want to follow that old codger all the way to Tennessee. Has anyone in your family ever lived to be a hundred before?"

"Not that I know of. How about your family?"

"Had an uncle who lived to be ninety-six, but that's as close as we got. He seemed a lot older than Amelia, though."

"She's pretty amazing. Abigail says she still works in her yard and takes long walks through the woods."

Lorna took out her ear buds and joined the conversation. "Grandma Amelia is going to live forever. Mom, what did you put in the trunk right before we left?"

Miranda turned in the seat so she could face her. "You noticed that, did you?"

"Yeah, it was in such a pretty quilted tote I thought it was a present."

"It *is* a type of present."

Darryn scowled. "So, you didn't follow directions?"

"Oh, yes, I did. I did exactly what Granny told me to. I am taking Bluebird's stone back to Oklahoma."

Lorna gasped. "Do you think she wants to give it to someone because she thinks she is going to die?"

Miranda patted her hand. "Don't worry. I'm sure she will let us know when we see her."

THE OLD FARMHOUSE was bursting at the seams with young, old, and middle-aged. The June weather was pleasantly warm, and family groups enjoyed picnicking on the grounds of the old homestead. Lorna stood in front of the cornucopia of desserts, staring at a multitude of pies, cakes, breads, and various other delectable dishes. "There's so much that I don't know what to choose."

Byron took a small slice from several offerings. "I know what you mean. Even I can't sample everything."

Having finally decided on some fresh strawberry shortcake, Lorna took her place beside her mother. Her dad looked over at her plate. "Are those Stilwell strawberries on that short cake? I haven't had Stilwell berries in a coon's age."

Grandma Amelia, who was traveling from picnic table to picnic table, heard him. "Do you have to ask? Of course, those are Stilwell berries. We bought them from John's Produce yesterday, and Abigail cleaned and sugared them up last night. She just took the cake out of the oven this morning."

Darryn jumped up and broke into a jog. "In that case, I better get me some before it's all gone."

AFTER THE DISHES had been cleared away from the tables, Grandma Amelia sat on the front porch in her rocking chair with her children gathered around her. Uncle Zack stood up and gave a shrill whistle. "Now I got your attention the way Ross used to get ours." He and his siblings all grinned at each other.

He waved his hand at the crowd. "Everybody come on over close to the porch. You can bring your cards and put them in the basket sitting here. Ma, do you want to say anything?"

Grandma Amelia held out her arm, and Aunt Abigail helped her to her feet. "Yes, I do. I want to thank all of you for coming to help me celebrate my hundredth birthday." She chuckled. "I never dreamed I would live long enough to see the changes I have seen. When I was young, we raised stock and grew our own food, and we never went hungry. We had our troubles, but we managed all right. My father Sam Clay told me that Granny Bluebird experienced hunger, fear, and suffering, but she still made a good life for herself and for her family." Grandma reached into the quilted bag at her feet and drew out the reddish stone.

"Granny Bluebird brought this stone all the way from Georgia on the Trail of Tears. She wanted it kept in our family as a reminder of where we came from and what we have overcome. It has been in Georgia for the last two years, but now it is time to come home to Oklahoma. Just like I hope it is time for Miranda and her family to move back home."

Lorna's heart skipped a beat. Oh, no. She didn't want to leave David or her mountain home. This fall she was going to attend Duke, and not even Grandma Amelia could stop that.

AMELIA WAS TIRED that night, more tired than she had ever been. Abigail bent over and kissed her on the forehead. "You had a big day today, Ma. Better get some rest."

"I'll do my best."

She did try, but her brain wouldn't stop turning. She heard a rustling movement in the corner of the dark room.

Suddenly a little figure stood beside her bed. Her hands shook. "Who are you?"

"Ha. You're a Cherokee, and you don't know who I am?"

She fumbled a bit but finally picked up her glasses from the nightstand by her bed and turned on the lamp. She thought he would disappear, but he didn't.

His chuckle was low and pleasant. *"I'm still here, Amelia. Lame Bird, Bluebird, and Ross knew who I am. Why don't you?"*

She raised herself to a sitting position and took in his appearance. "You're one of the Little People. Are you the man Ross saw under the house the night I almost died?"

"Yes, I was the one who warned him of what was going to happen."

"So, you saved my life?"

"I gave the warning, but he chose to heed it."

Amelia's tone turned bitter. "So, why didn't you warn me so I could save Ross's life?"

He hesitated a moment and mumbled something in Cherokee.

She glared at him. "You will have to speak in English if you want me to understand. I forgot most of my Cherokee a long time ago."

He shook his head. *"Some things are hard to explain in English, but I will try."* He took a deep breath and began. *"The Creator only lets me give warnings, and I can only warn those that He allows. I liked Ross, but I wasn't allowed to interfere with his fate. You were meant to live a long life, so I did what I was allowed to do in your case."*

"I would have traded my long life in a minute for a few more years for my son."

He sighed. *"I know, but neither of us had a say in the matter."*

Amelia wiped a tear from her eye. "Maybe so. What did you come to warn me about tonight?"

"You will soon be joining Bluebird, Ross, and all of the others."

She shrugged her shoulders. "That's all right. I'm ready, but I need to pass on Bluebird's stone."

"That's what I came to warn you about. It needs to be done very soon."

"Well, thank you for telling me. But I can't help wondering why you care what I do with my stone?"

His black eyes glittered, and he grinned. *"I had a feeling you would ask me that question. I think the best way to explain it is to show you."* He motioned with his right hand. *"Give me the stone."*

As soon as Amelia placed the stone in his hand, she flinched. "Something shocked me."

When she looked up, he had vanished. All that remained was the stone, lying on the floor, bathed in a pool of green light.

In alarm, Amelia called out. "Where did you go?"

She heard his chuckle before she saw him. Then he was beside her bed again, and the stone was back in her hand. *"Do you understand now, Amelia?"*

"You're tied to the stone somehow?"

"Yes, what else?"

Amelia frowned. "I think maybe when Bluebird picked up the stone, she picked you up, too."

He fairly danced around the bed. "Very good. I knew you would get it."

"So, as long as we have the stone, you are tied to our family."

"Exactly." He patted her hand. "And I like being part of your family, so please don't lose the stone."

"I don't intend to." She was suddenly overcome with fatigue. "This has been a very interesting experience, but I don't suppose I can tell anyone about it?"

His black eyes glittered again. "I would rather you wouldn't, but you are going to die, anyway, so there's really nothing I can threaten you with. Will you keep it to yourself as a favor to me?"

She stifled a yawn. "I suppose."

He reached out and took her hand. "Wa-do, Amelia. It has been good to meet you in the flesh."

After the little man faded away, Amelia spent a few minutes considering what she should do with the stone. Once she made the decision, she passed into a restful sleep.

THE FOLLOWING NIGHT, Grandma Amelia summoned the entire family. Lorna had never seen Grandma Amelia look nervous before, but tonight, as Amelia sat at the head of the table waiting for her family to gather, she repeatedly twisted and smoothed a small, floral handkerchief between her fingers. She waited until the last arrival, Uncle Ross's daughter, Rose, had taken her place at the big oak dining room table before she began to speak. "It is time to set my house in order."

Several gasps were heard, and Aunt Susan spoke up. "No, Ma. That can't be."

"Whether you believe it or not, it is time. Now I wrote my will years ago, and there is a copy lying here on the table which you may read if you want. It basically says that all of my assets will be divided among my children or their heirs, except for the house in Georgia, which I have left to Abigail for caring for me. We've discussed this before, and it is pretty straightforward, but if you have any questions, you are welcome to ask. Lying beside it is my instructions for my last rites."

Lorna looked around the table at her family's shocked faces.

Grandma turned to Abigail. "Bring me the stone."

As they waited, she prepared her audience. "Now some of you aren't going to agree with my decision, but I have thought and studied on it. It's funny, but I don't think anyone who ever was given the stone actually asked for it. My father was surprised when Bluebird gave it to him, and I didn't expect him to give it to me. "

Abigail came back with the stone in her hand. "Here you go, Ma."

Amelia held it up for them all to see. "It's time to pass on Bluebird's stone to a new generation. Come here, Lorna."

Lorna shook her head. "Not me, Grandma. It should go to one of your children. Besides I'm not staying in Oklahoma. I am going back to the South to attend Duke this fall."

Amelia chuckled. "It doesn't matter where you take the stone as long as it is with you. In fact, it may be time for it to return homeward for a while longer."

Except for a few eyerolls from the aunts, no one objected to Lorna's taking the stone.

THAT NIGHT AFTER she had finished a long phone conversation with David, Lorna fell into a deep sleep and found herself back on the ceiling of Grandma Amelia's bedroom. It was exactly like her dream two years before, only tonight she was staying in the same house as Grandma. This time Grandma Amelia opened her eyes and smiled at her. "I knew you were special, Lorna. That's why the stone chose to go to you. Now listen closely to what I tell you. Someday you may see one of the Little People. If you do, don't be afraid. Sometimes he is sent from the Creator to warn our people of danger. Now promise me you will never forget where you came from and who you are."

Fighting back tears, Lorna placed her right hand over her heart. "I promise."

"Good girl. Just be the strong woman you were created to be, and everything will be fine."

She smiled again and gave a little wave. "Goodbye for now, Lorna. Keep this experience to yourself, at least for tonight. Remember, I will see you again someday."

Amelia Clay Stone closed her eyes and stopped breathing.

THE NEXT MORNING the loud wails of Aunt Abigail woke Lorna. Her dream flashed through her memory, and a few minutes later her mother came in to tell her the news, but she already knew. The house soon filled up with people again, almost all of them sobbing and crying.

Grandma Amelia's instructions for her leave-taking surprised everyone. Four days later, after a traditional Cherokee wake was held at the homeplace the night before, a funeral service was held according to her written instructions. The sermon was delivered by the minister of the church Grandma attended, but the eulogy was given in Cherokee and English by a long-time full-blood friend of hers. The hymns were all sung in Cherokee and English. Present in the large crowd were both conservative Christians and traditional Keetoowah Cherokees. Lorna looked around at her family and saw all shades of color present—from the rosy Irish skin of Cousin Ronnie's wife and children, to the various shades of beige and brown, and all the way to the ebony skin tones of Cousin Micah's wife and sons.

Lorna smiled at a new discovery about herself. She was going to be just like Grandma Amelia and live and die exactly as she pleased.

WHEN MY CHEROKEE ancestors arrived in Indian Territory, it was not a choice. Their names are included on a muster list of the Trail of Tears, and their strength has inspired me to write the stories that they might have told.

My own story began in the small town of Stilwell, Oklahoma, where I have lived most of my life. By twenty-four, I was married with two children, teaching language arts at Stilwell Junior High School. I diversified my career, eventually retiring as the librarian of Siloam Springs Middle School in Siloam Springs, Arkansas, in 2010.

Even though I returned to work temporarily as a part-time library clerk at Stilwell Public Library, I found time to pursue my passion, writing. For the next seven years, I was published in *Guidepost Magazine, the Oklahoma Genealogical Society Quarterly, the Green Country Anthology, the Starwatch Anthology 37, Saddlebag Dispatches,* and in various newspapers and newsletters.